THE BOOK OF BRUCE
BY JESSE C. BRUTKIEWICZ

DORRANCE PUBLISHING CO
EST. 1920
PITTSBURGH, PENNSYLVANIA 15238

The contents of this work, including, but not limited to, the accuracy of events, people, and places depicted; opinions expressed; permission to use previously published materials included; and any advice given or actions advocated are solely the responsibility of the author, who assumes all liability for said work and indemnifies the publisher against any claims stemming from publication of the work.

All Rights Reserved
Copyright © 2024 by Jesse C. Brutkiewicz

No part of this book may be reproduced or transmitted, downloaded, distributed, reverse engineered, or stored in or introduced into any information storage and retrieval system, in any form or by any means, including photocopying and recording, whether electronic or mechanical, now known or hereinafter invented without permission in writing from the publisher.

Dorrance Publishing Co
585 Alpha Drive
Suite 103
Pittsburgh, PA 15238
Visit our website at *www.dorrancebookstore.com*

ISBN: 979-8-89341-065-5
eISBN: 979-8-89341-564-3

PREFACE

Around the time I began to write this story, I was beginning to undergo a massive awakening within my own mind. I looked back at the experiences in my life and realized that I have a story to tell. The contents within are highly autobiographical, but they are as they pertain to me. Many people have their own version of an awakening that takes place in their life, and this is very much my own.

Since the completion of this story, my life has continued to drastically change. My awakening has essentially continued non-stop, and I am writing this to you today as a direct contactee with Valiant Thor, and then eventually the Galactic Federation. This organization is the governing body of the Milky Way galaxy. I telepathically communicate with them on a daily basis. Following the completion of this book, my actions afterward cast me into their immediate attention. They are here to assist with the mass awakening of the entire human consciousness. I cannot say exactly what I have done since the completion of this book, but it is of Galactic importance.

I wish to emphatically and genuinely encourage all of humanity to take some time and reflect inward. There is a massive change potentially on the horizon for all of us. We have dreamed so many times, in so many ways of living in the stars, but the fact of the matter is that it is a reachable reality. We are well on the verge of achieving this dream, but the vast majority of us simply feel cut off from outer existence. This could not be farther from the truth.

The Acturans, Andromedans, Draconians, Ebens, Felines, Greys, Mantids, Pleadians, Reptilians, Sirians, and Zeta-Reticulans are the largest groups that make up the Galactic Federation. Each has their own society and message, but the united cause is one in the same; to assist with civilizations like ours to reach our destinies. First contact is upcoming. However, to those with a pure heart, genuine spirit, and a curiosity to reach out and make contact…. It can happen as soon as you are ready.

JUNE 18, 2013

My name is Benjamin Bruce. I've never kept any kind of documentation on the daily events of my life. Hell, I hardly ever get on social media anymore. But it seems the decision to start this, journal, or diary, or whatever you want to call it, is being made for me.

Some of the things that have happened to me so far are, for lack of a better word, peculiar. It's unclear as to why I am to write, or for whom. It's certainly not for anyone in the Army. If they got their hands on what I have to say here, I'd be kicked out in two weeks. I suppose I'll start with who I am, where I am, and what's happened so far. But before I start, I swear to myself, swear to whomever reads this, that the things I write in this journal are exactly as I have seen them. These events are written exactly as they have happened without any bias, exaggeration, or anything of the sort. Again, I'm not sure why this is happening to me, or for what end. All I know is that I am to write this journal. And I can only guess what will happen in the near future.

So, about me and where I am. As I write this, I am sitting in one of the many dusty tents in Camp Warrior. Camp Warrior is a transitional location in Bagram Air Force Base for all troops coming into and leaving Afghanistan. Now when I say all troops, I'm talking Army, Marines, Polish troops, French troops, and anyone contributing to the war efforts in the Stan. My tent is about the width of an average house, as long as a football field, and filled with hundreds of double bunk beds with shitty mattresses on top without sheets, or pillows. Literally hundreds of different people have slept/sweat on these things, making them the prime culprit for illness. (Though I suppose it's better to be exposed to the germs here early on so as to start building immunities) Each bunk has a double wall locker for you to put all your gear into, and there are poles running down the middle of the tent every 15 feet or so with a power outlet, which is usually daisy chained with 2 or more power strips, creating a natural fire hazard, not to mention the arid climate. Soldiers can stay here anywhere from a day to a few weeks before they finally get a flight out. The base itself is set in a Russian minefield, surrounded 360 degrees by mountains. As for the mines, it's mostly safe. Most have been removed by experts, or by the poor bastards that discovered the ones that were missed when driving. But rest assured, the routes around the base are clear. For me, this is day two out of who knows how many that I will be here before I start the trip back to the States at the end of this 9-month deployment.

Now, the reason for this journal is as follows. Before I came here, I was stationed at Forward Operating Base (FOB) Fenty aka Jalalabad Airfield, or JAF. In the last two weeks before my flight to Bagram, I had several dreams about… well, this very notebook I'm writing in. The dream was always the same; I would enter the USO here on Bagram, and it would be empty, save for a bookshelf, about as tall as my waist, across the room. As I walk across the room, I notice there is a box on the top shelf that appears to be glowing or on fire; I can't tell. When I reach the shelf, it stops glowing. I grab the box, open it, and it's empty. Life changing… right? Well, I had this very same dream a few times in the last two weeks I was at JAF, as well as on the very last night I was there. After taking the flight to Bagram, I ventured as soon as I could to the USO, telling no one of my intentions. Once I entered, I looked across the room, and the very same bookshelf from my dream was there. The room itself was full of people on computers, watching movies, calling home, etc., but that bookshelf was exactly where it was in my dream. I visited this very USO during the three weeks when I first arrived in the Stan, every day in fact. But I took no notice of it. But now, there it was, just as I had dreamed. I walked over to it and spotted that very same box. Extreme flashes of adrenaline surged through my body, and I got goosebumps so hard that it made me shiver. I reached the box, definitely not glowing, opened it, and found a notebook. One of those classic black and white splotchy ones, with the cover similar to the black and white static of a TV without an input. This puts me into deep thought...

Where did it come from? Why is it there? What does it mean? ... Who cares... it's just a notebook.. The supervisor of the USO probably thought it would be a good idea to stock this bookshelf with free writing materials for Soldiers that wanted to write. I looked at the other contents of the shelf and confirmed that thought. There were envelopes, bags of new pens, more notebooks, and the rest of the shelves were filled with board games and novels. Why would I dream about a notebook… As I continued to ponder this thought, I realized the answer was simple. *I dreamed about a notebook, because I am to write.* But write what? What did I have to write about? The daily life and routine of a Signal Soldier was nothing special to write home about. But wait.. I was forgetting something. It was almost as though I wanted to forget. But that wasn't going to happen. Something won't let me. I do have something to write about.

Then I proceeded to recall the chilling experience I had one night at JAF, about a month and a half back. That was worth writing about. But it would only last a few pages. Unless… there was more. Or, there *would be* more. This thought was nearly as eerie as the event I had experienced.

All of this happened about 35 minutes ago, which brings me to now. Here on this disgusting bed. Don't flop down on it too hard or you'll kick up dust in a 4 foot diameter.

What happened a month and a half ago… Well, I can't just go into it. I have to start with a man. A man named Dos Muhammed. Dos, which he enthusiastically informed me means "friend" in Pashtu, a dominant language of the Jalalabad region, was a member of the Afghanistan National Army. Pretty much the equivalent of our Army, except, far less funded, and basically a shitshow of organization, discipline, and every other moral or standard our Army puts emphasis in. This includes drugs. I cannot tell you how many times I've seen an ANA soldier smoke Hasheesh. Hasheesh is what they call a substance that is essentially concentrated Marijuana. Through some sort of refining process, using who knows what as tools and such, (Thought interrupted by incoming... every now and then Taliban likes to shoot mortars at this base... happens several times every day, but the mountains are so far off that they rarely get close to hitting the camps. Standard procedure: put your armor on, grab your M4, sprint to cover, await the all clear alarm, link up with your people, and get an earful of the schedule of events again for the 40th time, just in case your weren't paying attention for the first 39... But the most common practice the enemy uses for these attacks is to setup a mortar tube, put ice in the tube, then the mortar itself. That way when it melts and the mortar drops all the way to be fired, or reaches the primer or something... I don't know, I'm not combat arms, it fires, and they are hours gone. Clever, yet, cowardly) they cook usually around a half ounce of weed down to the size of a cookie. It becomes a hard Play-Doh-like substance; very sticky and keeps the same classic smell. Now, as a Signal Soldier, our primary mission was to support the communications backbone at JAF with our own equipment. However, what is being used every day was already here when we got here, and rarely has any problems. This means, we sit around and monitor comms equipment that never fails... which means... we essentially do nothing. This "nothing" is filled with playing X-Box, movies, tv shows, and just about anything you can think of that isn't pornography, or a violation of our own human rights. To give you an example of our boredom, we have come up with a game called Ball Ball. It's where two (male) opponents stand about 20 feet from each other and softly lob racquetballs across our workspace with the intentions of striking the other in the testicles. First one to yield loses. Generally, each toss is a miss. But, given a long enough span of time, there's going to be that one that is right on target, and drops you to your knees. Anyway... I digress..

Right, so, Hasheesh... Besides electronics, we also have good old-fashioned conversation as another form of entertainment. This is mostly done outside of the workplace with a cigarette in your mouth. Now, I'm not a smoker, but spend some time in a combat zone, and you will become one during your time there. It is the best way to find an excuse to separate yourself from your job, relieve some stress, and talk about anything and everything interesting you may have encountered during a tower guard shift, or Entry Control Point (ECP) Shift. Ahh... so, while we do spend most of our days doing nothing, our higher up leaders know this, and therefore, we get assigned to details across the base on a regular basis. These details, which I write the schedule for, include a 12-hour shift in a tower, where you sit and observe/report any suspicious activity in your immediate vicinity. Of course, you have various powerful weapons systems at your disposal, but let's not get into that now. The other detail option is ECP. The ECP is located on the other side of the airstrip and is about a 25 minute walk if you miss the bus ride @ 0515. ECP is basically..

(Random thought... Why am I explaining everything so much... who is going to read this? Any Army person knows what I am saying... perhaps it is for those not in the service. Who knows.)

(Consecutive random thought... I'm actually enjoying this. It's quite satisfying to write all this down..Perhaps that is not an accident... Sorry, I'm trying to get to the point.)

Anyway, ECP is basically the area where local nationals enter our base from the outside. There is a location where foot-traffic enters, and they get full body scans. Whole lotta penis if you're stuck with that station for the day. And there's a section for trucks to enter, which also gets full x-rays done in an attempt to find bombs/weapons. There's a whole lot more to it, but in a nutshell, both duties have potential for rather interesting things to happen to share with your fellow Soldiers during smoke breaks.

So.. Hasheesh… one of the things brought to my attention by a Soldier of mine during a smoke break, was a guy named Dos Muhammed. He was an ANA Soldier down at the ECP that openly smoked Hasheesh during the day. My Soldier went on to explain that if you befriend him, he is willing to share some with you. Now, as a Sergeant in the Army, and ironically as the assigned Unit Prevention Leader, or UPL of my company (the person that performs the drug tests), this should have been a red flag. I should notify my higher Chain of Command immediately. But I like this soldier. He undoubtedly is one of the most genuinely funny people I have ever met. Plus, I am not a tattling asshat. This is one thing most wouldn't understand; regardless of what you do in the Stan, when you're there, you're there. And it's terrible for so many reasons. Soldiers snap, or commit suicide, or purposely get into career-ending trouble to escape it. It's truly no place for the weak or mild-mannered. Given this, I understand that we all need to find a way to cope and deal with the unbelievable amount of stress we encounter. Some of them, like their Afghan counterparts, do this through drugs. So, I tell my soldiers, "Look. I know some of you are smoking hash. I'm not going to rat you out; however, I'm also not going to take you off the drug test list if your name comes up. Don't be stupid, don't get caught, and do it at your own risk." And I left it at that. Luckily, no one tested positive… though I may or may not have let them know when the tests were going to be.

Anyway, my Soldier tells me that Dos smokes nearly every day, or at least, he has seen him smoke every day. He then goes on to admit that he has taken part with him in his spliffs and has even gotten him to give him small amounts to take back to his room and conspire to smoke elsewhere. This I find fascinating, and yet, there is an opportunity present.

Now, when I joined the Army, when they asked me if I ever smoked weed during my entry exam, I stated that I had never smoked it in my life. While this was true up until the first time that I did, I was generally against it until about halfway through college. I suppose I bought into the DARE programs I was involved in during my youth and always viewed Cannabis as bad, or something that bad kids do. This opinion was quickly changed in college when I discovered that it had a rather positive effect on me. I consider myself to be an intelligent person, and while high, my mind would race with endless thoughts, humorous quips, and my generally shy and reserved demeanor would disappear, and I became a "social butterfly." Anything that makes you happy and helps you get laid, in my book, is a good thing. So naturally, one would find it quite difficult to pass on an opportunity to feel genuinely happy in a combat zone. Obviously, it's bad in the eyes of the Army, and also bad to have an altered state of consciousness during duty, so where and when I was to do it would have to be carefully planned. At least that's what I told myself after the first time that I tried it…on duty.

So, writing the duty schedule for ECP, and Tower Guard, I came up with an ingenious system. My soldiers would be on duty for five days straight, with the middle, or third day, being completely off and free of duty. This was possible because I would work their middle day of duty. During all my other days I was generally in the office, being in charge of the daily tasks. And when I say office, I'm referring to an oversized wooden hut about the size of a large living room, hidden behind a ten-foot chain-linked fence with cloth completely covering the fence and barbed wire at the top so as no one can see into or get into our compound within the base. We've all got Secret clearances, and our equipment is Secret as well. Nothing too fancy though; basically, it's just a bunch of routers and switches and various other radio/internet performance enhancing equipment with a few dedicated generators attached to a mobile satellite dish. We can provide internet and Ip-phone service anywhere in the world. (Hence why we are in the Stan) Some of our Soldiers would be sent off to other smaller bases to help support the overall mission at times, thus making my detail force smaller, and occasionally, I had to step in for a 5-day shift with no one taking my day off. But I didn't mind. This system allowed me to befriend Dos Muhammed.

After learning of Dos, every opportunity I had to work at the ECP, I was searching for him. Since all Afghans look pretty similar, which I suppose sounds racist, all I had to go by was a first name. (Although I have heard an Afghan interpreter honestly say that he thought all white people looked alike, thus it's a two-way street) So I made it a point to meet and greet as many ANA as I could while on duty at the ECP. When I first spotted him, I approached him to introduce myself, and it was pretty obvious I was talking to the right man. While he wore the dark green, black, and brown speckled camo uniform of his countrymen, his eyes were that of someone that is high 24/7. They were fairly sunken, overly wrinkled for his age, and seemed to be permanently bloodshot; but his dark features hid these aspects well. He tried quite hard to communicate with me, and his English was about the equivalent of a child just learning to speak. Most of our interactions would be quite on par to that of Neanderthal men, using single words, and lots of gestures. Though I noticed that as the deployment went on, his English improved drastically, pretty much every single day. Eventually it got to a point after about a month or so that he was generally quite happy to see me and greeted me as a legitimate friend. It was around this time that I decided the level of trust had been established, and to inquire about Hasheesh.

As I've already stated, smoking hash is a big no-go in the eyes of the Army, so this needed to be carefully planned. ECP is generally worked at two separate stations for six hours at a time, spanning a total of a 12-hour work shift. At the completion of the first six-hour block, you would then rotate with another Soldier and work the remaining six hours at another location to ease the monotony of the job. The ANA had an entirely independent schedule for their own soldiers, and it just so happened that Dos worked at the Exit Lane all day, every day. (Much like it sounds, the exit lane is primarily responsible for checking to see ANA or locals aren't trying to smuggle things off-base, and to note US mission departure times and their units.) It also just so happened that the Exit Lane was an exception to the si- hour shift rule, in that it's workers stayed there for the full 12 hours, which would allow for minimal interactions from higher ups. Coming onto shift at the exit lane at about 0600, the first three hours are usually completely dead. All of these factors combined to allow for the perfect opportunity to smoke Hash on duty, granted you were not attacked during this time. Naturally, this is always going to be a possibility, however, JAF rarely gets attacked. This is mostly due to the fact that it's the largest air base on the eastern side of the Stan, and there are literally a dozen fully armed attack helicopters standing by and ready to blast the shit out of anyone dumb enough to attack it. (Seal Team 6, which is just a name given to the group of individuals that carried out the infamous mission, departed from JAF) The Non-Commissioned Officer (NCO) in charge of ECP generally posts the station schedule two weeks in advance, which allowed for me to figure out what day I would be at the exit lane next with Dos. (Being an NCO myself, I generally only worked a couple of stations where an NCO presence was needed, Exit Lane being one of them) Once I had that figured out, I informed him to have a spliff ready for the both of us that morning to make for, as he put it, "Good time pass". Being a fairly large, 6'2", entirely solid 250 lbs, I added the request that he made it strong, anticipating that it would be needed, especially since we were to share the spliff. I also requested that he supply me with $20 worth of Hash for my own private stash to be had in the downtime between my ECP shifts.

On the morning of February 23rd, 2013, I arrived at the ECP, ate my breakfast of eggs, sausage and bacon delivered from the dining facility, and headed out to the Exit Lane. It was about a half mile walk across nothing but large rock gravel in a seemingly open gravel field that would be used as parking by the local nationals in the hours to come as they entered the FOB, after having gone through security. Once I arrived at the small shack at the exit lane, I relieved the nightshift, got their outgoing brief and sat by the benches next to the tiny metal hut. Afghan early mornings can be quite chilly, especially in the winter, so there was a makeshift fire pit consisting of a metal trash can next to the exit lane hut. The fire was already going from the outgoing night shift, and they had been nice enough to restock the firewood supply before they went off shift. I broke up a few more pallets and added to the fire as I waited for Dos to arrive.

About ten minutes later, a dirty brown and beat up Chevy truck comes rolling along carrying the ANA shift change. Out jumps Dos along with his other current shift ANA Soldiers. He greets the outgoing shift and talks with his current shift mates for a spell, then proceeds to head over to the fire. I stand up and take off my gloves and eye protection to greet him. (Afghan culture is big on skin on skin contact during hugs and handshakes, as well as making actual eye contact.) This is an important gesture, because all American Soldiers on duty, whether it be on base or off, are required to wear eye protection and gloves at all times. Once off shift, the eye protection remains, and the gloves can come off. The only places where eye protection was not required to be worn were while showering, while in your room, and while in a hard building. (A building made of metal/cement and not just wood) Some Soldiers care not for little customs and courtesies like this, but I say they go a long way. It is not unheard of for ANA to turn on an American soldier. Nine out of ten times you hear later that the American soldier killed had a blatant disrespect for Afghan people and their culture. I am a firm believer that if I embrace their customs, and show respect to their ways at all times, I am far less likely to get a bullet in my back when walking away.

After the initial greeting, I grabbed the twenty in my empty grenade pouch on my body armor and proceeded to hand it to Dos. He smiled at me and retrieved a plastic bag from his pocket. I took my newly acquired Hash and put it in the almost empty cigarette pack in my shoulder pocket. I then motioned to my lips with two fingers, making the universal sign for smoking and said the phrase, "Good time pass." He then smiled at me yet again and brought out a pack of cigarettes, and proceeded to hand me one that was slightly wrinkled and shorter than all the rest. I flashed him an approving smile as I inspected it and noticed that it was oddly odorless.

Just then, the call for prayer goes off. There were loudspeakers all around the FOB, and they went off at all hours of the day and night. Dos leaves the fire and heads to the ANA tower close by where his ANA shift counterparts are hanging out. I suppose calling it a tower would be generous. It's more of a glorified telephone booth, reinforced with cement and sandbags. Anyway, prayer can be pretty lengthy at times because they often eat and drink immediately after, making the break last upwards of 20 minutes. I wait for about 10, lose my patience, and decide to walk a ways away from the Exit lane shack to smoke the spliff. I do this because it is not just me at my station as far as US personnel go. You are always paired with at least one other Soldier. The Soldier I was paired with was square and would not be let in on what I was about to do. I took out the spliff, looked it over again, and lit it up.

The flavor was not at all what I expected. It had a very light taste of Cannabis, but it mostly tasted like nothing and had essentially no odor. It burned far quicker than I anticipated and before I knew it, I had smoked the whole thing. A few minutes later, Dos returns from prayer and asks to smoke the spliff with me. I gestured to him that I already had it and that it was gone. His eyes became wide, and his jaw slightly dropped. It was the first and only time I ever saw an Afghan man display the expression of shock. I thought he might have been upset at first, but he simply took out his stash, rolled another one, and smoked it all to himself. There seemed to be no harm done, and we returned to the fire.

At this point in time, I hadn't really felt any effects from the spliff. Dos started a conversation about a recent gift that I had given him. On top of the $20 I handed him for the hash, I had also given him a pretty nice pair of bullet proof eye protection during our previous encounter when I arranged for him to bring me the hash, and I wanted him to accept it as a token of gratitude. I figured this was a great idea because the ANA are always trying to get our equipment and show particular interest in the eye protection we wear. Also, I had about 5 brand new pairs just sitting in my room and figured I wouldn't miss a pair. Dos starts this conversation with the fact that giving him those glasses was to be seen as shameful. This took me by complete surprise, and I was genuinely concerned as to why this was as he continued on with the explanation.

It was at this point that the spliff hit me. I received an extreme head rush. It was somewhat similar to the best high I had experienced up to that point, only greatly magnified. The rush kept getting more and more intense until my state of consciousness left the current situation and I was transported in my mind to a memory I hadn't thought of in years. It was the memory of the greatest play I ever made during my high school football career. It was late in the 4th quarter against Upper Arlington, our biggest rivalry team, the score tied, and I was playing defensive tackle. They had been killing our secondary with a simple five-step drop and lob play that their star receivers could easily catch over our uncharacteristically short corners. As a D-lineman, this play was particularly frustrating because there was next to nothing that I could do; the ball was away before I could put any pressure on the play, every time. So, I made the decision that the next time their offensive line stood straight up at the snap of the ball (which signified passing protection) I would make a quick glance to see which way their quarterback was looking, and I would sprint toward that sideline at a 45 degree angle. The ball snaps, the O-line stands straight up; it's that god damn play again. I see their QB is looking to his left, my right. I turn and sprint like a bat out of hell towards the right sideline. I'm careful not to trip over our linebackers and I look for their receiver that is running down the sideline ahead of me. I notice he is looking up into the air, signifying the ball had been thrown. I give it all that I've got, knowing full well that the only way this would work would be to run faster than I had ever run before in my life. The corner and receiver slow down for a moment as the ball comes down in their immediate vicinity. I adjust my route and aim for a few yards ahead of where they stall. The receiver goes up over our corner and tips the ball. They both come down and the ball makes a short hop back into the air, then falls back again towards the outstretched arms of their receiver. Our corner trips and falls during the landing while the receiver bobbles the ball one more time and then catches it. Their crowd goes wild, and he turns to run the remaining 20 yards towards their end zone to essentially win the game. I reach the receiver right as he turns to go downfield; I lower my shoulder and plow his scrawny ass towards the sideline. We both go airborne, and I make sure to use him as a landing pad as we both hit the ground. The receiver makes a loud and pitiful whimper from the force of my hit, hitting the ground, and being used as a landing pad. I immediately stand up, look down at him and triumphantly say "I don't think so". I turn to run back towards the soon to form defensive huddle, having prevented their winning score, and pretty much saving the game on instinct alone.

Right then, the rush fades, I regain awareness of where I am, feeling somewhat normal again. I notice Dos is staring at me having just finished his explanation of why my gift had brought him shame. I proceed to apologize and tell him that I zoned out and make a general wavy hand gesture around my head in the hopes that he understood. He gave me a head nod and proceeded to explain again why I had brought him shame, and again, legitimately caring, I try to listen. I make it a bit further into his explanation until I'm hit by another extreme head rush that rapidly escalates until my consciousness goes yet again to another distant memory within my subconscious.

This time, I'm in a crib and looking straight up at the ceiling. My crib is in the far corner of the room, and I glance through the crib bars over towards the two doorways in the opposite corner of the room to see that they are both empty. It's early evening, as is evident by the light coming through the blinds of the window next to the crib on my left. I either just woke up from sleeping, or suddenly stopped crying after a long bout of being upset because I have the feeling of having just emerged from a thick storm of black only to discover loneliness. I am overwhelmed by loneliness, and simply long to be held.

I snap back to reality. That rush didn't last nearly as long as the first, and again, I notice Dos staring at me having finished the second and apparently shorter explanation of why I had brought him shame. Feeling even worse, I try to apologize, only this time he gets up and walks away to his ANA buddies. I really wanted to hear that explanation, but I will never know because after he walked away, neither of us ever brought it up again.

As for the effects of the spliff... Well... I continued on a roller coaster of head rushes for the next half hour or so, but each one was less intense than the last, and only the first two had... well, I guess they can be labeled as out of body experiences. (Damn, now that I think about it, there's probably a good chance that there was more than just Hash in that cigarette. Dos did mention doing Heroin before, and it may be possible he laced it with that or some other readily available opiate from the surrounding area. I didn't want to let him know just how hard it had hit me. I never asked him, so I suppose I'll never know.) Once the head rushes stopped, I experienced the traditional high feeling normally felt from smoking weed, only far more intense, and it lasted every bit of four hours. During that time, I wisely decided that I would never do it again during my duty shift. And there was only one notable incident that happened during those four hours. The incident was a visit from the NCOIC of the Base Defense Operations Center (BDOC). I was already familiar with how much of a complete asshole this guy was due to hearing him bitch out Soldiers over the radio during Tower Guard shifts. When he pulled up, I could tell that he was particularly pissed off. From the moment he and his subordinate Soldier stepped out of their truck, he was griping at how he could not believe they came all the way out there and his subordinate forgot it. It turned out to be a memo stating that a certain local national with ID# so and so was permitted to take wood off base for a carpentry project that would benefit his village. Simple. But holy shit was this guy digging into his subordinate's ass. He used every swear word in the book putting this guy down. What started as mild entertainment turned into me realizing as the Exit Lane NCO, I would have to intervene and actually speak coherent sentences despite my current state of mind. Somehow, I managed to get out something along the lines of me knowing exactly who he was, and that if he cared enough about this Afghan coming off base with said wood so much that he came all the way down here to let me know; I did not need a memo. I stated I would take note of the Local National's name and ID# and permit him to leave base with said wood when I would have otherwise confiscated it without a proper memo authorizing its removal. I must have spoken well enough because he did not appear to suspect anything. In fact, he didn't say anything to acknowledge what I had just said. He just continued to lecture his subordinate as they both climbed back into the truck and drove off. Holy shit was I thankful for my dark eye protection right then. Bullet proof, indeed.

After that duty day was complete, thanks to Dos, I had my own stash of Hash. I developed a plan of execution to smoke it again during the upcoming evenings that I shared with my Platoon Sergeant.

(Quick Rant) Now my Platoon Sergeant was the one that was supposed to be in charge of the office and all the other Soldiers. But from the get-go, it became fairly obvious that he gave no fucks about actually doing his job as the Platoon Sergeant. I was first annoyed and frustrated with this, since this also translated into him making poor decisions when making the duty roster for our Soldiers. I confronted him about it, and he pulled the old 'if you think you can do better, you do it' number. So I did. And I did. The duty schedule was flawless despite constant adversity, and I unofficially took over his leadership responsibilities as well. Like I said, I was pretty sour about the whole thing, but I would later learn that this was his fifth deployment, with two of the five being yearlong tours to Iraq, and this was only my second. I would probably be acting very similar had I been forced to come over here five times. Eff that noise. Also, it was my first real acquisition of legitimate leadership responsibility. I rose to the occasion, proved my worth, and my superiors noticed. In a way, I owe him. He may claim that was his plan all along, but… I call bullshit… Mostly.)

During our time in the office at JAF, we had become good friends, and would usually hang out after the duty day in his room and watched some TV shows saved on his external hard drive. Now, we could throw Hash into the mix, and make the experience that much better. Our plan of smoking it eventually evolved to be pretty bold.

Our equipment was mounted on the back of an Armored Humvee that had to be placed and removed via crane within our fenced-in compound. The truck sat in the same place for 9 months, and was generally out of sight and airtight, making it the perfect hot box. We would climb in, take out our wine Black & Milds which we had just mixed in with hash a few minutes earlier, and smoke them right there in the Humvee as we watched people walk by the fence of our compound less than six feet away. Once we were done, one person would get out, give the all clear to the other and head back to his room, while the other usually got out and cracked one of the windows open before smoking a cigarette to mask the escaping smell and then went back to his room. Considering we were never caught, the process worked. This was the way it went until it was time to pull our equipment out and head home. We must have done this around 20 times or so and every time was a success without incident, with the exception of one.

The one night… The one night I've been leading up to this whole time. Everything was going as planned, he got out first, I followed a few minutes later. I climbed out, cracked the window and silently closed the door and lit a cigarette. I was about to turn around and head over to join my Platoon Sergeant who was waiting for me on the other side of our building when I heard a voice. I didn't physically hear it, like you would hear a person speaking to you a few feet away. It was an intense whisper inside my head. I heard the sounds of cymbals crashing twice, a bird's caw, (though I'm not sure what kind of bird) and my name., 'BRUUUUUUUCCCEEEEEE'. I froze. I was unable to see myself, but I'm pretty certain that I turned a pale white. I looked around, and there was no one. I dare not say anything in return, and then figured that it was my Platoon Sergeant playing a prank on me. I turned and walked over to him on the other side of a small wooden hut where our satellite equipment was housed. I asked him if he had said anything just now or heard anything. He said he hadn't, and then noticed that I looked shaken. I made him swear that he was not in fact messing with me, and he swore that he was not. I described what happened, and he gave me a half smile saying that maybe I had heard a ghost. I chuckled and suggested we go back to his room to watch our shows and retire for the evening.

And that was it. It has yet to happen again, and after some research into the effects of Hash, it is not uncommon for users to experience auditory hallucinations. But that's what gets me. The voice was inside my mind. We can all think to ourselves using sentences in our heads, but nothing is heard. This was nothing even close to what it's like to do that. It was hearing without hearing. I can't really describe it in any other way.

After I left his room and went back to my own later that evening, I laid down in my bed and just thought. Thought about how strange the events of that night had been and how nothing like this had ever happened to me. And then I realized... *that's not entirely true*. In fact, that's just plain incorrect. Strange things have happened to me when I was younger. It had been over ten years since something strange like this rocked me to my core. I hadn't forgotten them... I just... hadn't thought of them in a long while. The Army has a way of preoccupying your life to the point where it's all you do. But why here, and why now? These were the thoughts that ran through my head as I fell asleep, putting a cap on that particular evening.

Now, the events that happened when I was younger... I've told a few people about it. Some find them fascinating, and some shrug it off as me making things up to try and get them going. I've never actually written about these particular instances, but I assure you that they are true.

I would love to get into them now, but I am pretty done writing for the evening, seeing as how my hand is starting to cramp, and its pretty much time for dinner. I'll most likely pick up where I left off tomorrow.

JUNE 19, 2013

It is day three of the returning home through Bagram stint, and we are no closer to getting a flight out of here. This means I pretty much have the entire day to write, or at least, as much as my hand can take. I suppose I will get used to this after a while.

The happenings in my childhood… There were two. I want to say there was a third, possibly even more, but for the life of me, I cannot remember any more right now. The first happened right after the only party I ever threw in my house while my parents were away. I want to say that they all went on a road trip for a baseball tournament for my younger brother, and for some reason I stayed behind. I believe it was because I was working at a video store at the time and couldn't get off work. It was *the* only time I was ever home alone over a weekend during my entire youth, and you know I'm going to throw a party!

At the time, I was under 21, so I had a co-worker at the video store buy about $100 worth of booze from Sam's Club. The party itself wasn't really noteworthy... We did the usual things; swam in the above ground pool in the backyard, jumped off the roof into said pool, played pool on my stepfathers pool table, and got wasted until all the booze was gone. Someone did end up breaking one of the pool cues, which I addressed the next day; it was nothing some wood glue and paint couldn't handle. The evening ended when a fight broke out in my basement, and I got fed up with the stress of hosting and kicked everyone out right after that.

The next morning, I spent several hours cleaning up after the party, searching everywhere so as not to miss any empties that would have given me away. I mean, I looked EVERYWHERE. And I'm glad I did, because I found a full bottle of beer behind a bunch of food in the freezer of the fridge in my garage. Someone thought they would be an ass and hid it there knowing that it would explode, and my parents would find it one day, and I would get in trouble. Some friends I had. But the event I'm getting to happened at the end of clean-up.

All of the empty cans and bottles that I found, I put on the dining room table as I went along. Once I was

100% sure that I had looked absolutely everywhere and there were none left, I put them all in a large, black and thick trash bag, and tied that sucker tight. I then proceeded to thoroughly wipe down the table to be rid of all the sticky residue that may have been left behind by the empties. Once that was done, I wiped the table with a dry cloth, and put everything that belonged on top of the table back in its place and proceeded to head out to my car to put the trash bag in my trunk to be taken to a dumpster out of sight from my parents, thus leaving zero proof that anything had ever happened while they were away. When I closed my trunk, and went back inside my house, I noticed there was one single empty bottle sitting in the middle of my dining room table. I stopped dead in my tracks and stared at that single bottle for a good five minutes. Had I left one bottle behind? No.. I don't think I did… When I wiped down the table, I removed everything from it. Is it possible I left one thing behind? No way. There was absolutely nothing left on that table.. I wiped it from end to end without any obstructions… I am absolutely 100% sure I did not leave it there.. I put every one of the empties in the trash bag… Waves of adrenaline surged through my body, and I got goosebumps just as I had when I heard the voice in the Stan. I've got them even now as I write this down and do every time that I tell this story to anyone. I don't really go around broadcasting this story, but every now and then at a party or in general conversation, the topic can touch upon ghosts, or the paranormal, or whatever. I would like to add to the conversation with this story. I don't really know what else to say about it… That shit happened. And I did not leave it on the table. Blows my mind.

Now, I used to readily tell this story to most new people that I befriend, at least, eventually. But one of my good college friends, whom I still consider to be one of my best friends, changed that. While being intelligent and athletic, like myself, he was also these things in a different way. He was very skinny, Indian, (the ooh-ooh kind, not the oooh-ooh kind; tapping a finger between our eyes for the first ooh-ooh, and patting an open mouth for the second, as went our joke) and the kind to go on to get a P.H.D. He tried to solve this story using the scientific method. Maybe one of your friends snuck back in and put it there when you weren't looking… Maybe you just put it there and you forgot it… No. Just no… I fucking know I didn't forget to grab it, and I was THE ONLY person in that house for the entire day. I mean, I understand where he's coming from. I place high value in logic and deductive reasoning and apply it to solve most problems and I experience great success in all aspects of life. However, as much as I hate to admit it, there are some things that science cannot explain. This event is silly. It's simple. But that doesn't change the fact that I cannot come up with a logical explanation as to how it happened.

That was the first incident. The second happened while everyone was home. I was in my room, and my Mom had brought up some of my clean clothes from the laundry room, and placed them on my bed. I went to hang them up, but per the usual, I had zero hangers on the rack in my closet. When gathering our dirty clothes to take down to the laundry room, she liked to grab all of our spare hangers so she could hang them up after they were dry down in the laundry room. Again, zero hangers in my closet. Double checked. I then went out of my room, made a left towards my brother's room at the end of the hallway, and found him sitting at his desk working on some homework. I asked him if it was alright if I took a few hangers to hang up some clothes Mom had just brought up. He didn't care. I looked through his closet only to find that he too had no hangers. Mom had cleaned us out, meaning I would have to either go down to the laundry room and retrieve some, or put them away folded into my dressers. I went with the lazy latter and headed back to my room. When I got there, there were two hangers on my bed, propped up and leaning against each other, like a teepee. Again, I froze. What the hell? And again, I retraced the events that had just happened. Had I left those hangers on the bed? No.. You had none. You double checked that shit. Possibly someone came up in your room while you were in your brothers room… I went downstairs to investigate the three other people present in the household. My sister was in her room playing boy band music as loud as my parents would allow, doing I don't care what, and Mom was busy doing dishes while my Stepdad was in the basement mostly likely with a beer in his hand, watching some baseball game. Just to double tap, I asked my Mom if she had recently gone upstairs and left some hangers on my bed. Looking kind of puzzled, she said she hadn't. And it wasn't my brother, because I had eyes on the whole time. All family members eliminated. Queue the adrenaline and goosebumps.

Now, I also told this story to my Indian friend, and he replied with the same in the box thinking… Your mom must have put them there, or you put them there and forgot you did. No... No man.. there's no way. I can't explain how that happened. I can't explain how either of these things happened. And neither can you. He would go on to insist I was wrong, and I had to drop the topic because he was seriously starting to piss me off. The fact of these matters is that I do not know how either happened.

And that's it... I'm not saying these events are related to what happened that one night in the Stan. They're all strange, and years apart between them all. I don't know. I try not to let it bother me. The main conclusion I tell myself is that I get so deep in thought sometimes that I completely forget what I was doing just moments before and find I have no memory of it when I try to remember. *That*, is the most logical explanation. But deep down, I know it's not true. I don't have the answers, and I probably never will. Really, it's not a big deal. I mean most ghost stories you see on TV make these events look like farts in the wind. Oh well...

I've been trying to remember the third thing, and I just did. Well, there's actually three more things to mention. The first of the last three was a dream I had. I don't remember how old I was, or any other detail that would be useful. But it was a dream unlike any other I've had, and all I remember is a snapshot, maybe five seconds of it. As is common knowledge, a majority of dreams cannot be remembered once a person wakes up, and memories of dreams that you can remember fade by the minute the longer you are awake. This dream, however, I will never forget. I was in a park, sitting on a bench. A booming sound, or voice came out of the sky and seemed to penetrate my mind. There were no words, or sounds that I could identify… It was similar to the sound that would be produced playing a few seconds of a dozen different songs all once, as loud as you could imagine. It was so loud that it startled me at first, and then paralyzed me with fear as I shrank under the park bench and got into the fetal position. I'm not sure if I woke up immediately after, but I do remember that scene going black, and I'm not sure what happened from there.

The second thing that I just remembered was that I once woke up underneath the bottom bunk of a bunkbed when I slept on the top. This was when my older sister was still living with us, and my younger brother and I were sharing the same room. I don't have a history of sleepwalking, and this only ever happened once. Kind of strange I suppose… I don't know. I just remember being really confused, waking up my brother to ask him if anything had just happened, and he looked at me, and rolled over.

And the last thing is less of an event, and more of an ongoing characteristic that resurfaces from time to time. The best way to put it is.. I know things. I'll know when a certain song is playing on the radio, or I'll just know what is being served for lunch one day without any prior knowledge. It's kind of a sixth sense I suppose but it's not always active. Although sometimes I also get a strange feeling from this sixth sense, and it ends up being wrong. I don't know. It kind of sounds like any other idea anyone has ever had about something.. either it will be right, or it will be wrong. Fifty/fifty. But I did bring it up to my mother when I was on leave from the Army one holiday weekend. I told her for the first time about the bottle and the hangers, and that I get feelings sometimes about things impossible to know. She smiled at me and said that sometimes she gets them too. Apparently, whatever it is that I have, is passed down on my mother's side, because she went on to explain that Grandma also has it. That was kind of odd to hear her say, because Grandma is getting pretty old now, and it's hard to imagine her being anything other than on the verge of senility. But the one story of her own that she did share with me was interesting.

My mother once had a dream about a bridge collapsing, and people dying from the event. The very next day, a bridge collapsed in Cincinnati Ohio, The Silver Bridge. Just looked it up, it was in 1967, which would have made her ten years old. She mentioned that it was linked to the Mothman Prophecies. I'm familiar with them, and it's somewhat interesting, but I take ghost stories with a grain of salt, as well as all other similar things. Most of the time, people are just making them up to become published or famous. Some of the Ghost based TV shows out there are so lame that it's any wonder that they get any viewers at all. Science is the language of life, and it explains things far better than religion can. Science goes hand in hand with logic, my favorite problem-solving tool. But, upon rare occasions, it doesn't explain everything. And I've been fortunate enough to have first-hand experience on some of these things. Granted, they are small and trivial I suppose, but any authentic brush with the supernatural, paranormal, or unexplainable, is a gift. Very few people I have encountered can share stories similar to mine. And when I do find someone, we usually end up becoming good friends.

Oh! I just remembered a great example of my sixth sense at work.. New Years Eve, two years ago, my wife and I were in Columbus, OH, visiting a different college friend of mine. We pre-gamed at his place, and then went out around 10pm or so to find the right bar to be in when the ball dropped. We left his place, crossed the street and started down the sidewalk towards our car that was parked two blocks further. On the way, we passed an oncoming group of three twenty-something year olds headed in the opposite direction. My wife and I, clearly holding hands, clearly "together" to any bystander, heard the lead male say (to my wife) "Hey baby, you are looking good tonight. You should come on home with me." This was the first time anything like that had ever happened to me (us) before. It was like a scene from some movie. I was a half second from telling this guy off when I stopped. I was overcome by the strong feeling that he had a concealed weapon. I could visualize this guy pulling out a gun from his jacket and pointing it at me. I broke eye contact with the group and kept walking and holding my wife's hand.

A part of me will always regret that decision. This punk thinks he's all big and bad saying shit like that, and I let him get away with it just so he can do it again to someone else. It wasn't a matter of being outnumbered three to one. That's not it at all. I consider myself to be a pretty humble person and will always be the last to toot my own horn, but trust me, I had their asses. All of them. I'm 6'2", 280, solid muscle. I can sprint like the wind, bench over 400 lbs, and have taken quite a liking to the Modern Army Combatives Program, which is basically mixed-martial arts. I've fought at least a hundred different people, and only lost twice. (The first loss was to an enormous black John Coffee mother fucker that made me feel like an infant, and the second was to some crotchety Special Forces Sergeant Major that turned out to be a third degree black belt in Jiu Jitsu; he couldn't tap me out, but he did beat me 20 points to zero) Everyone else, I dominate with ease. But that feeling I got was so sudden and strong that I literally could not ignore it. I'll never know if I was right.

Hand starting to cramp. That's enough for today.

Ok I lied, one last update. Just received word that our flight leaves tomorrow! We will fly to Manas Air Force Base in Kyrgyzstan, which still sounds bad I suppose, but it's significant because it's not a war zone, and we don't have to walk around in fear that a mortar or RPG could land next to you at any moment. Once there, we will wait yet again for another flight, but this time, it will be the flight that takes us back to the U.S. My wife Michelle, and my two-year-old, Colin, will be waiting for me. Not going to lie, I'm most likely going to cry. I've tried to convince her to teach him how to do a "big hug", where she puts him on the ground, and he runs up to me for a hug.. but we'll see how that goes.

JUNE 20, 2013

It is now night-time in Kyrgyzstan. Our flight here went off without a hitch. This is significant, at least to me, for two reasons. The first being our plane was not a commercial passenger plane built for comfort and ease. This was an Air Force passenger plane. On the inside, there is absolutely nothing there designed to ease your mind. The average person takes commercial airliners for granted. You don't see all the wires and lines, and the skeleton of the plane. It's all hidden from sight. But the Air Force cares not for your peace of mind. You literally see all of the internal workings of the plane right up to where the wings are welded to the backbone of the plane's frame. Also, commercial airlines fly gently and minimize discomfort felt from takeoff, landing, and also during flight. Not the case in the Air Force. Takeoffs and landings are quite steep, as well as the midflight turns, especially at lower altitudes. I mean, of course this is all necessary due to having to mitigate the risk of being shot down by the enemy, but still.. It doesn't help my secret fear of dying in a plane crash. These differences may not sound like a big deal to some, but for me it's a reminder of my mortality and all the systems in place that could fail at any time. Plus, if that were to happen, it would literally happen before my eyes. The other reason getting here safely is a big deal has to do with something that happened in history. On December 12, 1985, fellow 101st Airborne Soldiers were flying from Cairo, back to Ft. Campbell, with two stops along the way in West Germany, and Canada. Well, shortly after taking off from Canada on their way to Ft. Campbell, the plane stalled, and crashed about a half mile from the runway, killing all 248 Soldiers on board, as well as 8 crew members. There is a memorial on base dedicated to all the people that lost their lives on this flight in line with gate 4. You go in gate 4, and about a mile later, the road splits and there is a field in the middle with rows of trees neatly planted. Each victim had a tree planted in their honor, complete with a plaque at the base with their name on it, and a small American flag posted into the ground next to it. For me, this always serves as a grim reminder that your deployment, no matter where, is not over until you touchdown back home.

This time around, since we are on our way home, we are allowed to visit the local bar on this base and have two beers. Every military member that visits this bar is limited to two beers. Considering I haven't had any alcohol for nine months, they gave me a decent buzz that I complimented with my last few cigarettes before I have to go cold turkey. Michelle would leave me if I became a smoker. (Notice how the word "probably" is not in the previous sentence.) Outside of the bar one can find pool tables, ping pong tables, and cornhole boards... This is an actual overseas location where Air Force members are often deployed. And to think that some of them write home about how hard their lives are or something of the like. Get the fuck out of here! This place doesn't see any action... EVER. I mean, I'm not going to pretend to be some combat hardened bad ass, but still. We took incoming regularly. AND, we were attacked at JAF on December 2, 2012. The worst thing these Airmen see here is their dining facility running out of their favorite candy bar. Hahahahaha, I'm mostly kidding. I mean, there's some truth to what I'm saying here, but I respect our other branches, and do not hold one over the other. We all need each other and support each other. Plus, each branch has its fair share of bad asses. Case in point: I have seen some unbelievably fit Airmen during my career. Granted they have the freedom to work-out on their own and have free reign to improve upon their weaknesses, but still. Some of them can run circles around people in the Army that would consider themselves to be in good shape.

So, the attack on December 2... at JAF, at exactly 0600 in the morning, there is a ground shaking explosion that seemingly hits the wall right outside where I sleep. I wasn't supposed to be getting up for another half hour, but I got up anyway, put on all of my combat gear, grabbed my M4, and walked out of my room for accountability. We were all staying in a hard building as opposed to the wooden huts most had to stay in a little down the way. I always thought of it as an old dorm building from the 70s or something. It had hot running showers, nice toilets, and two to a decent sized room. We were living large. Anyway, we all stay by our rooms until 100% accountability is established, and then proceed to head outside towards the on-base marketplace, which we were tasked with guarding during attacks. There had been machine gun fire from our side, going your deployment, no matter where, is not over until you touchdown back home.

This time around, since we are on our way home, we are allowed to visit the local bar on this base and have two beers. Every military member that visits this bar is limited to two beers. Considering I haven't had any alcohol for nine months, they gave me a decent buzz that I complimented with my last few cigarettes before I have to go cold turkey. Michelle would leave me if I became a smoker. (Notice how the word "probably" is not in the previous sentence.) Outside of the bar one can find pool tables, ping pong tables, and cornhole boards… This is an actual overseas location where Air Force members are often deployed. And to think that some of them write home about how hard their lives are or something of the like. Get the fuck out of here! This place doesn't see any action… EVER. I mean, I'm not going to pretend to be some combat hardened bad ass, but still. We took incoming regularly. AND, we were attacked at JAF on December 2, 2012. The worst thing these Airmen see here is their dining facility running out of their favorite candy bar. Hahahahaha, I'm mostly kidding. I mean, there's some truth to what I'm saying here, but I respect our other branches, and do not hold one over the other. We all need each other and support each other. Plus, each branch has its fair share of bad asses. Case in point: I have seen some unbelievably fit Airmen during my career. Granted they have the freedom to work-out on their own and have free reign to improve upon their weaknesses, but still. Some of them can run circles around people in the Army that would consider themselves to be in good shape.

So, the attack on December 2... at JAF, at exactly 0600 in the morning, there is a ground shaking explosion that seemingly hits the wall right outside where I sleep. I wasn't supposed to be getting up for another half hour, but I got up anyway, put on all of my combat gear, grabbed my M4, and walked out of my room for accountability. We were all staying in a hard building as opposed to the wooden huts most had to stay in a little down the way. I always thought of it as an old dorm building from the 70s or something. It had hot running showers, nice toilets, and two to a decent sized room. We were living large. Anyway, we all stay by our rooms until 100% accountability is established, and then proceed to head outside towards the on-base marketplace, which we were tasked with guarding during attacks. There had been machine gun fire from our side, going out for a bit over by the explosion, but it had since stopped as we ran to the marketplace. Once there, we spread out among the buildings and looked to the sky to watch the already flying attack helicopters. They were heading across the airstrip, towards the opposite side of the base where the Special Forces compound is located. Just then, another massive explosion, much larger than the first, goes off at the ECP site. I would find out later that it was a fuel truck that had been driven into the old ECP truck entrance gate with hopes that it would be destroyed, but it easily withstood the blast. This left the Special Forces compound entry gate as the only other way onto base from that side. From where we were in the marketplace, we couldn't see anything going on on the ground, so we turned our eyes skyward and watched the helicopters work. They were laying out long .50 caliber strafing runs in front of the SF compound, along with firing hellfire missiles. With each explosion and gun run, we cheered and flashed huge smiles at one another. The fight lasted about 45 minutes, and it was later reported that 13 or so Taliban, armed with suicide vests, entered the SF compound and each one detonated their vests. There was one ANA fatality and two ANA wounded, zero American deaths or wounded. The best part, however, was seeing the arrival of an Air Force A-10 Warthog. We beckoned for it to do anything lethal, but it just screamed by a few times as a show of force. Now, I personally think that reporting this attack having only 13 Taliban involved is a lie. It would have taken at least 20 to pull off what they tried. Granted, they were all mowed down.. but still.. The first explosion that acted as a diversion had to have at least 4 involved. This can be assumed because I heard machine gun fire for several minutes after the initial explosion coming from one of the guard towers. What were they firing at? A burning vehicle? Unlikely. And then on the other side there were at least 12 that made it through the gate and onto the base before killing themselves via their suicide vests. I could be wrong, but I'm fairly certain that I'm not... Why lie about that sort of thing? What is there to gain from putting out false information? Especially when the actual number is only off by 10 or less... Makes no sense to me. But that was actually not the first lie I stumbled upon.

The other lie I came across was one of a larger and more significant nature. I heard it from a contractor while I was having a "thank you lunch" one day. I call it a "thank you lunch" because that was about the only thing that I could do to repay him. At one point during the deployment, a few key leaders were sent to Bagram to attend a training session on some equipment. I was one of those key leaders. We left, spent a few days there, and came back. Now weight is a very important consideration for aerial vehicles; especially for helicopters, which was our mode of transport to and from Bagram for this shindig. If there is too much weight to be put on the bird, either the passenger, or his luggage, will be put on the next flight out. This exact circumstance happened to me. My main backpack, with all my electronics and toiletries got placed on another flight on my way back to JAF from Bagram. I didn't find this out until after we landed, from the Crew Chief. He informed me when the next flight was coming in, and I returned to the landing pad when it did, only to find that my bag was not among the pile of luggage that was sitting there, having already been taken off the flight. I was crushed. I was looking at a potential loss of hundreds of dollars' worth of electronics, and my main mode of communicating with my wife back home, besides using a telephone in the base USO. This contractor, saw me standing there… he approached me and asked if I had lost a camo backpack. (Most backpacks are camo, but the gear that was sitting there was mostly tan, commonly used by contractors) I told him that I had, and he led me to a random spot not too far from the landing pad in-between some buildings where some additional bags had been brought, and my bag was among them. This guy had just saved my ass. It was only a matter of time before someone took it and claimed it as their own. So, I thanked him by doing the only thing that I could think of... having a meal together.

The contractor turned out to be a fairly interesting guy. He had been at JAF for over 5 years, making 300k a year. He was headed back home soon to his wife to take a few years off, the lucky bastard. I'd love to spend a few years doing nothing with over seven digits in my bank account. Who wouldn't? But then again, he earned it being out here. These contractors get paid what they do because so few are willing to accept such harsh work conditions. But the thing about it that really chaps my ass is I'm out here too, with the added responsibility of pulling the trigger should the occasion come, and our government pays me 10% of what civilians are making. That is just downright bullshit. I wonder if people actually care about that gross inequality. Many Americans are stuck on which celebrity had a nip slip or is going through rehab or about local sports teams to care or realize what they do not know about on a daily basis. But that's a topic for another time...Back to the lie.... So being there for five years allowed this contractor to run into a wide variety of both military personnel and other contractors. He told me about a time that he spoke with a Special Forces member who shared with him, which was quite literally, Top Secret information. Apparently, this SF member, along with his squad, had gone out in search of Osama Bin Laden, physically spotted him, aka had weapons pointed at his person, ready to kill on command, and were ordered to stand down... AND, the SF member knew that it had happened more than once. When he told me this, I was.. pretty shocked. This is big time. President Obama would be in on this, and probably was involved in the decision to stand down. Why?? Bin Laden was public enemy #1, or at least so he was labeled. What the fuck were we waiting for? Was it not a convenient time for him?? (I suppose it is possible that our leaders had the safety of the men on the mission in mind and they may have thought that they would not have been able to safely return. But to that, I also call bullshit; I have seen firsthand and up close, the skills, technologies, and capabilities of American Special

Forces, and it is without a doubt, one of the greatest forces ever known to man.) That information just blew my mind, but eventually the most logical conclusion that I came to was that they would have it happen at a time that would most likely benefit President Obama in terms of getting re-elected. Politicians, regardless of level, are involved in some pretty shady and secretive business. Unfortunately, this has become the norm. I'm sure there are scores of conspiracies and cover-ups that we simply do not know about. That was the main highlight of that "lunch". I thanked him for his deed, and never saw him again.

… One last thought on that Bin Laden information… If the U.S. put so much emphasis on hunting this man down and going to the extent of creating an entire war campaign just to find this guy using the guise of "eliminating terror" and we don't complete the mission given the opportunity…. There is obviously a hidden agenda that our government doesn't want us to know about.. Which means it can be assumed that hidden agendas exist on other war campaigns as well. Hell, it doesn't even have to be limited to war campaigns… Pretty much anything the government tries to do as a supposed service for the American public could and through rehab or about local sports teams to care or realize what they do not know about on a daily basis. But that's a topic for another time…Back to the lie…. So being there for five years allowed this contractor to run into a wide variety of both military personnel and other contractors. He told me about a time that he spoke with a Special Forces member who shared with him, which was quite literally, Top Secret information. Apparently, this SF member, along with his squad, had gone out in search of Osama Bin Laden, physically spotted him, aka had weapons pointed at his person, ready to kill on command, and were ordered to stand down… AND, the SF member knew that it had happened more than once. When he told me this, I was.. pretty shocked. This is big time. President Obama would be in on this, and probably was involved in the decision to stand down. Why?? Bin Laden was public enemy #1, or at least so he was labeled. What the fuck were we waiting for? Was it not a convenient time for him?? (I suppose it is possible that our leaders had the safety of the men on the mission in mind and they may have thought that they would not have been able to safely return. But to that, I also call bullshit; I have seen firsthand and up close, the skills, technologies, and capabilities of American Special

Forces, and it is without a doubt, one of the greatest forces ever known to man.) That information just blew my mind, but eventually the most logical conclusion that I came to was that they would have it happen at a time that would most likely benefit President Obama in terms of getting re-elected. Politicians, regardless of level, are involved in some pretty shady and secretive business. Unfortunately, this has become the norm. I'm sure there are scores of conspiracies and cover-ups that we simply do not know about. That was the main highlight of that "lunch". I thanked him for his deed, and never saw him again.

… One last thought on that Bin Laden information… If the U.S. put so much emphasis on hunting this man down and going to the extent of creating an entire war campaign just to find this guy using the guise of "eliminating terror" and we don't complete the mission given the opportunity…. There is obviously a hidden agenda that our government doesn't want us to know about.. Which means it can be assumed that hidden agendas exist on other war campaigns as well. Hell, it doesn't even have to be limited to war campaigns… Pretty much anything the government tries to do as a supposed service for the American public could and most likely does have a hidden objective that goes unknown to the American people. I hate the fact that I just wrote that down. I am a proud American citizen, and love to live free, especially considering what the state of living is like over in the Stan… But come on… America didn't always used to be like this. We were founded by the thoughts and efforts of great minds and leaders many years ago that wouldn't have dreamed of doing some of the things our government currently does. Greed and power have driven those that already have it to seek more. And then it just so happens that these people also have to make important decisions concerning the welfare of our great nation and have allowed their judgement to become poisoned. If our current leaders create massive campaigns costing millions to billions of tax dollars, not to mention American lives, and base said campaign around a clear-cut end goal, and then choose to NOT accomplish said goal when given the opportunity, then something is wrong. The current system we have in place has become corrupt. Instead of closing the file, or pushing the "complete button", if you will, to end a mission, our leaders turn to see how they can acquire more personal gain from the situation at hand, instead of keeping promises, and following through on a mission with pride and mother fucking dignity. And if the system is here to stay, then we need a whole new breed of leaders. The kind with vision and morals. Leaders independent from corruption and who genuinely have the betterment of the country as their main objective. Leaders that will say NO to the temptation of corporate greed and the allure of incentives from those that would seek to influence decisions that should be made by the leader and the leader alone. Leaders of the caliber of those that founded our country. I've no idea what needs to be done, but it's got to be something.

Alright, I'm done with my rant. It's getting late, and most everyone in my tent is asleep. Hand cramping like hell yet again. Possibly more tomorrow.

JUNE 20, 2013

Three topics to write about... Firstly, good news! Our flight to the US leaves tomorrow! But it's very early tomorrow, so we will technically begin the process tonight.

Secondly, there was an aspect of the flight from Bagram to here sort of worth mentioning... War trophies. A term used to describe souvenirs that in some way reflect the conflict going on in the Stan. They come in many shapes and sizes, and I'm sad to say that I had to leave both of my better ones behind. The first was a piece of shrapnel from a Taliban mortar. At one point, a mortar landed about 40 yards from where I sleep, and about a quarter sized chunk flew up and got lodged in a nearby cement wall. You could see round spiral grooves on the fragment and could tell that it was once part of a disc shaped piece of metal. That baby would have been a perfect little memento. I tried to pry it out with my multi-tool, but it had been so hot when it hit the wall that it fused itself to it and made it very difficult to retrieve without specialized tools. By the time I left and found something that may have been able to do the job, it had already been removed by someone else. (Most likely performed by some intelligence Soldier with part of their job being to collect things like that.) After all, things like this are technically illegal, at least in the eyes of the Army. My other decent object was an 8' by 6' map that was classified SECRET. It was just a map of the Stan, and every U.S. base in the country. In the hands of the Taliban, it wouldn't have really been *that* useful. When you're there, it's pretty obvious where we are stationed. Just look for the giant cement walls and guard towers with Americans in them. Not rocket science.. But still, being caught with a map like that could have ended my career. The mortar shard they never would have found, but all it would have taken is a curious x-ray tech to wonder what the large paper object was in my bag. Wasn't worth the risk.. So I took it out and dropped it in the amnesty box right before the baggage search. I was pretty disappointed. Some of my Soldiers were bold enough to smuggle hash back in their bags. Not in the bags that went on the flight mind you…

There are definitely drug and bomb dogs that go through all of our shit. They put it in their spare bags that got put in large metal equipment containers to be shipped by boat back to America. They wouldn't see it for months. Though, even these bags were supposed to be inspected item by item by customs inspectors prior to being sealed. That took some balls. A risk I would never take.

The third thing is a thought I had last night after finishing my entry… Why am I writing in this journal? Because of a dream? That's ridiculous. I can't deny that I have enjoyed just writing down the thoughts and feelings that come. And reading over them again is somewhat enjoyable as well. But why? It all seems pointless. A couple of my Soldiers have already called me out on it. They have apparently noticed me writing in this thing at night and have jokingly started calling me "The Frank". I suppose that requires some explanation.. In the military, everyone is generally referred to by their last names. This is because it is our last name that appears on our uniform, and the last name is generally more unique than a first name. (I don't really know, I made that up, but it does make sense) Anyway, my formal title is Sergeant Bruce. Some people think they are clever by calling me "The Bruce", as a reference to the character from the movie "Braveheart". Great movie, not that funny of a reference. So swap out Anne Frank's last name with my usual nickname, and they have a new running joke that is, I will admit, funnier than "The Bruce". People's opinions usually don't get to me, but in this case, I think I'm tending to agree with them. Besides, it's much easier and faster just to hold conversations with people. I could read aloud everything I've written here in minutes compared to the hours I've spent making my hand ache. The fate of this notebook is kaput. This will most likely be my last entry. There is some incriminating shit in here, so I suppose I will keep it to be burned when I get a chance. To quote Stewie Griffon, "Fare thee well, Broccoli!"

JUNE 21, 2013

I have decided to change my mind about this notebook in light of a new discovery.... While getting our bags searched a second time (I am currently writing this on the plane while flying to our first stop in Germany) the Airmen searching through my bag picked up this notebook, briefly flipped through it, and tossed it back to the pile of things that were pulled out of my duffle bag and moved on to inspect the next bag. When it landed, the back cover popped open and exposed the back page. When I bent down to pick it up and close the back cover, I noticed there was some writing in it that I had never seen before. Someone had written a short little blurb on the back page in some Arabic language. Shit! I dream about a book after experiencing some strange shit in the desert only to find there's a message in it that can be easily read by many in a place I've already left. I scanned through it for anything I recognized, and then I saw it. My name. The word "Bruce" appeared towards the bottom of the inscription. The Arabic part of the inscription looked flawless. I'm no Arabic expert, but I've seen my fair share of signs with English and an Arabic translation written as well, and it's fairly noticeable when the writing is messy. This was crisp and seemingly flawless. My name, however, was not. The letters of my name were sloppy and unconfident when compared to the rest of the writing. I think it's safe to say that the person that wrote the passage was not proficient in English. But that's not the point. The point is this: I heard a voice in the desert and dreamt I would find this notebook which apparently already had my name written in it. That's it. I'm writing. Whatever happens or will happen. After I heard the voice, I was so sure I would hear it again, or something else would happen, but nothing ever did. That can only mean that whatever is going to happen hasn't happened yet. It's going to happen… back home. My family… Holy shit, what will I tell my wife?? She's going to think I've lost my mind. I have no idea what I'm going to do. I need a moment to think.

I've come up with a general plan of action. I will continue to write when I can. If my wife pries, I will tell her that it's just something I picked up over in the Stan to help deal with stress and PTSD or some bullshit. If she asks to read it, I will tell her that I wouldn't mind if she did, but I want a bit more time to make more entries to make it worth her while to read. If things stay normal, the entries will taper off I guess, and I suppose I will stop writing. If they do not, obviously, I will continue to write. Priority #1 will be to find someone that can read whatever's written on the back. I know the Army offers Pashtun and Dari classes to soldiers that are deploying if they are lucky enough to get a spot, so I guess I will start with trying to find a teacher of one of these classes and see if they can and would be willing to translate.

The pilot just announced to the plane that it will be another six hours before we reach Germany. It's nap time.

Just woke up to fairly large roar of laughter. One of the "Madea" movies is apparently being shown. That entire series is just the worst. I refuse to give any of those movies a moment of my time. I'll just pass time on paper.

Ideally, once I get back to America, I'd like to spend time with my family, relax around the house doing a whole lot of nothing, and have copious amounts of sex with the Mrs. to make up my 9-month stint of celibacy. Is that what's going to happen?? Nope. We did have an apartment in Clarksville, but my wife decided not to renew the lease and moved back home to Ohio to live with her mother at her house. This means once I get back to the States, instead of relaxing at home, I will be holed up in a hotel for however many days it takes to find a new place. I don't know about you, but one of my pet peeves is living out of a suitcase. I prefer to be established, comfortable, and have my own furniture. I just spent 9 months living out of duffle bags in a region where the air compliments your living space with a fresh coat of dust every couple hours. (That is, if you clean.. otherwise, the current one just gets thicker)

Speaking of cleanliness in living spaces, I suppose I can tell the tale of Daniel Stuebenwicz. Besides, anything to keep my mind off of Madea. This guy was a Soldier in my company during this recent 9-month stint to the Stan. Twenty-four of us deployed, two stayed at Bagram as travel liaisons, and the rest of us went onward to JAF. Stuebenwicz was essentially a 27-year-old child, that had a face that resembled a naked mole-rat. Now you may be able to picture a naked-mole rat, and think, that's not possible. Trust me, he did, and it was. (If you cannot, look it up) Anyway, laziness often takes over people, and they do not feel like going out of their room, walking down the hallway, and urinating in the appropriate and delegated area. As an alternative, they instead get up, find an empty water bottle, uncap it, and use it as a makeshift urinal. I've done it before, but I always throw it in the trash on my way to my duty location the next morning. This guy did not. Pretty much ever. During a room inspection one time, he was found to have 27 bottles of urine under his bed. TWENTY-SEVEN. Gag-city. His roommate just happened to be the Soldier that told me about Dos. I felt pretty bad for him for that, but he ended up having the room to himself towards the end of the deployment, thanks primarily to my efforts.

One day working at the ECP, I was shooting the shit with another NCO, when the topic of Stuebenwicz came up. The NCO then went on to mention how he almost got into big trouble one day down at the Search Lane. (The station where soldiers wait for the all clear from the bomb-dog handler, and then go forth and physically search every truck and vehicle entering the base for anything the x-ray machine may not have been able to detect. They mostly look for drugs, or things that could be used as weapons, or anything suspicious.) Well, another part of that station is a computer that has a connection to the main database where information on every person that tries to enter the base is kept. If they are not already in the system, they get their picture taken, and they get entered. Every person gets looked up to see if they are flagged, or wanted for questioning in relation to Taliban activity, or even just to see if they are known Taliban. My fellow NCO goes on to tell me that it was found out that he had not been looking up the ID numbers of the local nationals coming in through his station, because it was supposedly "too much work". As soon as he said this, my jaw dropped. He what?!?! The NCO went on about it how it was called over the radio because apparently someone was found to be on base that wasn't supposed to be at the last point before, they freely enter the base and roam around. (Luckily, it wasn't anyone dangerous, but he was still flagged nonetheless) The NCOIC of ECP physically went down to the search lane, to see what was going on, and apparently just gave him an ass chewing, and left it at that. HELL TO THE MOTHERFUCKING NO, I said. What kind of person doesn't have the common sense to realize that looking people up to see if they are known for actively trying to KILL YOU, might be just a little bit important? Stuebenwicz. How he made it through Basic Training is an absolute mystery to me. In fact, his Drill Sergeants did their country an injustice by letting him slip through the cracks and enter the Active Duty Army. This guy was the definition of fuck-up. He was already in hot water for being late to his ECP shift on Dec. 2, the only day we were attacked... That caused two people to come all the way from the ECP to retrieve him in order to wake his ass up and take him to his shift. The attack happened while they were out trying to get him, and per base protocol, during an attack you seek cover wherever you are, no matter what; continuing to move is a serious offense. This caused the ECP, already relatively thin on Soldiers as far as defense goes, to be three soldiers short during an enemy attack. Had that huge fuel tanker bomb been a success and blown down the old entry-door, three additional Soldiers down there could have meant the difference between life or death for many people. Any way you look at it, that was a serious incident, and now this..... No.. I was not about to let him get away with this one. I took that information straight to my Chain of Command. They were just as shocked as I was. The next day, I, and another NCO went down to the ECP to get sworn statements from the people that knew about the incident. They were used as evidence to justify sending him back to the States before the deployment was over. This was a slight victory for him, because hey, you're leaving a combat zone earlier than you were supposed to. But it was a career ender because you endangered the lives of your fellow Soldiers and failed at doing the one thing that you spend all of your time training to do; your job while deployed. He was sent home and kicked out of the Army a few weeks later. I did that. Put that on my Resume.

And that's the Captain announcing initial descent into Germany. That's probably all for today. Getting excited about getting closer to home. Next entry will be after having seen my family!

JUNE 29, 2013

Took a bit longer than I expected to make this entry, but I have been ridiculously busy during the last week. Looking over my last entry, I see that I left off just before arriving home, so that is where I will start.

One of the best feelings that a human being can have is the feeling that one gets the moment your plane touches down on home soil after a deployment. Granted this is my second deployment, and the feeling wasn't as strong as the first time.. but nevertheless, I will try to describe it here. The daily grind of wearing 50 pounds of gear, always carrying your weapon, always wearing eye protection, sweating your balls off, and forcing yourself to drink more water than any human being is used to is *taxing*. Place on top of this burden the fact that you are surrounded by people that very well may want to kill you, mainly due in part to your religious beliefs. This can be especially confusing/frustrating when you do not necessarily have any religious beliefs, as is the case for me. (I suppose I can touch upon this subject in a bit) But the potential for hostility from people that surround you and the fact that mortars and bombs are fired and placed at random add to create a pretty damn stressful experience. The simple fact of just being in America frees you from this burden. You become surrounded by your American brethren knowing that they whole-heartedly respect the fact that you are most likely different from them. They respect that you may have different religious beliefs, and accept you for that, as well as your race, gender, and skin color. There are no roadside bombs to worry about, no children carrying knives in large crowds hoping to get a chance to shank you in the neck, and no rockets or mortars being fired in the hopes of killing anyone. You have returned home to a land of peace, freedom, and prosperity. A land where your close loved ones reside, and you want nothing more than for them to embrace you in their arms once more. Whether these thoughts are realized by each individual Soldier or not, we all feel it. And it is amazing. It's better than any drug, orgasm, adrenaline rush, or good feeling that you have ever felt. And it is in this moment that you realize just what it means to be an American; what it means to live free, and why it is worth fighting for. You realize that you took your life here in America for granted, and vow to never do so again. All of these things felt at once, and then you realize that you have absolutely no chance of not crying in front of everyone that came to welcome your home.

When an average person disembarks from a flight, they are in a hurry and want to leave the plane as soon as they can so as to continue moving towards whatever goal or end destination they may have in mind. Not so in this case. As we all leave the plane, we all suddenly have the most patience in the world. Our love for one another blossoms and kindness, politeness, and overall happiness is pouring out of everyone. When you eventually do get off the plane, everyone is smiling. EVERYONE is happy! You stare at the crowd that is up against the fence barrier and scan the faces for ones that you can call your own. After a few seconds, I see that my wife and two-year old son are not there, and must be inside the hangar, sitting in the bleachers. We all go to a gravel area and put our bags and weapons down and proceed to gather in one mass formation. We are all wearing the best uniform we have left from the deployment and have all showered and shaved within the last 24 hours, per orders of the Brigade Commanding Officer. The hangar doors open in front of us, and once wide enough, we march forward until all 200 or so of us are inside the hangar. As we march, I try scanning the crowd for Michelle, but cannot find her due to having to keep my head and eyes forward. We listened to a speech given by our Commanding Officer that I'm pretty sure only the families heard, because we all couldn't care less about what he was saying. It was just one last formality we had to go through before being reunited with our families. After several pauses and rounds of applause, we are at last released.

Most families rush down to the floor and seek out their already spotted Soldier. I just kind of stood there and looked around for my wife. The scene unfolding is one of pure chaos and love as people are crying tears of joy, giving the biggest of bear hugs, and living in the moment. It was probably only about 20 seconds or so, but it seemed like an eternity before I finally spotted her having just hit the ground floor of the hangar from the stairs of the bleachers. I rush over to her, abandoning the "Big Hug" plan I had arranged with my wife and proceed to grab my son from her arms. I wrap my arms around him and seemingly wrestle with him in the air as my torso twists back and forth. I let go so he can pull away and I can look at his face again. I say out loud that "He is so beautiful!" and begin to cry as I grab the back of his head with my right hand and give him a big kiss to his forehead. Now when I say this, I actually mean it and it's not just an automatic reaction.. you see.. one of my greatest fears before he was born would be that he would be ugly. My wife and I are fairly attractive people, definitely not model material by any means, but there's always that chance that lightning could strike and she could give birth to the second coming of the Elephant Man. Thankfully, this was not the case. In fact, this kid was damn near perfect. He was right on par with the cuteness level of the Gerber baby, even though he wasn't really a baby anymore, and this kid was going to be BUILT, just like his daddy. I pause from embracing him and turn to my wife to give a PG rated kiss and gave her a long embrace as well. Arranging what I really wanted to do would be difficult later on that evening in a hotel room with my son around, but I'm sure we'll manage.

They only give us about fifteen minutes of family time before we have to leave them and get on buses that will take us back to the area on base that has been designated as HQ for my unit. Not everyone from the unit deployed, as is the case with every deployment, so the few that stayed behind, otherwise known as the Rear Detachment (Rear D), were waiting to take all of the serialized sensitive items and place them properly back into vaults to be stored until the next time they would be needed. This process usually takes several hours because you never know if there's that one person that lost something and never told anyone, or that one Officer that thinks they're special, and decides to take hours of family time when the rest of us are doing what we're supposed to. You see, none of us can leave until our unit has 100% accountability of all sensitive items. This is how it is, and how it always has been.

As expected, it takes just under three hours before we are allowed to see our families again, and everything is gathered. You'd think we would be off for the next month or two as well-deserved R&R, but you would be wrong. We are to go through a process dubbed "Re-integration" into the stateside life that is the Army. We are to report every day at 0800, where they will take 100% accountability, and then we all get on buses to be taken to this center where all our vitals will be checked, records updated, and those that came back with a little extra trauma done to their psyche will be identified and treated accordingly. That last bit doesn't really apply to anyone in my unit due to the nature of my company's specific mission, but there are those that had to perform some pretty heinous duties or saw the aftermath of terrible events. This is of course, nothing new in the business of war. My first deployment, however, someone did see a bit of action. The story itself isn't all that glamorous, but the person it happened to is none other than yours truly.

My first deployment can't really be classified as a deployment since it was only four months long. When I got to my unit at Ft. Campbell after completing the nine months of training it took to teach me how to perform my job, I discovered that they had already been deployed for 7 months. It was decided that I would go and join them, which took about a month to arrange since I had to take some classes and do the whole Soldier Readiness Processing (SRP), which is pretty much the same thing as what you do when you get back, only it's all in preparation. There are a few more grim things added like making a Will and Power of Attorneys, should you need them. Anyway, I was to go join my unit stationed....... at....... JAF. The very same place my second deployment took place. (And the best part about that whole situation is that we already knew we were coming back before we left the first time.) When I got there, my main responsibility was to essentially be a detail bitch. My company had split up into two platoons, and my platoon (2nd) was to be the backup node to 1st platoon. 1st platoon was the main backup to the communications backbone already in place that, if you recall, never went down. Since my skillset was unknown to my unit, and since we were the backup to the backup of a system that never failed, I suppose the role of detail bitch came as no surprise. After having been on JAF for only one week, I was placed on the tower guard roster, and on my fourth day of Tower guard shift, my tower was attacked by a Vehicle-Born Improvised Explosive Device, or VBIED (pronounced v-Bid), and approximately 20 Taliban on foot, armed with AK-47s and RPGs.

In the minutes right before the attack, nothing out of the ordinary took place. I do remember there being literally no one on the road, but it wasn't a highly traveled road to begin with, and it was not unusual for hours to go by without seeing a single person walk by. (All of this based on four days of experience) The tower itself overlooked acres upon acres of crop fields. I'm not entirely sure what was growing there, but there was vegetation, nonetheless. About 20 feet directly in front of the tower was a creek that went from left to right. Once it was about 30 feet to the right of the tower (looking out from the tower) it banked 45 degrees to the creek's left and went on as far as you could see. On the left side of this creek was a road that ran alongside the creek, and also banked left 45 degrees. Somewhere off in the distance, that road goes over the creek, and comes back towards the tower, on the right bank of the creek. This road then goes all the way up to the gate located directly below my tower to the right, and also continues to the right around the perimeter of the base. It was this road leading up to the tower that the Taliban used during the attack. The attack itself only lasted about 10-15 minutes or so, but I can remember it as though watching a war-movie in half-speed.

The first thing I noticed was a white truck approaching on the road to the right of the creek. I thought nothing of it at first, until I noticed that it was gaining speed as I continued to watch it approach my tower, I became highly alarmed, stood up off of my stool and pointed the 240B machine gun directly in front of me right at the approaching truck. According to the rules of engagement, having drastically changed since Iraq, I am supposed to show, shout, combinations of both, but am not allowed to shoot unless I can 100% confirm that the enemy is showing intent to kill or harm, without any doubt. And of course, I can always simply shoot freely if fired upon first, but I am not supposed to attack first, else be faced with a Court Martial. (Though I am fairly confident I would have been able to get off on self-defense without charges if I had been able to shoot before they did first) But by the time I realized that the truck had no intention of stopping, it was already too late. Even if I had aimed the gun early enough at the approaching truck and started to fire upon the engine block, it still would have reached the tower on momentum alone. The truck smashed into the HESCO barriers at the base of the tower and blew up. The blast violently shook the tower as I fell to my knees, and the concussive blast left me momentarily stunned and deaf. A few moments later, I remember feeling small pieces of the wall of the tower behind me begin to fall on my helmet as I at first thought the tower was collapsing. (It took only short while to realize these pieces were from bullet impacts on the wall directly over my head) As I reached up to pull the charging handle to chamber that first round (because yet again, we are not authorized to have a round chambered unless under attack) I peeked my head barely over the waist high tower wall I had been ducking behind, and through the smoke of the burning VBIED at my tower base, I could see a second white truck had pulled up. There were MAM's (Military-Aged Male) positioned all around and on top of this vehicle, aiming AK-47s directly at me and my tower. Ducking back down, I pointed the machine gun in the general direction of the truck and began pulling the trigger in 3-5 sec bursts. After each burst, I quickly and blindly pivoted the aim of the gun until I had traced the outline of a small rectangle, several times. At first, I noticed no change in the rate of fire hitting directly above me. But after a few traced rectangles, I noticed the fire going overhead was significantly less, which meant at least some of them were ducking for cover, which gave me the best chance to take another peek at their positions. I quickly scooted several feet left of where I had taken my first peek over the wall and spotted three bodies in various positions around the truck that I must have apparently hit as they had been trying to run away. A few of them had run from the truck and taken cover in the small tree line on either side of the road, and another few had run towards the base perimeter wall and were taking cover by way of being out of my field of fire. I ducked back down and guessed that there were at least three different areas from which they could be shooting at me from. I crawled back to where I could reach the trigger and began blindly firing again. This time, I was aiming for the tree line on either side of the truck. I would fire a few bursts on one side, then swap to the other. I continued this pattern until I had run out of ammo. As soon as that happened, I quickly reached up and grabbed the ammo box and threw it I don't know where. I picked up a full box directly at my feet. I could hear them shouting to one another as I did this, and soon after, their AK fire picked up again. There is a large metal baseplate attached to the metal arm that supports the gun that acts as a built-in shield for incoming small arms fire. As I attempted to reload the ammunition box, I could hear the baseplate tinging over and over again as they were trying to shoot my arm as I tried to reload the weapon. This instinctually made me rapidly pivot the gun and plate on the arm back and forth so as to not give them a still target I managed to get the box in position, but I still needed to pull the strand of ammo out of the box and properly place it in the feed tray. It was ugly, and seemed to take forever, but I blindly was able to do it. I pulled the charging handle again and resumed my blind cover fire. I thought I was getting close to hitting them again, because their rate of fire slowed down yet again. But after my first peek, I saw that this was not the case. The men that went to hide behind the trees could no longer be seen, which meant that they had either joined however many were huddled up against the base wall, had gone back to the truck, or were currently low crawling somewhere out of sight. Whatever the case was, I did not see a single person out there, which gave me the confidence to get on one knee and bring my face to the left side of the gun, allowing me to look down the barrel, and actually see what I am firing at. (There was a small two-inch space between the gun and the baseplate on either side of the gun, but at that moment, I did not have the luxury to think about 'what-ifs'.)

This began the end of the conflict, or what I like to call, phase two. Instead of poking my head up in random locations to check enemy positions, I was able to pivot the weapon back and forth while looking down the sight to scan. After pivoting side to side several times and not being fired upon, I found the confidence to get on my feet, and huddle my face next to the 240, allowing me to simply lean one way or the other in order to aim, all while being able to use the sight. But a few moments later, two of them popped up from the middle of the truck bed with RPGs resting on their shoulders. I was able to put the sight on one of them, and watched as the rounds went through his chest, up his neck, and several through his head until most of it had been shot off but was not able to pivot in enough time before the second fired his rocket. Now, at the top of my tower was a room with open windows directly in front and to the left and right. All around the perimeter of this room was a ledge that stuck out about three feet, with a waist high wall at the edge of the ledge, aka what I had been standing on and using for covering this entire time. The rocket that the second man fired, went through the front window of the tower room, and out the left window as you face outward. I remember ducking down after killing the first man and thinking that was the end. I remember the rocket made a sort of SCHZEEEW sound as it flew a couple feet over my head, kind of what a laser sounds like being fired in a movie. But, to my surprise (and great relief) no explosion followed. I was still alive. I went back to aiming down the barrel of the gun and resumed scanning. After not seeing anyone for a few seconds, I raised my head ever so slightly to see what was left in the ammo box. Just as I had feared, I could not see the ammo chain. I reached my left arm into the box to feel it, and my hand touched metal. The ammo chain appeared to go down into the box, but that was apparently the extent of its length, which left me around 20 more rounds to fire before being out again. I scanned for a few seconds all of the places they had been, and decided to empty what was left into the back of the truck, where the second man may still be hiding. Once out, I ducked down, grabbed my M4 and proceeded to crawl to the left front of the tower. It was at this point, once I got to this left front corner, that I realized my ANA counterpart was not in this very corner, where his PK machine gun was mounted. I have no idea exactly when that guy left the tower, but I had been, and currently was up there by myself. I stood up again, this time placing my cheek on the Afghan machine gun, (which was actually Russian made) and aimed for the bed of the truck again and pulled the trigger. As I expected, and to my delight, he had a round chambered, and the gun fired immediately upon the first trigger pull. This turned out to be the difference between me still being here and not, because right as I pulled that trigger and put more rounds into the truck bed, the second man stood up yet again from behind the truck bed, having loaded another rocket into his launcher. All I had to do was slightly adjust the spray to be centered in the middle of his shoulders, and slightly raise my aim. I put at least a dozen rounds in that fucker's chest before he fell backward, dead. I immediately scanned for Taliban yet again and did not see any. I pivoted his gun as far as it could go to the right to see if I could hit the perimeter fence, and I made it about ten degrees further to the right than I could on my 240, but the wall itself, and the unknown remaining number of hiding insurgents, were just out of reach. It was at this point that I remember noticing that the base attack sirens were going off. I'm not sure if they had been for a while, or if I had just regained some of my hearing from the initial VBIED blast, but they were screaming, which meant help was on the way! I grabbed my M4 and crawled to the back of the tower. I chambered a round and toggled the safety lever from safe to semi. The back wall of the room in the middle of the tower had no windows, so I was able to stand with my back to the wall and slowly creep my way over to the right edge. I quickly peered out and around the right corner to look and see if I could see anything from the Taliban still hugging the barriers. I spotted one of them doing the same, scanning for me, and we both quickly ducked our heads back into cover. I slid my back down against the wall, and shifted over to the corner once my entire self was hidden by the ledge wall. I quickly popped up again with my rifle up, ready to fire, only to be met with no one doing the same. That was the moment when I noticed a third truck of insurgents pull up, and Taliban started jumping down with AK's raised toward my general direction. I quickly leaned back into cover and made the decision to leave the tower.

    I flew down the 24 steps leading to ground level, and looked for any sort of advantageous position from which I could fire my M4. The immediate space at the base of the tower was mostly open with gravel, but about 20 feet out was the start of the train car storage yard. The tower itself was located at the edge of the Motor Pool of the FOB and had a small little gate beside it that convoys sometimes liked to use as a back door out of the FOB when leaving for missions, but this particular section was where all the empty train cars were kept, stacked only two high at most, and side by side like they would be on a freighter shipping them overseas. I ran behind the closest one, and turned to expose my rifle, the right side of my head, and my right arm and shoulder as I leaned out to shoot anything that tried to enter the FOB through the now relatively unguarded gate. The Taliban fired one, then a second rocket in succession at the right side of the gate, which made the hole created in the barrier fence by the VBIED that much bigger, now about eight feet wide. Immediately after, four of them came running through the gate, AKs raised, ready to kill all Infidels in the name of Allah. Without fear, doubt, or much of anything really, I placed the wedge of my ACOG sight in the middle of their foreheads and fired one shot at a time, moving forehead to forehead. I dropped the first three and missed the fourth. Immediately after missing the fourth, I lowered my sight to his chest and did two double taps. The fourth man dropped, and I placed my aim back to the hole. Right at that moment, a tan, armored, and sexy as fuck MAT-V rolled up directly to the right of my position and came to a quick screeching halt. A second wave of Taliban came rushing into the blown hole. I don't know how many were in that wave, but before I could take aim and try to take them out, the mounted .50 caliber gun came to life on top of that gun truck. The sound of sweet victory rang through the air as round after round tore those terrorist fucks to shreds. Three of them exploded in the process due to the gun igniting the apparent suicide vests that (I would come to find out afterwards) nearly all of the attackers had been wearing. As this decimation was taking place, the back door of the truck lowered, and a quick reaction force, comprised of actual infantrymen, whose actual job was to kill, came rushing out, along with two medics. They immediately came over to me and insisted that I drop what I was doing and come with them. I looked towards the hole in the gate, and reluctantly ran over to the dropped truck door. The medics did not stop at the truck, and instead kept running back towards the interior of the base, towards another armored vehicle (a HUMVEE) that had also apparently arrived. This truck, however, was green with the universal Red Cross symbols painted on the sides, front and back. It was a medical HUMVEE. I ran to the back and climbed into the truck. I remember the medics taking my vitals and not too much after that. Shock finally caught up with me, and really the next thing I remember was coming to again on a gurney inside the medic station.

From the medic station, I was sent to the main hospital on Bagram Airfield for a few days, just in case. I had not sustained any life-threatening injuries from the attack, but the initial VBIED blast ruptured both of my ear drums, and they had been bleeding the whole attack. The BAF medical staff informed me that I would be facing an unknown amount of permanent hearing loss as a result of the blast. Other than that, I was fine. I ended up staying at the hospital for nearly two weeks. (Which was actually terrible, because I did not get a chance to bring any additional clothing along with me when I was flown to BAF. Luckily, our two designated BAF travel liaisons were able to provide me with a clean/fresh uniform) Meanwhile news of the event spread across theatre, and I was visited by dozens of high-ranking Army personnel that made it a point to specifically seek me out and congratulate me on my (small) victory. On top of the countless number of coins I received, I would go on to be awarded the Purple Heart, and a Silver Star with Valor for successfully defending the base and defending the lives of its inhabitants and being credited with 8 kills out of the possible 20.

As you can imagine, that story is eventually told to everyone that meets me, usually by someone other than myself. I suppose there are a few moments where I pull off some bad-ass shit, Jason Bourne style. But generally speaking, the whole experience was a bit of a mind-dump and certainly involved no small degree of luck. The story describes an extremely surreal sequence of events that come to life nearly every time I think about what happened or hear someone else describing it. Ultimately, it's great to know that I can essentially flip a switch and become a fearless harbinger of death, but at the same time, I would prefer not to think about it. For any thoughts on the matter inevitably lead to thoughts of how the deaths of 8 men were in reality 8 stories of hardship for their families. I realize that I sound sympathetic to terrorists here, but the fact of the matter is, they are people in the same way that I am. I have a life, beliefs, and a family, as did they, and I took that away. I'm not saying I regret it, because it was me or them, and I chose them. All I'm saying is that bearing the responsibility of ending the lives of other people is an enormous burden that most will never understand. The only way to make this burden as light as possible, and therefore able to deal with it on the daily basis, is to simply not think about it. But it is ok, and healthy, to once in a while, relive that one moment of glory. It is, after all, my own personal page in the history of the 101st Airborne Division. And I'll be damned if it's not made out to be the most god damned amazing true story that anyone has ever heard.

Holy side-tracked Batman… Where was I.. Ah. So it's been a week since we got back, and we have two more days left of re-integration in the upcoming week before we can all finally go on leave. Leave isn't an equal amount of time for all. It's a window the unit schedules during the year in expectance that many people *will* go on leave. Each Soldier is awarded two and a half days of leave every month that they serve, and generally save them to be used right after deployments, or during the holiday season at the end of the year. Some choose not to go on leave at all, which is smart, because when it comes time to get out of the military, you can take all your pooled days and either sell them back for thousands of dollars or take up to 75 days off in a row, paid. A nice chunk of time to get yourself situated with your next job, house, or to do absolutely nothing at all. The window itself was three weeks long. I would be going on leave for the last two weeks of that time period. During the first week, we came in, did PT, and were dismissed until the next day. An hour and a half was all that was required of us per day for that week. Pretty tempting not to take leave at all and just enjoy your free time locally. But I had plans to visit my Father down in Cocoa Beach, FL. *That* was a destination worth taking leave for.

In the meantime, I have been using my free time to search for a house for my Family and I to live in. We have done the whole apartment thing, and my wife and I have agreed to try out the house lifestyle for a year or two. We also decided that we did not want to live in Clarksville this go around, so the only other realistic option would be Hopkinsville, which was located in the state of Kentucky, some ten miles down the same road the base is on. Clarksville is just too busy for its own size. There are a half dozen accidents around town at any given time due to the main demographic of the population being young, testosterone driven, semi-psychopaths… Otherwise known as Soldiers. And the traffic… you'd think you were in an actual large city. It takes too long to get anywhere. No thank you. So, we went to Remaxx in Hop-town, and saw what they had listed. We ended up finding this cozy 1,600ft house for about the price we had been paying for an apartment. It was barely in Hopkinsville and had a corn field in front of and behind it. But it had everything we were looking for…

New washer/dryer, three bedrooms, two bathrooms, a porch, fairly large backyard, two car-garage, and quiet. It was only a mile down the road from I-24 and then it's a 10-mile drive doing 80 mph to Ft. Campbell Blvd. and then you're essentially there. Not sure about the neighbors though. In the big city where you have many neighbors, most people hardly get to know any of them. But in a rural area, where you have far fewer, they tend to play a more important role in your daily life. Funny how life works sometimes.

As far as the Strange Event Forecast goes, nothing new to report. I have mentioned this notebook to Michelle, but I only told her that I started writing during the deployment as a pass time and stress reliever, and grew to like it, and most likely will continue to write in it from time to time. She seems supportive and clueless as to its true nature.

The best part about being back; my son. He is simply awesome. He's super bright for his age and I love talking to him about everything. His range of speech is limited, as is any two-year old's, but man he sure understands what we are trying to tell him. He is most definitely a mama's boy though. I mean, he really can't help it since I've been gone for the last nine months. Plus, he was constantly around his grandmother, great grandmother, mother and aunt back up in Canton, where my wife stayed. That's a whole lot of coddling in a sea of Estrogen. He seems to be pretty sensitive and kind of wimpy, but hey, he's two. There's plenty of time to man up now that daddy's back. Plus, she will only be the favorite for so long. He'll realize that dad is awesome and will default as the obvious role model once he realizes just how much ass I kick. I'll teach him everything I know, and highly look forward to it. He's going to be a star Linebacker at THE Ohio State University. He'll go there free on scholarship, and pretty much do anything he wants to do because he'll also be brilliant like his father. Well, let's not sell mommy short I suppose. I wouldn't have married her if she wasn't a smartie as well. She does tend to be on the strict side though… I mean, as a military man, I am as well. But with me, as long as you are honest and everything you do is with good intentions, he's going to have a blast growing up. For example, he will drink his first beer with me at age 16 (… and smoke bud for the first time lol) despite what his mother says. One thing I came to realize is that children need to be shown that when used responsibly, these substances are not bad. And what is the best way to go about doing that? Well, I can tell you it's not prohibiting it until age 21. I wasn't allowed to drink at all while I was growing up. And what was the result of that?? I ended up nearly drinking myself right out of college. My upbringing was so strict and focused on academics that I was starving for a social life. Drinking is about as social as an activity gets, especially while in college. So, I drank. A lot. And I had a blast. But the point is, I should have been exposed to it prior to this point in my life so that I was better prepared. If I had the freedom to make mistakes, or to drink with my friends, I would have wanted to do it less. Michelle disagrees, but all I know is I refuse to make the same mistakes my parents made while raising me. I'm pretty sure that's what every parent says to themselves when raising their kids. But the difference with me is that I will also not force unreasonable expectations on my son. If he wants to be a musician, rock on. If he loves the theatre, go for it. If he turns out to be gay, that sucks for me and the grandkids front, but I'll still love him the same. Actually, that would suck on two fronts, because I am the only male Bruce in my family tree. My brother is only my half-brother and has his father's last name. So, yea, no pressure Colin, but our name rests in your…was going to say hands, but I suppose "loins" is a more appropriate word.

Ah, I just remembered, there is something a bit strange about my son. My wife informs me that he has an imaginary friend, whom he calls "Match". I have yet to witness him talking with "Match", but he supposedly does it while playing with a little finger skateboard one of my family members got him last Christmas. He also got a couple of toy cars, and I'm thinking someone called them Matchbox cars, and since he can't say that whole phrase, anything with four wheels he associates as a Matchbox car, and hence calls it "Match". I never had an imaginary friend at that age, but being a first-time concerned mother, my wife looked into it and found that it's perfectly normal. I have a feeling this is how raising him is going to go. She'll pull her hair out over a toy skateboard, and I'll shake my head and sigh knowing it's no big deal. Only time will tell.

Well, that about sums it up as far as updates go. Next entry should be from beautiful Cocoa Beach, Florida! Haven't seen my dad in a couple years, and the beach is sounding pretty amazing right about now. Plus, my dad is a character. But that's a story for the next entry.

JULY 7, 2013

This entry is coming to you from Cocoa Beach! I've finally come to a hot and sandy place worth visiting. It's Sunday on the weekend after the 4th, and it is finally time to take a moment and reflect upon the past few days.

Monday (the 1st) was the last day we had to come into work before block leave started. Block leave usually would not have started until Tuesday at 0000 in the morning, but since it's right after a deployment, and with the approach of a major holiday, they let us sign out right after formation on Monday, without being charged a half day of leave for the duty day that was still technically remaining. That may not sound like a big deal, but it is because it just doesn't happen. The Army isn't big on kindness, being "laid back" or being understanding. That may be the image we wish to portray to the world, but as far as the treatment of its own Soldiers…. There are many a good career's that fall to the wayside due to favoritism and apathy. But that is mostly just an opinion had by many. Currently I am fortunate to be a part of a good unit with few problems.

But let's not get into that, I'm here writing on the Beach, getting some actual sun to shine on my Vitamin D starved Casper-skin. Let's focus.

The drive down here took 22 hours. It would have taken several less if not for Colin. He did sleep a majority of the way, but his constant neediness makes us stop. As for the drive itself, pretty uneventful, just a lot of ugly, non-deciduous trees and swamps.

Since we have arrived, our days are looking to be pretty much the same day over and over; wake-up, eat, discuss when everyone wants to head to the Beach, eventually go back to his place, then eventually head to the Cocoa Beach pier. This sounds like a normal chain of events, but my dad's personality comes into play in that he mentions the pier so often that my wife and I secretly have started keeping daily counts of how many times he mentions it, and then we proceed to mention the pier out of context in our own conversations. I believe he kind of realized this rut he had created, so that's when the events of Friday come into play.

My father owns a longboard for surfing, (which I absolutely cannot ride… snowboarding, I got it. Surfing? Can't get it) and a paddle board. The Paddle board is similar to the longboard, only it's a bit wider and is meant to cruise along with its passenger standing on top with a long paddle. The person then gets about in a way similar to that of a canoe, and if skilled enough, can even learn to ride waves if they so desired. But it's mostly meant for cruising out on the water far enough from the beach so that the waves won't really affect the rider. Seeing as how I was unable to surf, my dad gets the bright idea to let me try this. So we go inland to the river, where the water is calm and sans waves, and should be an ideal place to learn to balance yourself and get the hang of it.

We pulled off to a tiny little bay just on the other side of the bridge leading away from Cocoa. There's a small sliver of land in the shape of a crescent moon jutting out from the roadway that creates a bay that naturally shields the water within from any current or wind that would prove difficult for this situation. We get out, and I attempt to mount the board in about 3 feet of water. I fail and fall the first three times and am finally able to stand on the fourth attempt for a decent distance and then proceed to fall again. Eventually I figure out that it's much easier to balance yourself when moving, much like the concept of riding a bike. Soon, I am paddling around, losing my balance every now and then, but I remain standing. Ready to really test my abilities, I turn toward the river and start to paddle toward deeper and rougher water. I was about halfway to where I deem to be the turn-around point when I spotted a black fin in the water, quickly headed in my direction directly in front of me. My first instinct was that it was a dolphin, and maybe I could get a chance to pet him, or ride him. But after looking at the fin for a few more seconds, I notice the fin is staying at the same level as it moves. Since dolphins move by moving their tails up and down, it gives their dorsal fin an up and down motion as they swim, much like a sine wave. Sharks, on the other hand, move their tails side to side, and their dorsal fins stay the same level as long as the shark is swimming at the surface. This was no dolphin, and judging by the size of the fin, I guessed this shark to be somewhere between 4-6 feet in length. It was at this moment that I knew exactly what I needed to do. I knew that if I fell for any reason, the shark would close in out of pure curiosity, and most likely bite me to see if I was worth committing the effort to kill. I decided it would be best to avoid any further contact with the water using any of my body parts. I proceeded to slowly drop down to my knees and lower my center of gravity in order to make it easier to balance. The shark hugged the perimeter of the crescent and went under. I slowly turned myself around and paddled back towards land. After a few long seconds, I reach the rocks at the shore. The water is fairly clear and shallow here, and I can clearly see he is not within striking distance. I step in the water, and then onto the rocks. For the first time, I felt a slight stinging sensation somewhere on my right leg. I looked down and notice that I have a small gash on my knee, and blood was running down the front of my leg. I must have landed on a shell during a fall when I was learning to balance. No wonder why all that shit just happened. I looked at my dad and proceeded to sarcastically thank him for the good time, but I was pretty sure that I was done. As we drove away, I spotted that same fin yet again doing another round in the bay. Noticing just how large it was now, even further away, I couldn't help but feel like I had been slightly off on how large I thought it to be.

Michelle had opted not to go with us, and instead decided to stay at my father's place to take a nap with

Colin. As soon as we got back, I proceeded to tell the story of how I nearly became fish food. I showed her the gash in my knee, and we all laughed at the close call. I proceeded to ask if we should then go to the Pier and tell my story to anyone that asks. My father, unbeknownst to the joke said that tonight my older sister was driving in, and we could do whatever we all decided to do. I mentioned maybe going to fish on the beach for a while. My dad seemed to like this idea and asked me to come out to the garage to show me this new fishing pole he just got. To me, a pole is a pole, and I could really care less… But I humor him and head out to his garage. To my surprise, he ignores the stash of fishing poles, and proceeds to go to the top drawer of a dresser. He opens the drawer and pulls out a purple sack with gold trim, a Crown Royal bag. From inside he pulls out a contacts case and what appears to be a homemade pipe. He tosses me the contacts case and tells me to carefully open it. I do, and upon doing so, my nostrils are immediately greeted with the light and pleasant smell of Marijuana. I take a closer look and notice the color is a very light green, and there's also a good amount of red mixed in as well. It looks and smells *amazing*, and I proceed to ask my father how good it is. He motions for me to toss him the case back, and I do, and he proceeds to pack a small amount into his pipe. He shows me how much he put in and proceeds to smoke it. He then hands it to me, and I easily finish the small amount off. It works almost immediately, and I quickly feel that head rush coming back that I haven't felt since the Stan. But this strand is rather smooth, yet strong. It turns out to be very good stuff, and I pack another small amount into the pipe as my dad informs me that I can come and partake whenever I want while I'm visiting. I suspect this is his way of apologizing for my near shark attack.... Apology accepted!

I head back inside and proceed to join my wife and son who I find watching Finding Nemo for the 4th time, if I'm not mistaken. My buzz is going ever so well, and I sit back on my dad's couch and start to get lost in thought. Colin then proceeds to ask me if he can have a pouch. (Organic fruits and veggies blended into a paste to provide a healthy and mostly tasty alternative to not wanting to eat actual fruits and veggies.) I proceed to tell him to go into the bedroom and to look in the bag on the floor, grab one, and bring it back so I can open it for him. He nods his head, and as he walks away, I turn to my dad and bet him that he brings back the Blueberry/Banana pouch, which through trial and error we have discovered to be his favorite flavor. I observe him walk down the long hallway, reach the room, and find the bag. He bends over, picks one up, and puts it back. He then picks up another and starts walking back towards me. When he arrives, he hands the pouch to me, and sure enough, it is indeed the banana pouch. I flash my dad a smile and continue to watch the movie. Once the 4th showing comes to a close, my wife and I decide to put Colin down for the evening and do so by putting him in bed and lying down beside him. We pretend to fall asleep so that he sees us sleeping, calms down, and goes to sleep himself. This method usually works every time, and it's not uncommon for one of us to actually doze off for a bit as well. But that night, something different happened.

As I lay on my back pretending to be sleeping, I hear my son start to speak out loud. He is apparently imitating us by saying that it's time to go to sleep, and to close your eyes. He repeats the same phrases several times and then stops. I thought he had fallen asleep until I felt him softly caressing my arm. He pulls his fingers away and proceeds to do it twice more. After three times, he is apparently convinced that I am asleep and proceeds to place his hand around the face of my watch. He grabs the face as firmly as he can and tries to turn the dial without luck. He briefly explores the sides of the face for a little while longer, and then brings his hand back to his person. In my "heightened state" I realize that he was testing me to see if I was awake. This child has been two years old for a couple of months, and he is displaying cautionary behavior that was a precursor to executing a plan to explore my wristwatch. That's amazing! That is undeniably a sign of solid intelligence... Solid.. I'm thinking that is a bit of an understatement. I continue to ponder just how smart Colin is for his age when I realize that he is talking again; only this time, it's a whisper. It's so soft that I can barely hear what he's saying. I hear the word "No, and the phrases "It's time for bed", and "Daddy said so." He doesn't whisper for too much longer. I pretend to roll over towards Colin and crack one eye open to see exactly what he's doing. His lips are still moving, and he's looking up at the ceiling, towards the far corner of the room. I notice that he's clenching his little finger skateboard in his right hand. I can no longer hear what he's saying, but his mouth stops moving, and he continues to stare up at the ceiling. He does this for a few more seconds, smiles, nods his head, and then rolls over on his stomach to assume a comfortable position for sleeping.

He was talking to Match again… This was the first time that I witnessed it that close up. I waited a few minutes until I was certain he was asleep and proceeded to get up and head back out to the living room to rejoin my dad and older sister. Michelle apparently dozed off at some point during all of this and I gently tapped her on the shoulder to wake her up. She easily awakens, and smiles at me slightly embarrassed, and proceeds to sit up, stand up and then walk out towards the living room with me. I turn to her and ask her if she heard Colin talking to Match just then. She said that she heard him talking but did not notice he has his skateboard in his hand. I asked if she heard specifically what he was saying, and she said that she had. She must have noticed my growing intrigue because she attempted to quell it by saying that toddlers often repeat the things their parents say as a way to calm down and fall asleep. She then makes some sort of "if I had read the baby books" comment, I would already know this. This is a valid point I suppose, but I've already stopped listening to her and begin to think about the situation. What stood out in my mind during that whole episode, was just how intensely he was looking up at the ceiling. His attention to the corner that kept his gaze was so genuinely intense that I nearly looked up to see if something was there myself. I continue to ponder until my sister asks me to join her outside, as she smokes a cigarette. I say sure and turn to Michelle to see if she wants to come along, but she says she wishes to stay inside. We get up to head outside, and my dad follows.

My sister, for as long as I can remember, has been one of the biggest pot smokers that I've known all my life. I knew very well what she was really asking, even though she does smoke cigarettes from time to time. We go outside and head over to the garage to retrieve my dad's Crown Royal bag. I'm still feeling good from having smoked not too long ago, but now it's time to add fuel to the fire. We pack a bowl large enough for the three of us and pass it around until it's gone. I'm growing very fond of this strand, and I asked my dad if it was possible to take some with me back home to Tennessee. He raises the point that sure it's fine to smoke while you're here, but don't you get drug tested in the Army? This is a valid point, because drug testing is a little different here in the states than when deployed.

Another part of the reason I was able to get away with smoking in the Stan was that I was the primary UPL without a backup. If there is a backup present that has also passed the class, then both UPL's can potentially appear on the random drug testing list since the one can take samples from the other. When there is just a primary, they are unable to handle their own specimens and must be removed from the list. Now that I was back in the States, however, there would be an alternate and that should be enough to deter anyone from smoking. But I made it a point to learn everything that I could on the subject while taking the online class overseas. It turns out, that a person that does not regularly smoke weed, like myself, would need to be tested within two days of smoking it in order to test positive. There needs to be greater than a .08% of the cannabinoid protein present in the urine in order for it to be deemed a positive sample. Several factors come into play when it comes to passing a potentially career-ending drug test: potency of the plant, water intake, and metabolism. The potency of the plant is really the only static factor. Either you're smoking dirty Mexican schwag, or you paid some decent money to smoke something good or are lucky enough to know someone that has some and is willing to share. Naturally, the more potent the plant, the greater the presence of Cannabinoid protein will be in the urine. So, let's say I smoke late on a Saturday night, or even first thing on a Sunday morning, with a drug test following on the very next day (Monday). I should be screwed, right? Not necessarily... If certain steps are taken and certain goals are met, one could potentially pass said test every time. (And no, I'm not taking about buying a prosthetic penis that pumps clean urine from a hidden bag.)

As soon as I'm done smoking, I start drinking water. I drink water non-stop for the rest of the day, well into the night, and if I wake up before I'm supposed to get up, I drink more then, and then drink some right when I get up. The goal is to reach about the gallon and a half mark. On top of this, once the main effects die down in the brain, I proceed to exercise. It doesn't have to be anything too vigorous, but one does need to sweat a lot. Of course, vigorous exercise is the best way to cause this, but again, it's not necessary. But usually I run about 5 or more miles, and if I'm not feeling up to the distance, I will do sprints instead with burpees, push-ups, and sit-ups in-between. When I'm done exercising, I should look like I stood in a shower with my clothes on. Now, this may be quite hard for some people to achieve, but for me it's quite easy because I naturally sweat a lot. In my opinion this is the *key* to passing the test. When you sweat profusely, your body will need to replace the fluids you've lost. This will create a natural thirst throughout the day and allow you to more readily drink a large amount of water. In addition to this, while you are sweating, the cannabinoid protein is rapidly leaving your body with your sweat. In order to pass the test, the protein needs to leave the body. Profusely sweating is essentially a way for your entire body to be rid of extra proteins currently traveling through the blood stream. This allows for a large majority of the protein to leave the body through the skin, instead of simply relying on the kidneys to filter it from the blood. Skin cells secrete water from themselves to try and cool the body down as a reaction to the raising core body temperature. Cells replace this lost water with water in the bloodstream, which means the Cannabinoid protein is being pulled from the bloodstream into the cell, and then being secreted out. If the bloodstream can be purified at the source via sweat, then this means that the large amounts of water you will be drinking will essentially fuel the cleansing process. Once exercise is complete, continue to drink water, and the rest takes care of itself. Now, there is another factor that I have yet to mention, because it does not affect me, but it may be a factor for others. If a person has an excess amount of fat on their body, then a decent amount of the Cannabinoid protein floating around in their bloodstream will also be stored in their body fat. Since fat is constantly being used as a source of energy, this means that the protein can be pumped into the bloodstream for quite a while as a by-product produced from the body using fat cells as energy, allowing for this fat person to potentially test positive over a far longer period of time. Sooo there… that is the science behind how I can pass a urine test at any time in the Army. As long as I follow those steps and meet those goals, I'm good. Last holiday block leave, my unit conducted a 100% drug test of everyone the very morning we all returned. Having smoked two days prior, and wisely sticking to my routine, my urine must have passed the screening because I was never approached about testing positive. This is why I love science. Given enough knowledge of how a complex system works one can accurately deduce the results of an experiment without having to actually conduct said experiment. Science is a mode of existence that bases its conclusions on sound factual data. It can provide the answer to all life's questions, as opposed to religion, which is unfortunately a much more popular means people use to get their answers.

And this leads me to the next topic of conversation that took place on this particular evening.

Somehow, the conversation between my sister, father and I turned to religion. We were all pretty baked, and being the oldest out of us all my dad was most likely the one to bring it up, because older people tend to think about religion more than younger people do since, after all, they are closer to their graves. During the conversation, my father focused primarily on re-incarnation, and thought he would come back as a sea creature, having spent most of his life around the ocean. I, on the other hand, thought that this might be possible. I went on to ask him what he remembers before he was born. He remembers nothing. A black, empty void. That, unfortunately, is what I believe could be possible that awaits us all upon death, but it is also possible to simply just not have any memories present from a previous life because after all, there are many people that actually do. My father then goes on to ask if I believe in an afterlife, to which I said that it could be possible, but just had no idea as to how that process could actually be conducted. Around this time, he got a bit tired which led to him excusing himself to turn in for the evening. As everyone was turning in for the night, I ended up getting a call out of the blue from a good friend of mine, Josef (he was my best man at our wedding) and went on to talk to him for over an hour. I had spoken to him only a few times since I deployed, and needless to say I had many stories to tell. Michelle and my sister sat outside for a bit longer and then went back inside to go to sleep, or so I assumed. Josef went on to say that he hadn't smoked bud in quite a while and just happened to have some with him at that moment. I went on to say that I also had some with me, and suggested we smoke on the phone together. So.. we did. We laughed at each other's stories, and it was really great to hear from him again. Eventually neither of us had anything new to say, so we promised to meet up in the near future, somewhere, and somehow. We said our goodbyes and I proceeded to sit back down in our chairs and think for a bit before I went inside myself to turn in.

As I sat there, I let my mind wonder over the evening's events, and found myself stumbling upon a memory that I hadn't thought of in a few years. (And one that I should have already remembered and mentioned here..) It was during the summer between my first and second deployments, down at the Joint Readiness Training Complex (JRTC) in Ft. Polk, Louisiana. I theorize this particular base was chosen as a host to this exercise in an attempt to replicate the misery experienced during the summers of Afghanistan. I must say that it was indeed quite miserable to the point where it was actually worse than the Stan. But this particular memory wasn't about the heat, or the mission. It was about a moment when I was outside, having just come on to my night shift. The sun was mostly set, I was standing there alone with no one else in sight, and the stars were just coming out for the evening. I reached into my side shoulder pocket and pulled out my away from home pack of cigarettes, and lit one up. As I'm taking my first few drags, I notice a star that's not a star, but an airplane. It is approaching my position, coming in from West/Northwest. For some reason, I like to imagine planes that I see flying in the sky are actually UFO's, and I imagined it doing zig zags in the sky. As I imagined it, the plane started to zig zag. At first, I smiled and thought I was imagining it, but this plane was making 90 degree turns with absolutely zero arc or bow in the flight path. My smile faded and I continued to stare. The plane did a few more and then stopped in mid-air. There were no flashing white or red lights as there should have been if it were an actual plane or helicopter. From where I was standing, it was simply a solid white glow, and had I not just observed it flying through the air, I would have assumed it was a star without looking twice. I stood there for at least fifteen minutes, waiting for it to move again, or do anything. It just hovered. I memorized where it was in the sky relative to the stars around it. I went back inside my tent, and poked my head back out an hour later to find that it was still there. I made checks continuously throughout my night shift to confirm that it remained there all night. At about 4 am, some clouds rolled in, and I was unable to see the stars anymore. The following evening, the light was gone from where it had been the previous evening.

As I finished recalling the event, I seemingly snapped back to reality. What had just happened to me? I was still sitting in a chair, outside of my dad's apartment, 3 blocks from the beach in Cocoa Beach, FL. Why did that particular memory come to my mind at that particular moment? I continued to ponder this for a few seconds when another thought came and punched me in the face. *What exactly had I witnessed in that memory??* At the time, I was pretty excited to have seen a genuine UFO. But I had no proof, no pictures had been taken, and I was the only one that saw it. I remember completely ruling out the helicopter possibility because it simply didn't move like one. A helicopter can bank side to side like that, but it has momentum to deal with, and there's a pause as it overcomes its momentum going right, stabilizes, and then proceeds to go left and vice versa. This craft had zero hesitation. It reminded me of the movement of a pinball bouncing off the walls in a narrow portion of a pinball machine. Granted it wasn't bouncing as fast as a pinball would have, but that thing seemed to bounce off nothing without delay. This was a legitimate UFO. I had been on the training grounds just outside of an actual Army base, which left me with two options. Option A: it was top secret technology being piloted by most likely an Airman near an established military base. Option B: ... Option B. Option B sent chills up and down my body. Option B. Option B was that it was an alien craft, being piloted by beings not of this world.

As soon as I had that thought, I felt dopamine surge in my brain as though I was being rewarded for thinking the right thought. I began to feel panic, confusion, uncertainty, excitement, bewilderment, and shock. I felt my heart racing and realized that I needed to calm down. I stood up and began to instinctively stretch, increasing blood flow throughout my body and relieving stress at the same time. It felt really good, and soon a feeling of calm was washing over me. I suddenly remembered my son, and how he had been looking up at the ceiling… as though something were there that could not be seen.

Pieces began to float around in my head, and slowly fell into place. This crazy scenario began to come into focus all at once. I don't wish to go any further about my thoughts on this matter at this point in time. Shit, I just remembered the inscription on the back page of this journal. What the fuck does it say!? That seems more important now than ever. I'm so confused right now. I'm not sure what to write.

For the time being, I am going to step away from trying to analyze this. Between now and my next entry I will observe my surroundings closely, attempt to figure out how to explain exactly what I think is going on, and closely observe my son. And somehow do all of this without arousing the suspicions of my wife. Not sure when the next entry will be, but, once I've figured at least something out, I will write again.

JULY 14, 2013

It's been a week since the last entry. As far as figuring out what's going on, I do believe I've made some progress, though I've honestly raised more questions than I have been able to answer. And those that I have answered are just answered by seemingly insane ideas. Allow me to illustrate:

It would appear that when I smoke Cannabis, something happens in my brain on a chemical level. I've always thought it was just racing thoughts and normal side effects of being high. But it would appear that this characteristic was a precursor for something else. Ever since I smoked the Hash while on duty in the Stan, it seems as though my brain chemistry was permanently altered. Every time that I have smoked since that time, I have been susceptible to spontaneous memory recall to nearly the point of losing consciousness. What exactly is going on while this happens? I've looked into how brain cells communicate, and it seems pretty straight forward; synapses on neurons release chemicals and bind with neighboring receptors on other neurons to pass along a message. I suspect that what I ended up doing was either damaging the traditional way the neuron cells communicate, or changing the way they communicate altogether. The communication is still taking place, hence why I can still walk, talk, and am not making sounds like a golden retriever. But yet, something has changed. The neurons in my brain behave differently when the cannabinoid protein is present. I suspect that it somehow allows my brain to achieve a chemical state that is similar to that of a brain going through REM dream sequences. When my brain reaches this state while still being awake, it apparently allows for something amazing. The voice. The voice I heard in the desert. I'm starting to think that it was not an auditory hallucination brought on by the stickiest of icky. It was a successful communication broadcast from….them. Now logic dictates that I'm having a psychotic episode, and I have been hallucinating on a regular basis and should most definitely seek psychiatric help. And that should hopefully be the course of action that someone would take having had these kinds of thoughts. But I won't seek help, at least, not yet, because of one reason. Colin. My son. I suspect this "Match" character is not an imaginary friend after all. I think it's also them. I believe he is able to freely communicate without the aid of Cannabis. I know this all sounds insane, and I should lock myself away in some institution. But the proof is there. It's been there the whole time. The strange things that happened to me when I was growing up, the phantom bottle, and the teepee hangers. Those were signs. Those were subtle indicators that there was more going on around me than appeared, and/or served as small training incidents to lessen the burden of the actual truth some point way in my future. But why me? I suppose being able to receive communications is reason enough to gain their attention, but why?

And what about these beings themselves… Why are they here? How long have they been here? Does anyone else know about them? It seems likely with all of the observational technology that we have that at least someone else has witnessed *something*. What about the lies I had come across, the false report on the attack to the public, and the Bin Laden incident. These lies were but the minute tip of the iceberg. If the government is aware of the presence of these beings, why haven't they told us? If that UFO I spotted during JRTC was actually being piloted by humans, where did we get the technology? Why is all of this happening now, and what is my part in it all??

There are so many scenarios and unanswered questions flooding my conscious right now that it really doesn't do me any good to go on writing about them. I suppose that time will be the tell-all, and I will continue to update this journal as things continue to happen.

I can, however, make myself a list of things I need to do.

1. Carefully observe my son and confirm these thoughts and ideas
2. Seek help if it turns out I'm going through a legit psychotic episode
3. Find a steady weed supply if it turns out I'm not
4. Figure out what the inscription says in the back of the book
5. Find out why all this is happening, and why me?
6. Try to somehow establish direct communication, most likely through Colin

There is much to be observed and much to find out in the near future. For the first time in my life, I am truly terrified of the unknown. I feel this is either the beginning of a great revelation, or, the beginning of a major psychotic breakdown that ends with me losing my wife, son, career, and everything else important to me. I suppose all I can do is stick to the plan and take it one day at a time.

JULY 19, 2013

A decently progressive week since the last entry. First, after returning home from block leave, I took this journal to the Base Pashtun teacher after work got out on Monday. I waited around until their last class let out, and did the whole awkward "Hi, my name's Bruce, found this book with some Arabic writing, was wondering if you could translate it.." spiel. Well, it turns out that they could not. But they did recognize that it was written in a very early form of Arabic. I thought that if they knew that much at least, maybe there was one word they might be able to recognize, and it turns out there was. A phrase meaning "the son of the father" appeared in the middle of the text. It was apparently a very old phrase still used today and has deeply religious connotations. They went on to ask if they could make a copy of the page and send it to a friend of theirs, but I said that wasn't necessary and simply thanked them for their time. As I was walking away, he casually asked where I had found that notebook. The sudden feeling that he knew more than he was letting me know came over me, and I told him it was a gift from a friend, and I left it at that.

As far as my son goes, I had an interesting conversation with him. On Tuesday, after work, I went home to our house and watched Colin as the wife went out to do some grocery shopping, and other odds and ends she needed to tie up. She still suspects nothing, and this gave me an opportunity to play with him and see what he would say about match.

At first, he was all about his Thomas the Train toys, and I humored him for a bit and played along. Eventually I brought up Match, and asked him if he knew where he was? He nodded his head and proceeded to walk over to his bed and pull the skateboard out from underneath his pillow. I asked him if he wanted to talk to Match. He shook his head no, he didn't. I then asked him if daddy could talk to Match. His eyes lit up and he said "Sure!" as he thrusts his skateboard into my hands. I hold it up to my face, taking a closer look for inspection. After a few seconds, and not really knowing what would happen next, I bring it away from my gaze and hand it back to Colin. Colin stares at me blankly and says, "Talk to Match". I hesitate, bring it back to my face and hesitate some more. If nothing else, I can always claim I was just playing with my son to boost his imagination when I'm in therapy. Feeling foolish I say to the skateboard, "Hello, Match. How are you doing today." I pause, look back at my son for approval. Colin looks at me with a puzzled look. "You no hear?" he stammers. I drop the skateboard, get down on my knees and get face to face with my son. I shake my head no and ask if Colin can hear him. He shakes his head yes, that he can. I ask him if Match is saying something right now. He shakes his head yes, again. I ask what… Colin enthusiastically says, "Hi daddy!" I smile at him, feeling a bit foolish. I stand up and start to walk out of his room when Colin says, "No daddy, I say 'Hi daddy'. Match says 'Hi boose' This raises an eyebrow. The only way Colin would know what my name is would be if he heard Michelle say it. I ask him what else Match says.. My son slowly comes out with "We are speh-shal, be kuh-hair-ful. Dane-ger." Colin looks up at the ceiling and nods his head after each word he attempts to pronounce. I wait for there to be more, but Colin simply averts his eyes from the ceiling to mine, seeking some sort of approval. I give him a big hug, and say "good job buddy!", trying to sound as unconcerned as possible. I ask if there's anything else Match says, but he shakes his head no, and remains quiet.

Needless to say, I'm fairly alarmed here.... What danger?? Damnit Colin, you need to grow up faster so I can better communicate with you. The words he used.. I've never heard him say them before. Most two year olds don't say words like that.. And now that I think about it.. It was as though he was just repeating what he heard. Repeating what he heard in his mind... Similar to how I heard my name being called in my mind. But if I need Cannabis in order for my mind to reach that state, Colin just did it right before my eyes. Which means, either he is in a constant state of dopamine/serotonin overload, or, his mind is on a completely different level than everyone, ever. I take a closer look at his face to see if he looks out of it, but all I see is his usual turkey self, staring back at me with his bright blue eyes. (I call him a turkey as opposed to calling him other names to his face) It seems like with all of these amazing and crazy things happening, I'm still having trouble believing them. The proof that my son is telepathically communicating with celestial beings is literally happening right before my eyes.

But it's as though I still need more proof. I'm not sure what it's going to take to commit, but whatever happens, I'm on board with it all. I suppose I fear this is all happening in my mind, and I'm having a mental breakdown. The only reassurance I'm getting right now is Colin. What I need to do is find out more information. And the only way to do that is to communicate. Colin will be a much more reliable source of what the fuck is going on further down the line, but the necessity for Cannabis is real. And coincidentally enough, I believe I may have already solved that problem.

On Wednesday after work, we went to Wal-Mart and bought a used lawnmower to use for lawn care. It turns out that this used lawnmower was an outright piece of shit and could not handle the task at hand. In all fairness though, it had been weeks since the grass had been cut and was up to three feet tall in some places in the backyard, thus making it a formidable task for any mower. What made it particularly tough though, was the humidity of the summer. The grass was so thick and watered that the remnants left behind started to build up on the inside of the mower and cause it to stall every ten feet. What made it worse was that the more I cut, the more of this thick remnant that was left behind. AND, worst of all, this large backyard of tall grass had become a mosquito breeding fest, and I was constantly wiping armfuls of mosquitos away as I mowed. Talk about misery. Luckily, my neighbor to my left spotted me going through this mess, walked over to my yard to open my gate and then proceeded to ride his riding mower right on over. I had my back turned when he first entered, so when I spotted him, I was rather surprised. The realization of what he was doing came next, and I got an idea right then and there. Once he was done, I went up to him and officially met my neighbor. He said his name was Fred. He was in his early 40s, but you could tell that he was still young at heart. He had a shaved head, and a long red beard. My idea was for him to ride his mower and regularly cut my grass while I would give him cash or anything he wanted in order to not have to do that again. He refused my cash and/or gifts, and yet still agreed to cut it every week anyway. That's a good neighbor.

I ended up getting him a bottle of Jack Daniel's as a token of gratitude anyway on the following day. I went over to his house in the evening and knocked on his door. Showed him what I had to offer, and he accepted, though I got the feeling when I handed it over that he wasn't the drinking type. He invited me in to open the bottle and share a drink, and I happily accepted. Once inside, I couldn't help but notice there seemed to be a rather faint lingering odor of Marijuana. I asked him if it was weed that I smelled, and he started to play dumb and tried to think up an excuse. I reassured him that I loved to smoke as well and if he was willing, I'd smoke with him right then and there. I must have come off as genuine enough, because he agreed and left the kitchen area for a moment to go get some and came back with a massive jar full of amazing looking buds. My jaw dropped and I immediately asked if I could smell it. He handed me the jar and I proceeded to remove the lid and inhaled long and hard. A-ma-zing. There's just something about the smell of Cannabis. It's as though my neurons have already changed how they work in anticipation of the protein entering my bloodstream in the immediate future. Fred rolls a couple joints and we smoke them both. Well, he smokes most of it, because it's pretty damn strong, and I suppose now that I think about it, I'm a lush. But hey, things are happening in my brain that aren't in most other people's when they do this…

I proceed to spend the next hour or so talking to him about whatever came to mind. I learned that he was a crane operator for a local construction company, played

Bass guitar locally in a metal band with a couple of his friends, and had smoked weed every day of his life for the last 25 years. I thought, 'Wow. My sister is no longer the biggest pothead that I know.' I inquired as to how he has so much, and he gestured for me to look out the window by his kitchen. I did, and noticed there were two marijuana plants, each about 5 feet tall, growing right outside his window. They were shielded by their own fencing on either side and were blasted by sunlight from pretty much noon to sunset. Perfect. No one would ever notice because they can't be seen by his neighbors, and no one ever walks around in the cornfield directly behind our houses. Not to mention, being out in the country, people regularly fire their firearms in their backyard, so you tend to stay indoors. I commended him on his growing situation and expressed my jealousy. This led to me asking if he wouldn't mind "supplying" me with bud on the regular, and if he would want to regularly smoke together. He said that he would, and that was how I secured my communicative future. I sent a text to Michelle and asked if it was cool if I stayed longer to watch a movie with the neighbor, and she said she didn't mind. Of course, I loved watching movies while high, but it was mostly to allow for the smell to dissipate off my clothing.

My wife's sense of smell is pretty damn good, though sometimes I get the impression that it's simply paranoia that rules her sinuses.

We watch the movie, he hands me a small bag of bud, and I proceed to head back to my place to retire for the evening.

This leads me to what happened today. Michelle works on the side as a Premier Consultant, hosting jewelry parties for other cackling hens, so I support her and stay home with Colin as she goes and makes money. These events allow for me to smoke while she's away, and more specifically, this would allow me to finally see if I could find out some more answers after smoking, or just to see if anything would happen. Well… something did. The shock has mostly worn off, and I'm trying my best to write coherently. This is what happened.

I put on a Pixar movie for Colin to watch as a distraction. I thought about inviting Fred over to strengthen our friendship, but I had a specific agenda this time around, and his company would have to wait. I put a decent sized amount into my glass piece with the intention of smoking it gradually until I reached that magic state of mind. I don't smoke very much before that familiar racing of thoughts feeling quickly returns.

I'm standing in my garage with the door open in order to let all the smoke alleviate. I start thinking about why this is happening to me and my son, and what's so dangerous about our lives. These are the thoughts I'm focusing on when my mind begins to wonder and images from memories and things that I've encountered begin to surface.

At this point, before I get into what I 'learned', I wish to express what I think was happening. When my brain functioning reaches the state that I've already described as close to REM sleep, I think this is the key to communication. This is hard to explain... Earlier this week when Colin was speaking with Match, it was fairly clear that he was hearing words. I did not hear any words this time around and haven't since that one time in the Stan. I'm beginning to think that my brain simply lacks the capacity to be able to consistently hear these words. But something still happened. When I was in college, there was a hypnotist that came to our school, and chose volunteers from the audience to participate. Out of the hundreds present in the crowd, I was chosen, mostly because I was wearing a tight and revealing shirt, and he most likely wanted to use that to his advantage to sweeten the show. Now, most feel that hypnotism is a sham. Well, it's not. The volunteer has to have an open mind and be completely submissive and willing to do the hypnotist's bidding. The whole point of the process of being hypnotized is to look inward and reach a high state of relaxation. When I volunteered, I was completely willing to do everything he said because up until that point, I didn't believe being hypnotized was possible. What he did, was put me in an extremely relaxed state; the most relaxed I had been without the influence of drugs. Once I achieved this state, his show began, and I was fully aware of what was going on. The kicker was, I allowed him to influence whatever I did and did everything without caring, or being conscious of how ridiculous I was acting. I didn't care, and just wanted to do my best. From what I can remember, I danced as though I was competing for a spot on an MTV music video, was a horse and gave rides to the other people on stage with me, Riverdanced to Irish folk songs, and pretended to be seven and told Santa what I really wanted for Christmas. At the end of the show, the relaxed state of mind persisted. I was in control of everything I was doing. But for the duration of that show, I let the hypnotist do the driving, and I didn't care.

This feeling of 'letting someone else do the driving' was similar to what happened. They were using images from experiences and memories to communicate messages, much like a plan or message would be conveyed during a slide show. They were somehow able to tell exactly what was stored in my brain from the experiences throughout my life and pull these images up into my conscious like a computer retrieves files from a hard drive. With each image that would appear, I would proceed to examine and interpret. Successive images would then appear, and I would proceed to figure out correlation, or causation, or just think until I correctly interpreted what the meaning was behind each image. I can't remember every image that was brought up, but I can recall the overall message that was trying to be conveyed.

The episode went something like this; (and again, I'm doing my best to put into words what I experienced, I will treat this like a conversation of thought, with me as the interpreter and them as the speaker), the first image that came to me was that of Jesus Christ, specifically scenes from *The Passion*. Jesus walking around, performing miracles, being the son of God, gets crucified. I don't believe in Jesus, at least, not in the sense that he was the son of God. Jesus may have existed as a man in history, but he was just a man. I do not deny the chances of there being a God or creator, but I feel that

Jesus was an exceptional leader that touched the lives of thousands through words of hope and inspiration, and not necessarily the physical son of God. Man then wrote the Bible as a lasting record of his deeds, spiced them up, and created a lasting legacy of moral values that everyone could easily follow. Following the image of Jesus was an image of the newly discovered double helical DNA from when I did a science report on Linus Pauling in the seventh grade. Jesus' DNA? What about it? Then the zig-zagging UFO I saw at JRTC. They saw me imagining the craft zig-zagging, and it proceeded to zig zag. They can detect my brain signals, and follow my train of thought, much like they're doing right now. Humans were not piloting that craft after all. It was them. They were watching me. They have been watching me for years. JRTC again, only this time it's Jesus looking up to the sky, staring at the UFO. Jesus could communicate with them as well. Back to the DNA model. Something in Jesus' DNA made him special? Well that seems obvious… But what about it. What was it exactly that made it special? And if they are showing Jesus standing where I stood, am I also to infer there is a connection between us? Next, an image of the classic 'Grey Alien', pulled from some documentary I saw once upon a time.

Something about Jesus' DNA and Aliens? Last image: The classic line of the humanoid evolution diagram, starting with chimps, progressing in various forms all the way to Homo Sapiens.

This is all I can recall from the episode. I snap out of my deep trance like state and realize I'm still sitting on the step just outside the door that leads to the garage. I step inside to check on Colin, and notice he's still watching the movie, and I notice, it's still at the beginning… in fact, I would only venture to guess that only a few minutes have passed since the start of the movie. What seemed like a half hours' worth of deep thought and drawing conclusions took place in only minutes. These 'episodes' are periods of rapid thought generation and advanced thought processing. It's… it's like time slowed down. Or time was stretched to seem longer. In fact, that sounds like a good code word for it. Time-stretching. I like it.

Back to the episode, I try to smoke some more in hopes of another Timestretch, but it doesn't happen. I'm left to ponder my own thoughts as to why it didn't work again.. I conclude that either it's a skill that I can work upon to build and strengthen, or it's a delicate state that cannot be abused, else damage the ability or even possibly lose it for good. Man, I hope it's the former.

Back to the point.. What does it mean? I've thought about it and can only come up with this explanation to which I have no proof or evidence to back. Something that I have always seen as a hole in the theory of Evolution, is why it was that if man supposedly evolved from Apes/Chimps, why are there still Apes and Chimps around today? Why don't all forms of man along its evolution still exist today? Each form would be more intelligent than the last, and if monkeys were the base and are still here, why don't all forms still exist? To me it doesn't make any sense that these species of man can evolve independently and alongside monkeys... Ok, let me put it this way. It is widely accepted in the scientific community that all of the continents were once one larger supercontinent, known as Pangea. Some enormous seismic event occurred which caused this large land mass to split and separate into smaller land masses which would eventually lead to how the continents are arranged today. Consider the inner coast of Africa, consisting of countries such as Nigeria, Gabon, Cameroon, and the Congo. These countries are all coastal and are all filled with tropical jungles. Now consider the northeast coast of Brazil. When South America, specifically Brazil, is placed right next to the inner coast of Africa, one notices that they essentially fit together like puzzle pieces. This would be because they were once connected in this region while Pangea was in existence. In addition to this, Brazil and the inner coast of Africa are both primarily comprised of tropical jungles. Today, the jungles of the two regions have become different over millions of years, but they were once directly connected, and were once all part of the same jungle. This separation of land masses will be the basis of which I use to discuss my evolutionary Timestretching point.

While these two continents were connected, there would have undoubtedly been many species of Ape and Monkeys present in this massive jungle region. The populations would then be separated with the split of Pangea, and the two continents would change as their positions on the globe changed in accordance to longitude and latitude. These changes would lead to changes in climate and vegetation, which would also undoubtedly affect all species of Apes and Monkeys in these regions. The Theory of Evolution would lead us to believe that these species would then go on to mutate, or in some cases, not mutate. Regardless of what happens, Evolution dictates that in both land masses, a majority of all populations on both land masses mutate and evolve as time progresses. These populations would exile their mutant population, and these exiled populations would then persist to continue to mutate into the eventual forms of early primitive man. We can assume that both land masses produce forms of primitive man due to the fact that there is human racial diversity on the planet. However, in both cases and on both land masses, in order for Evolution to be true, forms of original Apes and Monkeys would survive on both continents, and all forms in-between the origin species and eventual primitive man would not. How is it possible, that with each mutated/evolved form of man being produced, none would go to survive to today, yet all we see on the planet are ancestors of the original species, and homo sapiens? In my mind, it doesn't make any sense for there not to be at least one surviving species of primitive man that came between Monkeys/Apes and homo sapiens. Sure, there have been Bigfoot sightings, and this very well could be the answer that I'm looking for, but until we have one in captivity, and considering our currently technology, it can be safely assumed that all instances are hoaxes, and that they simply do not exist. I'm not trying to completely discredit Evolution here, because it is a sound scientific theory, and has already been proven to exist. My point is, if Evolution is the answer as to how we are here, it doesn't explain why many origin species persisted to today, and all other species between them and humans, did not. I believe the more logical explanation behind the Theory of Evolution is that the species of Monkeys and Apes found on the planet today *are* the result of millions of years of un-altered evolution. These primates evolved from much more robust and primitive forms of primates over thousands of years, but never to the extent of evolving into Humans on their own. The theory of Evolution explains why these species are here today, but when it comes to explaining why *we* are here, there is a hole in the theory, and we are left with pieces and a lack of evidence that no matter how you look at it, does not logically explain our creation.

This is where *they* step in. But before I get to that, let me discuss the possibility of other life outside of this planet. Let's assume the Big Bang Theory is correct. We exist today as a result of matter reforming from the Big Bang to create our galaxy, and thus cooling over billions of years to form stars, our Sun, and metal cores slowly gaining matter to form planets. It just so happens that our planet orbits our Sun the perfect distance so as not to be too warm or cold, the proper elements are found on this planet to potentially form life, and our planet is tilted on its axis at just the right angle to allow for appropriate heating from the sun for life to occur. All of these main factors (and various others I'm not going to mention) contribute to the reason why life can exist today. When you think about it, it really is quite amazing to the point where it inspires the thought that maybe it's not a coincidence, and these conditions were created in order for this to happen. Seems possible… enter God(s) and religion, created by those fortunate enough to experience the miracle of life from all of these events lining up. Now, let us look outside our galaxy, to everything else out there. There are an estimated 100-200 billion galaxies in the universe, with each having formed in a similar fashion to our own Milky Way. Life required quite a lineup of events to occur in order for us to be here, but we are here. From what we can see in our own galaxy, there are an estimated 40 billion Earth-like planets in the Milky Way alone. This means that we can assume there are roughly 150 billion galaxies besides our own out there, with each having around 40 billion Earth-like planets. When thought of in this way, Alien life loses the question of if, and becomes more appropriate to ask where and when.

Next, assume our own state of civilization. During the last several hundred years, technology has exploded and continues to do so. Ten thousand years from now, what will technology be like? One can assume that the need for food and resources will be greater than that which our planet currently yields, and we will have ventured outward and developed space travel out of necessity. While this may or may not be the case, the point is, our civilization on a global scale will be vastly different. Now assume the very probable chance of there being an earth-like planet that developed similarly to ours at around the same time, only theirs reached the ideal conditions needed for life a few thousand ranging to a few million years before ours did. (Because let's face it, in the history of the cosmos, a thousand years, even up to a million years of our time, is but a blink of an eye compared to the rest of its history) Both planets produce a dominant and intelligent humanoid species, only theirs has had what has now become a significant chunk of time to become more advanced. If it is safe to assume that we will venture out into space in a few thousand years, then they have already done so, and are currently doing so. On top of this, if they are already in space, then it can also be assumed that they already know what we know scientifically, and then some. (An understatement)

The Timestretching episode is seeming to suggest there is a link between their DNA, our evolution, and Jesus. What I believe they are suggesting is that they visited our planet to find it inhabited by a lesser humanoid species compared to where we are now. If we have the technology today to be able to splice animal genes and essentially genetically engineer animals, plants, and even ourselves, then it can also be assumed that they are familiar with these processes, since they have had a much longer time to develop their own technology to a point far beyond that of our own. I believe these images are suggesting that they took the humanoid form they found on this planet and spliced just enough of their own DNA into ours to make us more intelligent. Why would they want to do this? Well, what motivation do we have to do it to animals? Essentially it boils down to advancing our own knowledge base as a species, and because, frankly, we can. And as far as Jesus goes, well, that I'm not sure on. Last time I checked, the only thing Jesus and I have in common would be … amazing things are happening to us. Holy shit… No, I refuse to believe it. There has got to be more to it than this. I need more answers.

And what of this danger? I've suddenly become overwhelmed with anxiety. If everything I just wrote is true, and my son and I can communicate with another life form... then this is huge. This is.. life changing, no, this is significant to the point of affecting human history in its entirety. These are .. I guess the precursors to the most significant anything ever. The information that I have stumbled upon is.. dangerous. Oh shit. Why me? I just wanted to live my life as a normal man, raise a family, have grand kids, die happy and loved. This changes all of that. I will be lucky if I see any of my grandkids.. or even to have grand kids.

I understand why I'm writing this now. This is my story, should I not get to tell it. These theories and ideas are actually closer to the truth than any other person has ever come before me. I don't know what's in store for my future, my family's future, or even the future of the world... But all I know is that with every entry into this journal, the truth can be remembered. I will write in it until I can no more. What a shitty and morbid thought.

I need to find a way to break this to my wife. I need to find out why this is happening to me. And I need to keep my eyes open more than ever before. I will write again when I've gathered more answers.

JULY 27, 2013

Just read over my last entry to remind myself of where I left off... If that can be classified as "ground-breaking" then this update splits the Earth in half.

First, no update on filling in Michelle. She is still clueless about our son, and just thinks he's the "brightest little man." I plan on letting her know when two obligations can be met; 1) I can provide proof to her directly, so she believes without any doubt. 2) This danger we've been warned of becomes real. The more I think about this aspect the scarier it becomes. Michelle needs to know asap, but not just yet. Colin should be at home hiding from those that would seek to do him harm in a secret bomb shelter built underneath this house. But that would raise suspicion with the wife, and the neighbors. And living in a low-key area, in the middle of a bunch of farmlands is about as off the map and safe as it gets. (Not to mention, daddy is a bad ass mother fucker, with an Ace up my mind)

Second, the work week was uneventful. The Army sucks, leaders are dicks, and I'm grossly underpaid. Nothing new there.

Third, I had an opportunity to Timestretch yesterday. Michelle went on a paid mini-conference trip to Nashville yesterday morning with Premier for being the top salesperson in the State of Tennessee for this month. I was invited to come along, but we've no way to have Colin watched, not to mention, I'd rather stay home and keep my eye on him. So, I encouraged her to go have fun and take lots of pictures. It was just a few nights out on the town and a paid fancy hotel room. She would be back in a day and a half on Sunday afternoon. Nothing too special.

Once she left, I fired up another Pixar movie, and let Colin become absorbed while I went out to the garage to smoke. This time around, I was going to focus on what I determined to be the most pertinent questions I came up with this past week; why me, what's next, my wife needs to know, and what do I have to do with Jesus?

The episode starts with a memory of the day Michelle told me she was pregnant. Once she told me, I remembered feeling very surprised. We had been told that she was unable to have kids due to having Poly-cystic Ovarian Syndrome. This is where a woman has many cysts on her ovaries that cause for complications during ovulation. Some cases are minor, but my wife was to the point where the doctors were 99% certain that we would never have kids. This was a pretty large hurdle to get over and caused a lot of stress and doubt between the two of us. But it did not last long because not even a month later, we found out she was pregnant. I remember thinking something along the lines of "It just goes to show that whatever a doctor tells you needs to be taken with a grain of salt." But apparently, I was wrong. The next two images they submit to my conscience are the moments when I found that single bottle on my dining room table when I was in high school after that party, and of the two hangars resting upon each other like a teepee. They did those things? But how... and why? Wait, I'm missing something... The pregnancy... They assisted with that too. I continue to ponder these thoughts, but no other images in relation are brought up. I move on to my wife and Jesus. The image of JRTC re-appears, with the UFO hovering in the sky. But when I turn to look where I was standing, or where Jesus also had been standing, I see that it is neither of the two, but someone new. My son Colin, stands there, grinning his little turkey grin. (Nothing follows)

I snap out of it and am left in my garage to contemplate, yet again, what it was I was just shown. Why can't they just speak to me directly? As I'm thinking this, I suddenly say out loud "Because that didn't work the first time." Did I just say that? Where did it come from.. I try to remember the moment as it just happened seconds ago.. I was deep in thought, and the words seemed to come from deep within my subconscious. I might have said them, or it could have been them as well. It was my voice, but it seemed distant, and wise in a way. I have no idea. But then I begin to think about the words themselves… it didn't work the first time? What is this in reference to? If I'm having trouble placing exactly what I'm talking about, how could it have been me? My first thoughts go to the voice I heard in the desert… but that doesn't make sense, because that technically worked. The first time.. I think I know. The dream I had when I was younger. Where a booming voice came down from the sky and scared the shit out of me. It was so loud and paralyzing. But it was them. That *was* the first time they tried to contact me.

The main two differences between then and now are A) I was much younger, and B) I was asleep. Ahhh, and apparently C) I hadn't been smoking. That's it! That's the key. They attempted to speak to me when I was younger, but I didn't receive it well because it scared the shit out of me. Not only does Cannabis allow for this communication, but it apparently numbs the sensitivity of certain areas of the brain in order for the communication to take place. Makes sense I suppose.

But what about the other things? They're claiming to be responsible for my wife's pregnancy, and those two events when I was younger. The only way my wife could have gotten pregnant would be if my sperm cells were physically placed in proximity of her egg. And this is related to the two events… The only way the two events could have happened would be if someone also physically placed them there. I need a moment to ponder this.

This is what I have come up with; these beings have the technology to manipulate matter, all the way down to the cellular level, and possibly even smaller. What I'm suggesting here sounds a lot like telekinesis, but it doesn't necessarily have to be. Another way this could be accomplished would be through a machine that has the ability to create and project powerful magnetic fields. The problem with this idea would be the lack of metal in the plastic hangers and glass bottle left on the table. Though, I suppose the objects themselves wouldn't have to be metal, if they used metal ions, or other surrounding metal objects, or atoms, to do the moving for them. Or perhaps they use their own metallic flat discs to act as a work force to move things. This kind of sounds a lot like a phantom Magneto flying around pulling pranks on everyone. But then again, technology we do not understand leads to confusion, ridicule, and more often than not, fear. Case in point: religious people not with the technology curve. But now that I think about it, the existence of this machine would explain a lot. It explains how my wife got pregnant. She got pregnant, because they made sure an egg and a sperm cell found one another in her Uterus. And it would allow for them to examine each individual egg in both her ovaries, as well as each of the millions of sperm. That's it! They were able to see the chromosomes held in each cell, and pick and choose the right combination to produce Colin. Colin… Colin standing in Jesus' place. I'm still not clear on whether or not my bloodline is in line with Jesus, but I'm beginning to think that's not the case. I think they were suggesting that Jesus came to be in the same way. Mary was most likely labeled as a virgin, because she was unable to birth a child, much like my wife was told. She most likely figured this out through trial and error, which would make her quite far from being a virgin. And unfortunately, if one knows they cannot get pregnant from sex, or cannot impregnate others, respectively, this tends to lead to many partners. This would explain why the father was unknown, and her getting pregnant in the first place would be seen as an act of God. Hence, her son being the son of God.

This means that my son is the equivalent of Jesus Christ, and I am his father. The inscription! The teacher said part of it meant "the son of the father". Whomever wrote the inscription already knew who I was? How is that even possible?? And I still know nothing concerning this supposed danger we're in. Although, I'm not too sure that I want to know. Examine the life of Jesus. It was normal until he found out who he was. He accepted his fate, tried to spread his message, and was killed in the process. Who exactly killed him.. Well, the Jewish I suppose… But more accurately, people that did not understand what he was, or did not want to accept that he was the truth and would defend their religion based on manipulations and lies to the death. Does this sound like anyone in the world today? Unfortunately, that description fits millions of people on this planet.

Suddenly I feel as though a massive weight has been placed on my shoulders. The responsibility of raising.. of protecting the Christ child. How am I to succeed? This has to be kept a secret from the world. I have been chosen. Colin is the truth, the way and the life now. Tears are running down my face now as I write this. I need help. Even when my wife finally comes on board, it will be the three of us against the world. They have to see this! Read my mind right now damnit! I NEED HELP!

I don't know what else there is to say. I think I will go inside and watch a movie with my son and show him love and security that he will hopefully know for as long as possible.

JULY 29, 2013

As I write this, I have just returned from being held at the Christian County Jail. It is close to midnight, and even though I am exhausted, there is no way I could possibly sleep right now. Michelle and Colin are currently asleep in the master bedroom. Michelle knows about Colin, and I learned the truth about the forces of good and evil on this planet. There's so much to say.. My life, and this world as I knew it, are forever changed. (I feel as though I could write that a lot lately) I'm dreading the cramp that awaits my hand at the completion of this entry.

Earlier this morning, (Sunday), Colin and I got up, and did the usual breakfast routine. I allow him to play in his room, while I contemplate if it's worth another Timestretch before Michelle gets home later today. I decided against it, and instead decide to clean up a bit around the house so Michelle will be pleased to come home to a clean home. I'm cleaning for a while when I get the idea that Colin and I should also be freshly bathed for when she arrives. So, I proceed to take a shower with Colin. A few minutes into the shower, I notice Colin look up at the ceiling, and then tap me on my butt to get my attention. I turn to him and ask what he wants. Colin proceeds to say "Daddy, someone's here. A bad man, in da grr-rage." I freeze. I ask him if Match told him this, and he nods his head yes. I proceed to turn off the shower, tell Colin that I want him to lay down in the tub and be very quiet. I order him to stay there until I come back. He looks at me with a mixture of fear and surprise yet nods his head. As quickly as I can, I get out of the tub, grab the clean pair of boxer briefs I was going to put on after our shower, and put them on as I darted into our closet. On the top shelf I have several pairs of ratty old jeans in the corner. I reach in-between the top two pairs and pull out my Springfield .45 XDM. I turn and sprint to the bedroom doorway and proceed to move using Army room clearing procedures, like one would see on a cop show. I remember feeling silly as I did it, but the technique works. I clear the other bathroom and two spare rooms to make sure we are still alone before heading towards the garage door. Once I reach it, I slowly reveal half of my face to get a glance of what's out there. The garage door is open, and there's my car in the garage. Behind it is a black SUV, which I've never seen before. Beside the SUV is a man in his late forties, looking down at something in his hand. I stare for a second longer to confirm… it's a revolver. Once he's done looking at it, he reaches behind his back and tucks it into his pants. I slowly move the half of my face out of sight so as to not catch his peripheral vision with a quick movement. This guy has a deadly weapon but is not leading with it out. I choose to put my .45 under the couch right beside me and crouch beside the corner of the wall. (The garage door opens immediately into the kitchen, and the living room is on the right with the garage door being in the corner of the kitchen just before the start of the living room.. see diagram) The plan is to use the element of surprise to quickly over- power, and subdue.

I reach my hand around the corner to quickly lock the door without making a sound. I think for a moment and suppose that a locked door may avoid this whole sit- uation. A few moments later, he is at the door, and I hear him trying to turn the knob to open the door. He then proceeds to break the glass of the lower window panel and reach inside to unlock it. This guy is committed, which means he most likely wouldn't hesitate to use deadly force. I must strike hard and fast. He opens the door and takes one step into the house. He pauses and looks around in the kitchen for anyone. He takes a few more steps directly into the kitchen, and towards the living room, coming into my complete view. I spring up and out from my crouched position at a 45 degree angle. With my right palm, I thrust upward and grab the bottom of his chin. I use my right leg as a base and my left leg to sweep him at knee level. I push his head backwards with my right hand and he goes sprawling backwards, landing with a loud thud on the vinyl kitchen flooring. From here, I quickly and expertly sweep my right leg over his torso, and achieve the mount position, quickly moving both of my knees close to his armpits to limit his upper body movement. I proceed to aggressively grab control of his right arm, and pin it down across his own neck, as though he were trying to choke himself. Once I have secured his right hand behind his own neck, I pull with it my left hand, and push his elbow with my right, making his own grip around his own neck, that much tighter. This guy doesn't like this and uses all the strength he has to try and buck me off or break free from my grip, or anything to relieve the feeling of me about to use his own arm to choke himself. I quickly lean forward as a response to this and pin his arm down with my chest, and free my right hand from gripping his elbow. I'm sure to pull even harder with my left hand to make sure he stays in this position as I use my newly freed right hand to quickly palm strike his nose three times in an attempt to quell his newfound energy. This puts him in immense pain and momentarily stuns him, and then I resume my grip on his elbow and start to use all my strength to push his arm as far behind his own neck as it will go. I know this is particularly painful, and he will respond by trying to roll with the direction of my applied force, allowing me to spin him over onto his belly. Once there, I use my chest yet again to pin him down and use my right arm to navigate between our two bodies, and pull the revolver out from being tucked behind his pants. Once I have it, I give it a hard toss directly in front of me to be dealt with in a few moments and proceed to completely release both of my hands from his right arm. I cock my right arm out to the side and deliver three 'You fucked with the wrong person asshole' strikes directly to the side of his right ribcage. With each of the last two strikes, I hear cracks both times, and the man screams in agony. I sit up and test the magnitude of his injury by essentially applying zero force to his person, and he remains on his stomach, displaying heavily labored breathing, and making long and loud groaning noises. It is at this time that I decide he is more or less subdued, and proceed to get up and walk over to his revolver. As I'm doing this, I get the thought that a couple of broken ribs wasn't quite enough. I proceed to hop back onto his back and pin his right arm down in a 90 degree angle. I use my chest to apply force to the upper corner of his right shoulder, pinning his entire right side to the floor. I use my left arm to pin his wrist to the floor, tuck my right arm underneath his right arm, and tightly grab my own left wrist pinning down his hand. With what seemed like divine purpose, I quickly and powerfully lifted my right arm straight up, being sure to maintain my tight grip of my own left wrist pinning his wrist to the floor. Like magic, we both heard a loud pop, and his shoulder easily popped out of its socket. This reset his moaning and groaning, and with this additional injury, I was then confident enough to stand up and retrieve his revolver.

Once I reach his revolver across the floor. I open the release and proceed to dump all the bullets onto the floor. Once this is done, I toss the gun into the sink, and turn back to the intruder, who is still whimpering on the floor about his shoulder and ribs. Your tax dollars at work, bitch. I grab his now bad shoulder and turn him over so I can see his face. I look over him for a moment, and then proceed to ask what he's doing here. He looks up at me coldly, seemingly unwilling to talk. What do I do now? This has never happened to me before, and my mind blanks for a moment. How am I supposed to make him talk? I think about it for a moment, and the answer comes... more pain. Torture. But before it comes to that, let me try with words again.

I look down at him yet again, and calmly say something along these lines, "Look, unless you tell me right this fucking moment why you're here, I'm going to break all of your limbs to the point where you will never walk again. And that's *if* I decide to let you live." This was apparently rather convincing, because he told me he was here to get my son. I ask why, and if he was sent by anyone, but again, he doesn't talk. For some reason, call it fatherly protection, his silent defiance this time around infuriates me. I crouch down and punch him in his broken ribs The man starts to scream again yet again. I'm about to continue, when I stop myself. Where does this end? With me killing this guy? I don't need that. I need to hide and protect my son. If the police come here, it will make the news since break-ins never happen around here. Then my whole family will potentially be on TV for the world to see which would pretty much be the opposite of what I'm wanting. So instead of continuing to batter him, I proceed to search all of his pockets. He at first tries to stop me, and I give him a quick jab to his nose again. I tell him, "No, you don't get to stop me. You won't talk, so I'll let your things do it for you." I confiscated two cell phones, and his wallet. One phone is an old school flip phone, and the other is an iPhone. I tap the top button on the iPhone, and his phone comes to life. His background picture is of a little toddler, playing at what appears to be the same place where my son goes to daycare at times. We don't send him every day, but we use it so he can spend some time with kids his own age, and Michelle and I can have a date every now and then. The iPhone is password protected, and I move on to his wallet. His name is Walter Cross, and he's sporting a Florida Driver's License. At this point, I'm starving for answers, so I walk over to my couch, grab my hidden gun, and walk back with it pointed at his chest. I calmly say to him "This is your last chance, Walter. If you don't tell me why you're here, you're done. I'll get off with self-defense, and your little girl will never see her daddy again.' I load a round into the chamber, 'Your choice." Walter thinks about this for a moment, and then proceeds to tell me.

He learned about Colin through his wife. His wife is apparently a teacher at Colin's daycare, Mrs. Cross. Her description of my son sparked his interest, and he came to visit his wife at work one day, with the intentions of observing my son. He goes on to say something about the boy fitting the prophecy, and if he brought him in, he would be praised, and rewarded. I ask where he was going to take him. He says "to they that have no name." I step over to him and punch him again in his broken ribs. I explain to him through his continued pain that I am in no mood for riddles, or vague descriptions; I want to know everything. Once the throbbing subsides and he's able to speak again, he goes on to say that he doesn't know their name because he has not yet been accepted. Knowing what I know about my son, had he gotten to him, this guy would have hit the jackpot. I ask him to tell me everything he knows about this "organization". Expressing a brief moment of surprise, indicating that he had known their name and I had just guessed it, he says that they've been around for a long time, they're everywhere, and know everything. He said they'd kill him if they knew he told me about their existence, and then they'd kill me and my family. I prod for more, but he swears that is all he knows. I ask if anyone else knows he is here, and if he came alone. He said no one else knew he was coming here, because he wanted to surprise the organization. I stand back and think for a moment and come up with an idea. I would keep him here until Michelle comes home and have him tell her everything. This could be the proof I need to bring Michelle up to speed. I'm feeling rather satisfied with this plan and proceed to hear a car door slamming outside in the driveway. I peer through the garage door and notice Michelle has just arrived. As she's walking up, she stares as the black SUV for a moment with a puzzled look, and then proceeds to carry her purse and a huge bag of luggage, far too big for a 36 hour trip. As she enters the house, her look has gone from puzzlement to alarm as she notices the broken window in the garage door, sees me holding my gun in my underwear, and sees this stranger on our kitchen floor. She immediately asks what's going on, and if Colin is safe. I realize that I nearly forgot about Colin and proceed to tell her that he's hiding in the bathtub, and to go check on him; I would explain everything when she comes back. We wait for a few seconds until I hear a loud and happy "Mommy!" Michelle proceeds to talk to him for a few seconds, and shortly returns, holding him in her arms wrapped in a towel. I turn to Walter, and command him to tell her everything he told me. Michelle listens to the story, and when he's done, she asks about the prophecy Walter mentioned. This part I have yet to find out myself, although I'm pretty sure I have an idea of what he's going to say.

Walter goes on to state that a prophecy was foreseen by someone in the organization; a woman, born in the sixth year, on the sixth month, and on the sixth day during an unknown decade, would immaculately conceive a child that would bring about the end of the world. Every woman that has been born on June 6 in the sixth year of every decade is assigned someone within the organization to observe and live nearby in close proximity, to see if they are the one the prophecy mentions. I think to myself, there has to be hundreds of women born on that day every decade, and that's just in the US alone. Plus, all that effort because of a prophecy?? There's got to be some key information missing here. I interject to ask about those born outside the US on that day, and he answers with the simple statement of, "they are everywhere". Michelle fails to see how Colin fits the prophecy, even though she creepily fits the birthday requirement; Colin was born naturally. Walter looks at her with a scrutinizing grin.. "You have no idea about your son do you…" He turns his gaze to me, smiles again and then adds "But your husband does… he's been keeping secrets from you.." Michelle turns to look at me and has the "WTF is he talking about" look about her. I proceed to tell her that I will tell her everything, but first we need to figure out what we're going to do with Walter here. I explain to her that if what he says is true, and there's this huge "organization" out there, if he goes free, he will tell them, and they will be back. But I also go on to say, that if we kill him, they will most likely investigate the cause of death to one of their own, even though he apparently hasn't been 'initiated' yet. I pause for a moment, and then add that it's possible that he could be lying or not telling us everything he knows.

Michelle, obviously shaken by the thoughts of people trying to take her child, stands there silently with a glazed look in her eyes, lost in deep thought. I look over her way and attempt to snap her out of it. After a moment she looks at me and says that she believes that letting him go would cause more trouble to arrive faster, and if he's dead, we would at least have some time to find help. She gets up and heads towards the back door, she turns to me, and says "You know what to do, NCIS." I give her a quick smile and slight head nod. What she's referring to is a show that we sometimes watch together on TV, the Naval Criminal Investigative Services. These government agents go out and investigate crime scenes and use literally everything in their power to solve crimes. What she means when she says this, is to think how they would approach this scene, and to make it look like he was shot in the heat of the moment in self-defense, and not so much us sitting and being judge/jury. I call after her and tell her to take Colin for a drive; this may take a good 20 minutes or so. She nods in agreement and proceeds to head towards the garage door. Just then, Colin looks at me from my wife's arms and says "No daddy. Don't hurt the bad man. Match says no!" All of us turn our gaze from Colin to Walter. Walter had apparently started convulsing on the floor. His eyes had rolled in the back of his head, and he was having some sort of seizure. I turned to Michelle to find that she was just as puzzled as I was, and I proceeded to walk over to Walter to get a closer look. I give him a swift kick in his broken rib, to test the authenticity of this "seizure". Walter has no reaction and continues to shake. I run into the bedroom and find my phone. I guess I wouldn't have to shoot this guy after all, and someone up above now has gotten my back twice today. I hesitate before calling 911 and think about exactly how this phone call is going to sound. I chuckle to myself and think 'this ought to be rich'. I dial the number, and tell them mostly the truth; the break-in, admittance of attempting kidnapping, and then the seizure. I change the details ever so slightly, and when I'm done with the phone call, and an ambulance and squad car are on their way, I go and tell Michelle the story I just told the police. Once that is done, I attempt to start the story about what I have learned about Colin, but I soon realize that there just simply isn't enough time for it wouldn't be long before I was being arrested as a pre-cautionary measure. I get an idea and tell Michelle to put Colin down and come and stand by me. I give Walter a quick glance, and he appears to have stopped convulsing and is now lying there, snoring ever so softly. Michelle walks over to me, and I motion for her to stand behind me. I bring both hands behind my back and hold up no fingers. I ask Colin, how many fingers am I holding up? He looks up and looks back at me and enthusiastically shouts "zero!" I turn to look at my wife and she seems slightly surprised. I get another idea and grab a piece of mail sitting on the kitchen counter and proceed to find a pen and write something on it. I hold it up to Michelle, so she can read what I wrote "The father of the son" I ask Colin if he can tell Mommy what I wrote on the paper. He looks up, nods his head, and looks at my wife and says "Da fah-ter uhf da son." I look at Michelle and tell her to think of a number and whisper it in my ear. She softly whispers "21", her favorite mall store. We both turn to Colin, and he says "Twenny-one!" I turn and look at Michelle to see if we need to go further, and her jaw has since dropped as she stares at her son with shock. She rushes over to him and gives him a huge embrace. I follow shortly behind and crouch down. Michelle pulls away and asks Colin how he knew all of those answers. He smiled at my wife and enthusiastically tells her "Match." Match tells me. I inform her that Match is what he calls *them*. It's not certain whether she understands exactly what I mean when I say *them*, and I'm about to start explaining when we all hear the sound of approaching police sirens. We both look at each other, and I tell her to head out into the front yard, and to tell them I am inside next to Walter, on the floor with my hands on my head. She nods and proceeds to give me a quick yet passionate kiss, as I suppose a 'thank you" of some kind, and she heads out to the front yard just in time as the first squad car pulls into the driveway. I proceed to do as I promised and lay on the kitchen floor and put my hands on my head. I glance over to Walter, and he seems to be stirring somewhat, as though all this commotion outside were disturbing his nap.

I hear male voices coming from outside, followed by the shrill voice of my wife. I can tell she's schmoozing the acting bit… Theatre majors. Le sigh. A few moments later an officer steps up to the garage doorway and asks if I was Benjamin Bruce. I confirm that I am. He then asks if there is anyone else in the house with us. I say there is not. He takes one hand off his pistol, and waves over his shoulder, signaling his partner to go ahead and sweep the house. The second officer brushes past him and proceeds to clear my house. The first one steps over to Walter, keeping his pistol focused on me, and does a quick vitals scan on Walter. Just then, I hear an ambulance pull into the driveway, followed by at least one more squad car. The second officer returns to my position and proceeds to say my Miranda rights as he arrests me and puts hand cuffs on me. He then brings me to my feet to be escorted outside to a squad car. I take a glance to my right and see Fred standing on his front porch with a look of concern on his face. I flash him a brief smile and try my best to shrug my shoulders. I then notice that all of my neighbors as far as I can see down the road are outside their houses, trying to get a gander at what's going on. Great. I got escorted to the back of a police car and placed in the back seat. A Police officer opens the front passenger door and proceeds to get in and turns around to look at me. He closes the door behind him and proceeds to get a statement. Before I start, I inform him that this could have been done inside my house so as to avoid the entire street seeing me in my underwear. I assure him that once he hears the story, he'll realize that this treatment is quite unnecessary. I proceed to bend the truth, ever so slightly, making sure to leave out the whole judge and jury part my wife and I went through. Whatever Walter ends up telling these guys shouldn't hold much water next to what I have to say. The word of a would-be criminal, vs that of an active-duty soldier having thwarted his criminal act sans use of deadly force… I'm practically Mother Theresa here. The police officer records my statement and then gets out to head over to Walter, who is now conscious and is currently hand-cuffed to a stretcher and being put in the back of the ambulance. The same cop climbs in the back with him, to get his statement. The doors stay open as he listens to Walter. The cop isn't in there for more than a couple minutes before he shakes his head and jumps out. The cop then proceeds to head over to my wife and son, who are standing with two other cops on the front lawn. He proceeds to say something informative about me, because he gestures toward my direction and turns to walk back towards the car I'm in. He proceeds to open my door, and to inform me that I am not being charged with anything at this time, but he would like me to come down to the police station for questioning, right after he takes off my handcuffs and allows me to go inside to get some clothes on. I tell him that sounds like a swell idea. I get out of the backseat and turn to have my cuffs removed. Once off, I hurry over to my wife and son and give them a big hug. I suddenly remember I'm mostly naked, and head back inside to find some clothes. Michelle and Colin follow me inside, and I inform them that they want to take me in for questioning, but I am not being charged with anything at this time. I told her that I would give her a call when

I was ready to be picked up. She agreed to this plan and reminded me that we still had much to discuss regarding our son. I throw some clothes on and head back out to the waiting squad car, and get in the back again, this time without cuffs. He backs out of my driveway, and speeds away to the station.

Once at the station, things went as I expected, paperwork, photographs, fingerprints… all standard procedure. Once it was time for questioning, I was taken to an interrogation room, just like you would see in a movie. The classic single camera in the corner, and the one-way mirror to one side, complete with a single table and four chairs for sitting. On the table was a laptop that had some sort of recording program already pulled up. I take a seat opposite the laptop per instructions of my escort. The escort then informs me that a specialist was being called in, and it would be a while before he arrived. I nod with apprehension. I sat there for four hours, before the door finally opened again. I had laid my head down on the table and was close to falling asleep when the man entered the room. He was wearing a black suit with a black tie. He proceeded to place his briefcase on the table, close the laptop, and push it over to the side. Once seated in front of me, he brings his hands together, and clasps one over the other, as he quietly studied my face. I'm not sure how long it was before he finally started to speak, but the tension I felt was among the thickest I had ever experienced.

(An app had been recently sweeping through the phones of my soldiers... one where you can record conversations with the push of a single manually programed button on your phone. I had recently been assigned to a new unit and this unit's leaders were apparently notorious for making unfair decisions and showing favoritism, so in response, they had countered by recording every key disciplinary conversation they were a part of, with the sole purpose of exposing blatant, unfair treatment. Thanks to them, I pulled out my phone on my lap, and was able to record the following conversation.)

Man: Hello Ben. My name is Thomas. I am with a top-secret sector within the FBI, but my affiliation with this sector is pure coincidence, and has nothing to do with why I am here.

Me: Uhh.. O...k

Thomas: (He makes a gesture towards my ring) I notice you are wearing a ring with a large red stone... Might it be a Ruby, Ben?

Me: It is. (Quick Sidenote: I bought jewelry as a souvenir from my second deployment. A large, 13 carat championship/graduation looking ring for myself, and a smaller, 5 carat teardrop shaped stone for Michelle. Never really thought to mention it, because this is the first time it's ever come up… The fact that I'm wearing it at this moment is pure coincidence. I just happened to throw it on when I went inside my house to throw some clothes on before coming to the station. Something inside me thought it might be a good idea to wear it, as a status indicator.. or for a "demanding respect", kind of thing.)

Thomas: Might I ask why you wear it, and where you got it?

Me: What does this have to do with me being innocent?

Thomas: Ah yes… your 'situation'. We'll get to that Ben. In due time. (He flashes me a devilish grin that makes him look similar to Tommy Lee Jones, despite his mostly bald head) Now, back to the question. Your ring?

Me: I purchased it in Afghanistan, during my most recent deployment. To me it represents my accomplishments overseas, specifically being crowned the unofficial "Strongest Man in Jalalabad". I won the bench press competition, three months in a row.

Thomas: Ahh impressive.. But why choose a Ruby Ben… Is red your favorite color?

Me: No… Green is, actually. A sapphire was my first choice, but they were a bit pricey.

Thomas: Of course… Well, perhaps you were drawn to a Ruby for another reason… Hmm?

(Thomas releases his clasped hands to reveal that he too was wearing a ring on his right ring finger. One adorned with a large red stone)

Me: (I stare at him in silence and give him a slight shoulder shrug)

Thomas: Men like us are drawn to Rubies Ben. They mark men of status, men of influence and power; they are the mark of a man with content. Do you know of what I speak of, Ben?

Me: (I raise my eyebrows and squint by eyes before honestly saying) Thomas, I haven't the slightest clue what you're talking about.

Thomas: (Thomas smiles at me with his evil grin again) Content, Ben. It is our content that defines us, our content that unites us, and our content that sets us apart.. I'm talking of course, about your DNA.

Me: (This guy has me literally guessing what the hell he's going to say next… I'm confused, and yet, have a very odd feeling about this man at the same time. All I can manage to say during this pause is) Go on…

Thomas: Ben… The man that attacked you today, this… (Thomas opens his briefcase, and pulls out a manila folder. He opens it and briefly looks over a file) this… Walter Cross. What did he say to you?

Me: He said he was there to kidnap… my son.

Thomas: Yes, indeed… Was there anything else?

Me: (I pause for a moment and debate whether or not to tell this man about "The Organization", or the prophecy Walter mentioned. I decide to casually drop it, to gauge his reaction) Yea, he mentioned something about some organization he was trying to impress.. (I then added to cover my ass) He wasn't really making much sense, and it was hard to understand him. I think he was in the process of having a stroke of some sort. (I decide to leave out the prophecy)

Thomas: Can you recall any details about this "Organization"?

Me: No. Just that they would be impressed with him.

Thomas: I see… And you're certain there's nothing else?

Me. Yes. Nothing more.

Thomas: (smiling) You see Ben, I'm not entirely sure what your 'content' allows you to do.. But my content has enhanced my sinus receptors. When people tell lies, they emit a certain type of pheromone that is, rather different, from those emitted with the truth. You are emitting both, which means you are with-holding information. Naturally, I don't expect you to trust me yet, seeing as how we just met, and I haven't told you what I know… yet. But if you want us to become friends Ben, then you are going to have to trust me. Do you think you can do that?

Me: (I open my mouth to try and say something, but I'm so stunned and not prepared for anything this man has had to say that nothing comes out)

Thomas: I will take that as a maybe. (Smiles) Your DNA, Ben. Are you aware that it is special?

Me: Yes.

Thomas: Ahhh good.. Then you do know what I am talking about… ?

Me: (I suddenly feel defensive) Three things; first, is this conversation being recorded, second, I'm not saying anything until you say it first, and third, is there anyone behind the glass? (I nod my head to the one-way mirror to the right)

Thomas: Spoken like a man with an agenda I see. (Smiles) To answer your questions, no. This conversation is not being recorded, and the hidden room is empty. In fact, this conversation never happened. I was never in this room, and you were never in this room. You were processed by the police here at this station and sent to a cell to await questioning. It would later come to pass that questioning was determined to be unnecessary. You were released.

Me: I see...

Thomas: The man that attacked you happened to be driving down the road and felt a heart attack coming on. He crashed into the ditch just outside of your driveway and suffered a broken rib and dislocated shoulder. He then stumbled out of his car, and broke into your house seeking help, in fear of death. You and your son were home, given quite the startle, and called 911... Walter is in stable condition, and should be released in a few days.

Me: He broke into my house to kidnap my son! Who's to say he won't try again?

Thomas: Walter Cross is of no threat to you, or your family. He has no memory of why he entered your home.

Me: Oh? And what makes you so certain?

Thomas: You saw it happen, did you not? The seizure... they were erasing his memory. The Organization will review the police report, look at his medical charts confirming a previously unknown heart condition, see his injuries from the wreck, and you should be in the clear.

Me: Why? Why all this cover up? Who, or *What* is the deal with this 'organization', and how do I know I can trust you?

Thomas: (Leans back in his chair, his tone getting low and serious) Ben.. I am member of a secret society, which goes as far back as this "organization" Walter told you about. Both exist in secret to the public, but my society exists in secret of the organization. It has been this way for centuries. We have kept our eye on you, suspecting that one day this day would come. You see Ben, you have proven yourself ready. Ready to join our ranks... Ready to know what we know. Ready to keep some of the greatest secrets of all time. It may be that you already have knowledge of some of the things I'm about to tell you... Before each member is initiated, it is always unknown just how much they've been shown. That's what I'm trying to find out, Ben. And you are being... rather uncooperative.

Me: Who has shown me what?

Thomas: *Them*, Ben. (Thomas makes a gesture up towards the sky as he says this) You see, we have been watching you for some time now... We have been waiting for you to prove yourself to be ready.. And whether you realize it or not, you have done just that.

Me: Proven what? How?

Thomas: Proven you are ready to join us, Ben. We, the ones chosen to do *their* bidding. They reach out to us, because we are the only ones with which they can communicate. Each of us has a different purpose. Mine, are to act as an initiator, and to determine the initiate's rank. I am called upon to bring new entrants up to speed, which is exactly what I am doing here with you now. As I was saying, you have proven yourself to be ready in two ways… the first is becoming aware of the Organization. The simple fact that you are aware of its existence puts you in danger.

Me: But I don't even know who they are, or what they're trying to do.

Thomas: Simply being exposed to the concept of their existence is grounds enough for them to wipe you and your family off the map. We are well aware of Walter Cross' recent efforts to join the Organization. But rest assured, they are not aware that you are aware.

Me: If you're aware, why don't they come after you?

Thomas: (Slightly chuckles) A few of them have accidentally come across me and attempted to pry their noses into my business, but they should know better. You see, being *their* servant comes with the benefit of *their* protection. *They* have their own agenda and are constantly moving their own pawns. I have easily been able to evade all possible threats and eliminate those that have gotten too nosy. The question is, where do you fit in? What have they shown you?

Me: I… I'm having trouble grasping all of this… You never mentioned the second reason why I'm supposedly ready, by the way.

Thomas: And so, I did not. You are quite bright Ben… Just how bright, remains to be seen.. The second reason is your Ruby ring.

Me: My ring? What about it?

Thomas: Every member of our society, without any prior knowledge of our group or being told to do so, acquires a large Ruby. We may not realize it at the time, but we seek them out so that they can fulfill a subconscious craving. As you most likely already know, communication with *them* does not come direct. We need the Cannabis plant to influence our brain chemistry, allowing for memory communication. Using words from our language, they have given the process a name… Time-stretching. Is this not what you know it to be as well?

Me: Yes... How did you (I get cut off)

Thomas: I didn't. You see Ben, on top of them using memory recall to convey messages, they also plant subconscious ideas. You think you're having a genuine thought that is your own, when in reality, it's happening because *they* want it to happen. This raises the paradox of knowing that you have no way of knowing if the thoughts you experience on a daily basis are happening because they're yours, or if they're planted by *them*. The memory recall portion only happens after Cannabis consumption, but subconscious thought planting can happen at any time; granted this process can happen in the first place.... All of us know this term, and we all think we have come up with it on our own. But in actuality, they planted it there. This word is sacred to us. It is one of the ways we identify our own.

Me: But how did you know to watch me? How do you know I'm special? And, how else do you know your own?

Thomas: The easiest way is through our rings. You see, your desire to acquire a Ruby, was not your own. Just like the concept of Timestretching, it was planted in your mind, by *them*. As you are most likely aware, most rubies are dark and not pure. They are not particularly valuable gemstones, and not popularly sought after. But what makes them so special, is that regardless of whether they are naturally occurring, or man-made, they have unique properties when in close proximity of their technology. Each member's ruby behaves somewhat differently from each other, and to be honest, we are not entirely sure why these 'unique properties' exist. It is up to you to explore the dynamic properties of your stone.

Me: When you say 'their technology' what exactly are you referring to?

Thomas: They have the technology to move objects of all sizes and masses on our planet. It is a technology that we have never been able to replicate, and one that they refuse to let us have for our own. They fear that we would use the technology in a manner that deviates from its practical purposes, building and manipulation. Using it for building is rather self-explanatory and as a matter of fact, there is evidence all over the world of its use. As for the manipulation aspect, it's more along the lines of using objects to achieve an outcome other than construction… This could include anything from moving an object out of place in order to bring your attention to it or moving cells around within our bodies to cure ailments, recall memories, or even to selectively reproduce. Most members are born naturally and tend to show up in certain prominent family trees, like yours and mine, for example. But every now and then, they selectively choose a single egg from a female, and a certain sperm from a male, both cells extraordinary in their own right. The cells are chosen in order to be certain that particular genes are present and expressed over others in order to maximize the person's abilities. Hence Jesus, Moses, Muhammad, Buddha, etc. Which brings me to the answer of your other question, as to why we knew to watch you... Well.. that's a bit complicated... You see Ben, every once in a while, certain members of our group are given special tasks to complete by our friends. These individuals do their best to complete their assigned mission in secret, and due to their exceptional talents, achievements, and worldly contributions, their names are forever marked in the pages of history. It then becomes our job to guard these chosen bloodlines, and ensure they continue on, until once again a descendant is called upon again to do their bidding. All of the religious figures I just mentioned were all actual people that existed and were all selectively created by *them*.

Me: You're saying I'm related to one of those?

Thomas: No. (Another light chuckle) Of course not. The descendants of these people generally do not stray far from their origin. The living relatives of these people are living on the other side of the world. Your distant relative, however, was Benjamin Franklin.

Me: Benjamin Franklin?? He was part of... whatever you guys are called?

Thomas: Ah, I apologize... We do not have a name. Not exactly sure of the reason why, but I suspect keeping a certain level of anonymity can do nothing but help all of our safety. But you may refer to us however you like. I usually refer to us as "The Society." But yes. Benjamin Franklin was a brilliant mind of our great nation, and was charged with being a foundational leader in our countries history. With a job as important as that, and accomplishing what he accomplished, it's no wonder that he had help. Is that so hard to believe?

Me: No I suppose not. And who are you related to? Thomas Jefferson?? (I say half-jokingly)

Thomas: ... That is exactly right Ben... It appears your level of subconscious suggestion is quite strong...

Me: I was mostly kidding...

Thomas: Whether that is what you think or not, the fact of the matter is you knew that because *they* told you, just now. Do you not often find that you know something, or are aware of something, and you're not entirely sure how that knowledge came to be…as in.. the presence of this knowledge seems to be planted by something or someone else?

Me: Actually.. yes. That explanation is quite refreshing. I know exactly what you mean.

Thomas: Good. And now, going back to your ring. When two members seek to challenge one another to see if they can be trusted, they place their rubies in close proximity to one another … Since those of us in our society are under constant surveillance by them, as a free security measure, they validate membership for both individuals. However, in my case, my main motivation to challenge you, is mostly to see how your stone reacts.

Me: … What happens during the challenge?

Thomas: Let's find out, shall we?

(We proceed to bring our right hands to fists, and place them palms down on the table, bringing them approximately two feet apart from one another. The rubies in our rings begin to glow like the magic stones did in Indiana Jones, and the Temple of Doom. Thomas glows whitish yellow, while mine seems to glow an unstable blue/violet, both colors trying to vie to be the dominant color, yet neither ever wins. We pull away, and they continue to glow for about 5 seconds more on their own, and in those seconds, we both notice that mine is considerably brighter than his)

Thomas: Interesting… This hasn't happened for quite some time.

Me: What do you mean?

Thomas: As I have already stated, all of us are generally being monitored, every day. Whether the being monitoring us is assigned exclusively to a certain individual, or if they monitor several, or even all of us; it is unknown. But, as it is my job to determine the rank of each new initiate, the glow of your ruby has indicated you possess a rank that has not been in existence for quite some time. Your rank is that of Guardian; guardian to the prophet, and second to only the prophet him or herself. It is unknown who the last person was to hold the rank of Guardian, but we assume they would have been tasked with being the guardian of Jesus Christ in his youth. The reason we do not know who this person was, is because we have no evidence that such a person ever existed, but I know such a position exists, because *they* have told me so. And as for Jesus, he held the rank of Prophet, the highest rank in our society. These two ranks only occur when they are needed, and it can be hundreds to thousands of years before they occur again.

The last time these ranks were seen on this plant, was during the lifetime of Jesus Christ.

Me: You're saying that my son is the… the Prophet?

Thomas: That remains to be seen. I'm afraid he is too young to know for sure, but you are most certainly the Guardian, and since one of the main tasks of the Guardian is to protect the Prophet, it would only be logical for your son to be the Prophet. However, it is entirely possible that your son is not the Prophet, and you will encounter the actual Prophet later on in your life. It is hard to say.

Me: I.. I don't know what to say.

Thomas: I don't expect you to Ben. But, I will tell you, that in light of this information, it is protocol for you to meet with the current highest ranking members of our society. I will arrange for you to meet the Grand Master tomorrow, and then eventually you will meet the High Grand Master. Seeing as how your outrank them both, they will want to meet you for themselves.… (a pause) You're looking quite shocked Ben. Tell me, is what I'm telling you really so hard to believe?

Me: I don't know. I suppose I've known for some time now that this was the case, I mean, I've been in denial.. I mean.. My son.. I thought I was going insane. All they've told me to do is to keep a journal. There hasn't been anything like… this.

Thomas: A journal? What journal?

Me: I'm not really sure. I just know they want me to write in it. Write about what's happening. I was under the impression that it wasn't a big deal.

Thomas: (seemingly offended) 'Not a big deal'… Ben, you are literally one of billions that an alien life form has chosen to communicate with, and they give you the task of documenting your own life, and you view this as 'Not a big deal'… I know people that would love to have your brain on a slab right now, in the name of 'science'. Hell, they'd love to have both our heads. And these are just normal people, never mind 'the Organization'.

Me: The Organization!... What can you tell me about them?

Thomas: I can tell you just what you need to know, for now. Once you have met with at least the Grand Master, I will happily divulge anything you wish to know. But for now, we will stick to the basics…. The less you know, the better, trust me… There was a time when 'The Organization' didn't even exist… We were one within the same secret society, until the coming of Jesus Christ. Jesus was given the mission of bringing the truth to light. The split happened when there was a disagreement on how to portray Jesus throughout history. There was a side that believed his way of life was his true message, and that should be how he was remembered. The rest of us believed, that his mission from *them*, should be how he was remembered.

Me: You mean 'bringing the truth to light'… (Thomas nods) What truth exactly?

Thomas: That would be the truth of the origin of man. What do you know about this?

Me: They've shown me.. well.. At least, this is what I believe it to mean, that they created us from the beings that were here when they first arrived.

Thomas: Precisely! Very good, Ben! Brilliant… And what exactly have they shown you that makes you certain of this?

Me: Because it came to me during my first few… Timestretches.

Thomas: And.. you're letting uncertainty cloud your judgement?

Me: Yes.. well.. no…. I figured it out, but, this is all so… forgive the pun… alien to me.

Thomas: (Smiles that seemingly evil smile) I completely understand. You just simply have to trust your instincts…. They are right.. you are right… Do not be so quick to doubt yourself.

Me: Yea.. ok.. thanks. So what happened with the disagreement?

Thomas: Ah.. Well.. a small scale war broke out. Those wanting to hide the truth believed it would cause too much damage to the world, and they proceeded to wipe out those that wanted the truth to be continued on. "Those" in this context, primarily refers to the devout Jewish of that day in age. Once they learned there was a man spreading the word that Man came to be from aliens, and not from the creation of their God, they silenced the blasphemer, and made sure none of his followers were left to continue on his true mission. Only a few recent initiated remained whose initiation went unknown by the "Organization". They persisted on in secret, and we have since rebounded, and now continue to serve their wishes in secret.

Me: The "Organization" knows nothing of our survival?

Thomas: There have been close calls, but no… Thanks to the efforts of people like 'yours truly' (gestures to himself) our presence has remained undetected, and we peacefully persist in secret. Which is another reason why I'm here with you today. Had I not intervened with the investigation and covered up the true nature of Mr. Cross' encounter, we very well may have been exposed to the "Organization". They would have sent more to finish the job. Your son would have been taken, and you and your wife would have disappeared off the face of the Earth, pending an unknown fate.

Me: I see… There was one other thing Mr. Cross mentioned that I've kept from you… I apologize, but I had no way of knowing you could be trusted…He mentioned something about a prophecy… What do you know of it?

Thomas: A prophecy? What is this 'prophecy' you speak of??

Me: He mentioned that someone within the Organization prophesized that a female born on the sixth day, of the sixth month, of the sixth year in an unknown decade, would immaculately have a child, and that child would bring about the end of the world.

Thomas: (Thomas brings his right hand to his chin, and falls into momentary deep thought) Your wife… if my memory serves, her birthday matches this, does it not?

Me: Yes.. How did you know?

Thomas: I told you Ben, we've been watching you. Whether you realize it or not, much of your past is due in part to efforts of those from our society. I do not wish to go further into this matter at this time, but I can tell you this… the tasks they have us do are often sporadic, and tend to depend on where the decisions of our own free will take us… often times we come into close proximity to someone they have identified as a future initiate that would allow for us to make an impression, or to influence the life of this future initiate… Does that make sense?

Me: (I ponder for a moment) You mean, like giving someone a gentle shove 'in the right direction'?

Thomas: Yes… Ingeniously spoken.

Me: But I thought you said that I've been watched because of my family history… that doesn't add up.

Thomas: Yes, there are many of us that are well aware of your potential, and you've unknowingly come into contact with several more prominent members of our society during your life… you simply did not know at the time. One thing *they* cannot control, is our ability to make our own choices. They can influence our thoughts, plant ideas, but it is ultimately up to the individual to decide what to do. The life path of each person is their own…. Their plans, much like our own, are dependent upon all of the factors present in this world that they cannot control. They simply take life, much like we do, one day at a time.

Me: But what about the Proph–

Thomas: The prophecy… This is the first I've heard of it… But it sounds like something not of this world.

Me: What do you mean?

Thomas: I mean, it sounds like something someone learned from Timestretching

Me: But you made it sound as though the Organization no longer communicates with them anymore…

Thomas: We don't know. We assumed they did not since their beliefs were not in line with the plan *they* gave Jesus. It has always been thought that they stopped, looking up to the sky, if you will. But this… this is not good.

Me: How so?

Thomas: If your wife fits this prophecy, then, you are already being watched by the Organization… And it's standard for them to send extra surveillance on a subject they're watching when an incident happens to one of their own.

Me: Shit.. you're right. He did mention they were aware of my wife.. and her immaculate conception.

Thomas: Immaculate conception?

Me: Well.. My wife and I were told that due to a medical condition, she would never have children. But, less than a month later, we learned that she was pregnant with our son, Colin.

Thomas: Explain this 'Medical Condition'

Me: Michelle has Poly-cystic Ovarian Syndrome. She has cysts on her ovaries to the extent that they could never successfully release an egg. Her ovaries can release all the eggs they want, but due to blockage, it would never make it down to her Uterus without the doctor's physically removing an egg from her ovaries, fertilizing it in a petri dish, and then manually planting the egg in her Uterus.

Thomas: And she got pregnant without a Doctor doing this process?

Me: Yes.

Thomas: Hmm… It does sound like *they* intervened, but there could be two possible reasons why… The first would be simply to continue your bloodline. As you are your Father's only son with your last name, you need a son or your family line dies with you. In this case, they would be doing you.. and I suppose themselves a favor by continuing a prominent blood line. But… this sort of thing has never happened for that reason before. It has always happened for the other reason..

Me: What's the other reason?

Thomas: The other reason would be to create a Prophet.

Me: Like Jesus?

Thomas: Not like Jesus. Jesus Exactly. Only, today's version. He would at a minimum be able to communicate with them freely. It's hard to say what else he could be capable of... They would have chosen specific gametes from you and your wife in order to produce desired results.... Gametes that would have many dominant genes of *their* origin, so as to grant certain abilities. Which reason do you believe it to be?

Me: (Needless to say, there is a long pause here) My son.. has already shown that he can communicate with them. I thought it was an imaginary friend.. but.. it's becoming more and more clear that he is... the Prophet.

Thomas: How certain are you that he is able to talk to *them*?

Me: I've seen him do it. He's done it for me, almost on command.

Thomas: Well, this certainly changes things.. I'm afraid our time together is nearing an end. I have an idea as to what I need to do. What is it you require of me?

Me: Uhh.. what do you mean?

Thomas: You are my superior... They hold you with higher regard. I have a plan of motion set in my mind, but before I share it with you, I'm asking if you have any orders, or instructions to me...

Me: N-no Thomas. I don't know.. need... anything.

Thomas: (Smiles) Very well then. In light of your apparent rank, the situation with your son, and the fact that the Organization will be following up on the incident regarding one of their own... I will be setting up a meeting between you and the North American Grand Master, tomorrow. I will try to make it so he will meet with you on your Army base. He is in the top ten of our society, and knows far more than I. He will provide you with further guidance on your state within our society... .. You seem Distraught Ben.. Do not worry, we have a considerable head start on the Organization.. It should be several days before any action is taken regarding the incident with Mr. Cross. I recommend you bring your wife up to speed on these matters.

Me: Y-yea.. that's ok?

Thomas: Of course... half of your child's DNA came from her, did it not? Just play her our conversation from your phone... that should be all she needs to hear. Also... if you haven't already figured this out, it would be wise to wear your ring every day. Forever.... Should you need to contact me, call this number and then the listed extension. (Reaches across the table and hands me a black business card) It's a secure mailbox, completely unhackable, so don't worry about mentioning sensitive information when leaving a message. And one last thing.. I wouldn't recommend recording the conversation with the Grand Master.

And with that, he smiled at me, grabbed his briefcase, and walked out the door. I was about to ask how he knew about my phone, but, I reminded myself that I wasn't the only one with "special talents" in that room.

After sitting in the room for another 20 minutes, an officer finally came in through the door and informed me that I was free to make a phone call to secure a ride home. I passed on the pay phones, and went just outside of the station and called my wife. From our house in the middle of the farmland, it would take her 30 minutes just to get here, and that's if she was sitting in the driveway, ready to go. I proceeded to sit down on a nearby bench, and ponder everything that had just happened.

It turns out, that I came up with many questions I wish I had asked before Thomas left. I will attempt to remember what I can up with during this time here, and refer back to them tomorrow, when I'm apparently meeting with the North American Grand Master.

Who else knows about these beings other than our society and the organization? It seems highly unlikely that they are the only ones that know. Surely the US government knows something about all of this…

Thomas mentioned something about sensing pheromones and how that was one of his special abilities that his 'content' allowed him to do… Does that mean he smoked just before talking to me? Or can he do that all the time? Do I have certain things I can do at certain times? I need more information.

If the Organization discovers the truth about what happened to Walter Cross… Thomas informs me that my whole family will be wiped off the face of the Earth… That is a scary ass thought. I'm not sure what it's going to take, but I need more protection than what I've got. I need to bring this up with the Grand Master. Thomas' reassurance, while confident and convincing, will be the last time I take words in place of action.

Thomas mentioned something about unknown properties, and how they pertained to my ring… Does the Grand Master know anything more on this subject?

If my son really is the new age Christ figure… What is it *they* hope for him to achieve? And why bring a prophet to this world now?

I feel like there's more to my ancestry than what Thomas mentioned. I'm The Bruce. If I am a living relative of Ben Franklin, why isn't my last name his? And I also wasn't a fan on how Thomas didn't expand upon him being related to Thomas Jefferson. He just casually brushed it off, as though we were talking about the weather or something. Something was off about the whole situation. He was a really strange guy.

I need to learn as much as I can about our society from whomever I'm going to meet tomorrow. Hopefully they will be a bit more informative. I'd like to know about this rank structure, and what exactly I am entitled to, if anything. Rank in the military does come with perks, and it would only make sense for rank in the society to do the same.

I also need to smooth out some facts about my ability to Timestretch. I was only able to do it regularly after the time I smoked the spliff on duty in the Stan. Was that the cause, and do others need to have a drastic experience in order to Timestretch as well? There has to be some sort of significance with this event, because I was never able to do it all the other times I smoked Cannabis prior to that moment, in the U.S.

Thomas mentioned something about me coming across several prominent society members in my past and insinuated they guided me to get to where I am now… Who were these members, and how did they guide me?

Tomorrow's meeting with the Grand Master will be one of the most important days of my life. It would probably be wise if I Timestretched tonight in preparation.

It was around this thought that Michelle finally arrived to pick me up with Colin in his car seat in the back. I immediately plugged my phone into the car charger and proceeded to pull up the recording of the conversation I had with Thomas. When it was done, she proceeded to bring up every question and concern she could think of, well into the night. I can't remember everything she brought up, but, she did raise a few good points which I will mention here.

If I am able to Timestretch, then her DNA should be prominent with Alien genes too, and she may be able to as well. I told her that this is entirely a possibility, but, I went on to explain to her that only after that spliff I had in the Stan from Dos, was I able to accomplish this feat. I offered to let her try with me that night with the stuff I got from Fred, but she shouldn't expect much from it. Most likely, she would just get a normal high like every other criminal dope smoker in the country, except for places that have already legalized, respectively.

Another point she brought up, was about this notebook. She suggested the reason I am to write about all of this is in case something should happen to me, or my family, and our story would be lost forever. She believes that this journal would speak for me, should no one be able to tell the stories contained within these pages. This idea does make sense to me, but I do not believe it to be right. Thomas mentioned something about being monitored by them as having its benefits. (Random thought: If they really have been watching me all my life… I apologize for my excessive masturbation during my younger years. That must have been fun for them) But, I hope for all of our sakes that she is wrong.

Once we arrived home, it was already past everyone's bedtime, and we took our sleeping son from his car seat, and placed him into our bed. I then proceeded to retrieve my secret stash and packed a large bowl into my glass piece and headed out into the garage with my wife. I must admit, that I was genuinely excited to smoke with her. She had been so adamant about being against all drugs in general, that this was new and exciting for me. I hadn't felt this way towards spending time with her since we first met and started dating. I let her take the first hit, and we passed it back and forth until it was all gone. The resulting Timestretch went as follows:

    I was sitting in the interrogation room again with Thomas. They reiterate two things that he mentioned… the part where he mentions the ranks of Grand Master and High Grand Master, and the part where he asks if I had any instructions for him. Once these are done, two separate images are brought to my conscious. The first is a snapshot of a man with wild looking dark hair, being interviewed for a documentary for some TV show I saw in the past. The next image is that of Walter Cross in the back of the ambulance, being interviewed by the Police Officer. That was all that I was shown… I came back to the garage with my wife and began to work through what these images meant. On the surface, these 4 images are either going to be co-related in an AA BB manner, or an AB AB manner. Since the two excerpts from the conversation with Thomas were not related, it should be safe to assume the latter correlation is the correct one. That would align the man with crazy hair as being the Grand Master, or the High Grand Master, which pairs instructions with Walter Cross and the Police Officer. Let's focus on the first pair first…. They are insinuating the man with the Crazy hair is either the Grand Master, or the High Grand Master. Which would it make more sense for him to be… If I am to meet the Grand Master tomorrow, would it make sense to reveal to me who he is prior to meeting him? Yes.. and no I suppose. It makes sense in terms of security and trust… But if Thomas is trustworthy, then the benefit of knowing who he is going to be is lost once the meeting takes place. However, if the man with the crazy hair were to be the High Grand Master, I would essentially know who he was before being told by the Grand Master… If he was going to tell me in the first place. Yea… it makes far more sense for him to be the High Grand Master… It's as though I'm to use this knowledge to impress the Grand Master… no.. Knowing who this person is would be a sign of.. status? Already knowing one of the biggest secrets within a secret organization is.. power… I think it could mean that they see me as higher than the Grand Master. Man I hope that's not right. This person is undoubtedly going to be someone of significant status, and here I come out of the blue, and trump their lifelong accomplishments and endeavors, and I've only known for days what they've known for years, not to mention the likely struggles they must have gone through to acquire said knowledge. This leaves me to try and figure out who the crazy haired man is, but before I get into that, let me go over the second pairing. The interaction between the Walter and the police officer... What was spoken between the two? Does it matter? Depending on what Walter said.. I suppose it does. Actually, what he informed the police officer is vastly important. Shit! I need to know what he said. In fact, as the closest Organization memb.. well.. almost member, I suppose he could potentially be used to find out more information on the Organization. And, depending on his state of mind after whatever it was *they* did to Walter in my house, he could have revealed some important information to the police officer. It would appear that I have two 'loose ends' that need to be tied. I don't really have the ability to look into this.. but Thomas.. he could. Yes, that's it! I need Thomas to look into these matters, and report back to me. I will give him a call, and have him do it for me. He should easily be able to access this information. That leaves one last thing... The man with the crazy hair... I'm trying to remember where I saw him.. where did I see him...

"Bruce!" My wife snaps me out of an apparent trance, and I'm back in my garage again, staring at my wife whom apparently has a rather worried look on her face. She asks me what the hell I was doing.. she went on to describe me during this episode. I had been standing there looking off into nowhere with a glazed look on my face. She described my eyes… She said it was as though I were flipping through a book, using my eyes to turn the pages. I had been mouthing words, but not actually making any sounds. She said she let this go on until she had enough and had gotten 'creeped out' by the emotionless look on my face. I smiled at her and gave her a big hug, and asked her how long I had been standing there doing that before she snapped me out of it. She proceeded to say that it had only been a few seconds, twenty at the most, and she thought I was having a seizure or something. I take a moment and marvel at myself.. all of that deduction in less than twenty seconds! That's amazing…. I proceeded to explain to her everything that I had just experienced, and as I went on, her eyes got wide and her mouth slightly opened. She seemed to be amazed that I had processed all of that in seemingly no time at all. Then after a moment of connecting the dots, she hesitantly asked if all of that was from them. I gave her a sly smile, and went on to explain that just the images that came up were their doing. I explained that I believe they have the ability to examine our brains and can see what we have stored in our memories. All they have to do is stimulate a certain area in our brain that corresponds to a specific memory using the slightest electro-magnetic stimulation, and we recall the memory. It is then up to me to figure out why they would show me the image, and to figure out correlation between successive images as interpretation of a message. I then went on to remind her that this is only possible due to a couple of reasons; the first is THC, or the active ingredient in the Marijuana plant. The protein being present in the bloodstream, and therefore the brain allows for certain brain waves to take place in order for this communication to happen. This however, isn't enough. (And as I'm saying this, I realize it's the first time I'm having this particular thought.. as though they planted it as I was explaining) Much like the relationship between the Hypnotist and his subject, there needs to be a certain amount of trust. You must clear your mind and be willing to accept what comes. The nature of our brains in terms of thought process is similar to that of a circuit; the brain can only process a certain amount of electrical signals at a time. If you sit there and preoccupy your brain with the electrical signals of your own thoughts, then it will be that much more difficult to discern what they are trying to say. I ask her if this makes sense, and she smiles and nods her head that it does. I then go on to ask her if she experienced anything, but she shook her head and through some slight laughter, she commented "Nothing like that".

At this point, I went back to the man with the crazy hair, and explained to Michelle that I was trying to recall where I had seen him before. She thought about this for a moment and said that it sounded like a guy that we had seen on that "one show" on the History channel. She then added, "The one about the aliens." I thought about it for a moment, and then it came to me.... Ancient Aliens... We had been browsing through Netflix one evening, bored out of our minds, and had decided to give a few of these episodes a gander.... I remember thinking that the show was pretty cheesy, and it often made assumptions that were ridiculous and not logically sound, but I do remember that it mentioned several interesting things that I found to be, at the time, rather shocking. Again, many of the claims this show makes are dumb, and over the top, but seemingly hidden between these, they present evidence that is pretty close to irrefutable on Aliens having visited the planet in the past. Now that I think about it… I'm not quite sure why I haven't thought back to this sooner. If the guy with the crazy hair.. (let me look him up really quick and put a name to a face)… If Giorgio A. Tsoukalos is the High Grand Master, it's fairly obvious what *they* have been instructing him to do. Giorgio has devoted his life to learning ancient languages, reading ancient texts, and traveling the world in search of evidence of *their* presence. Unfortunately, many people in the science community would attempt to discredit his lifelong efforts. TV shows can be created about using high tech equipment to decipher white noise or using thermal cameras and surveillance in the attempts of experiencing an ounce of paranormal activity, but mention Aliens, and all of the sudden the endeavor becomes a waste of time, or people brush it off as "stupid". Well, that was before I came along. I believe they brought up Giorgio from my subconscious because I am to contact him. I have the definitive proof that he would need to make his lifelong work a reality. He has already placed his academic reputation at considerable risk producing these shows on the History channel, and the only reason people have not completely written him off as a "spook", is because many of the things he has found and chooses to put into his show are truly groundbreaking. I can recall several of these objects and archaeological sites mentioned in the show, but to describe them so inadequately would be an injustice to the lifework of the High Grand Master. I believe I know what they wish me to do. I am to contact Giorgio and ask him to produce for me a list of the strongest evidence, items or locations, that prove *they* have been here. I am to include his contribution to this journal. But the ultimate purpose of why I am to write this is still unclear. However, and I can't help but smile as I write this, I feel this 'purpose', will soon be made clear. I just hope the means to whatever end lies in the future remains relatively smooth, as it has been in the recent past. The High Master may be able to provide more guidance when it comes to contacting Giorgio, or he may be able to clue me in on something that could change everything. Regardless of the outcome, I believe *they* wish me to meet the HM before the GHM for a reason. Tomorrow, I will know for sure.

    I took out my wallet and retrieved the business card that Thomas gave to me. I dialed the number, and it went straight to an automated voicemail. That familiar female voice stated "You've reached the voice mailbox of.." The voice went on to say the phone number I had just dialed, number by number. I was hoping it would be a recording of Thomas saying his own name, but I'm sure he chose the phone number read-back for maximum anonymity. I left the message as brief as I could, saying that this message was for Thomas, and that I needed him to do two quick favors for me. I asked him to look into the statement Walter Cross gave to the Police Officer, and to find out as much as he could about Walter Cross himself, in terms of his ties to the Organization. I asked him to please get back to me with this information as soon as he could.

Tomorrow, I will be taking this notebook with me, so I can refer to the questions I thought of a few paragraphs above, and to see if the Grand Master may be able to shed some light on the inscription in the back of my notebook. I have no idea what I will know by this time tomorrow, but all I can say is, I look forward to writing about it.

AUGUST 3, 2013

Well, I had every intention of writing about the meet and greet with the Grand Master, but the events of the following day happened, and we are still trying to recover… I will start with the morning of the 30th.

I got up around 0430 for PT, as I do every morning. I suppose I could get up around 5, but I like to get to the company area with around a half hour to spare to allow for a nap. Once 0630 rolls around, we were all in our company formation, when 2 Military Police squad cars pull up, and interrupt the morning announcements being given by our First Sergeant. They ask to speak to him in private, and head inside the company building. A few minutes later, one of the MP's comes out of the building, and asks to speak with SGT Bruce. I fall out of formation, and head inside the company area to see what was going on. Once inside, I am confronted with my Commander, 1SG, and apparently the post MP chief. The chief informs me that I have been summoned by "White House Officials", and that I was to report to the airfield at 0800, dressed in civilian attire. He informs me that people will be at the airstrip waiting for me, and not to worry about where to go from there. The chief then leaves the three of us behind in my Commander's office. The 1SG attempts to ask what the hell is going on. I look over at him, and lie to his face by saying I have no idea what's going on, and that I was just as surprised as they seem to be. These two individuals have been making life for me and my soldiers a living hell for months now, and I will be damned if I do anything even remotely close to helping them. (I suppose I can get into that a bit later) They both attempt to pry some more, but I inform them that I need to go back to my house to change since it's a 25 min drive, one way. They nod their heads and send me on their way. I race out of the base and take I-24 all the way to my house. Once there, I inform Michelle that I am apparently flying to Washington to meet this Grand Master, and am not sure when I will be back. I scarf down some poptarts, give smooches to the family, and I'm out the door. I'm in my car, about to speed towards the highway, when I look down at my right hand and notice that my Ruby ring isn't there. I quickly hop out of my car, and run back inside to get it. One more round of smooches for my family, and again I'm out the door and on the road back to base. I make a mental note to make sure I'm always wearing that damned ring.

Once I get off I-24, and onto Ft. Campbell Blvd, I head through the entrance closest to the airfield, and drive all the way back to the passenger processing center, the military equivalent to an airport terminal. Once there, there are men in black suits and black glasses waiting to escort me through the processing center. This entire time, I'm expecting to be flying on a small private jet, or possibly an air-force cargo plane, but once I show my ID to the people and the men in suits hurry me out the back door, I lay eyes on what was to be my ride for this trip. The White House, had apparently sent an F-15 fighter jet to pick me up. The pilot was leaning against the ladder leading up to his cockpit when he saw us approaching. I couldn't help but smile the entire walk to this aircraft and proceeded to get instructions from the pilot. He colorfully tells me not to touch anything, gives me a crash course on how to use the radio system built into the face masks we'll be wearing, and reminds me to remember to breathe. He motions for me to climb up into the empty co-pilot seat, and then climbs half-way up the ladder to assist with me putting on the seat harness. While I do fit inside the seat, it is very snug, and obviously meant for people somewhat smaller in stature. Once I'm strapped in to the point where I can barely move, the pilot then climbs into his own seat, straps himself in, and proceeds to seal the glass cockpit surrounding us. He fires up the engines and radios the control tower that he is wishing to depart Ft. Campbell. The tower acknowledges, and we start rolling toward the take-off end of the runway. We get the all clear to depart, and HOLY SHIT. We accelerate with amazing power and before I know it we are airborne and flying fast. The pilot adjusts course and informs me that it will be about a half hour flight to Washington over the radio. I do what any guy would do and ask if we have time for a quick demonstration of what this baby can do, and with a slight chuckle, he informs me that we may have time on the return trip. I inform him that it sounds like a plan, and that was the last we spoke the rest of the flight. When I was younger, I had aspirations to become a pilot, and when I was 15, I had the chance to fly a single engine Cessna at Don Scott airport. The flight was quite overwhelming and scary to the point I no longer wanted to be a pilot after that. However, sitting there, enjoying the scenery as we burned millions of dollars' worth of jet fuel on our way to D.C., I couldn't help but regret the fact that I never gave being a pilot a second chance. Ironically, if I had, the world might have been a very different place.

Once we land at Anacostia-Bolling in DC, more black suits are waiting for me at the location where the pilot parks the craft. He informs me that he will be ready and waiting for my return. I give him a universal head nod and thank him for his service. He gives me a smile and replies with 'likewise'. I turn and walk away with the suits, and they proceed to escort me to a black SUV, complete with police car, and police motorcycle escort. If this person has all of this at their disposal at all times… then I must be meeting someone of considerable status outside of the society. I begin to feel quite anxious and excited as we roll away and eventually drive off base. We drive for about a half hour until we stop in front of a large and very nice Hotel. I wasn't really sure where we were going to meet, but I did assume it would be a neutral area where people can be free to have privacy and away from the public eye. I suppose a hotel can fulfill those aspects, though I was hoping for the White House or something equally grand.

The suits walk up to the front desk and inform the woman that they are here to see 'Mr. Rogers'. I couldn't help but scoff at this.. One, what a lame and obvious cover for an actual name, and two, it's pretty awesome and hilarious at the same time. I find myself singing the Mr. Rogers theme as we head up towards the top floor in the elevator. Once there, we get out and I notice the space between hotel room doors is quite significant. These must be the "VIP suites". Sweetness. We come to the last door on the right where more suits are standing guard outside. They do a quick frisk for weapons, ask to see my ID, and proceed to open the door to let me inside. Once I step through, the room is quite elegant, decorated with an excessive amount of Marble, granite, and European architectural themes. I notice there is a room service cart complete with a mini buffet of breakfast foods. I realize that I didn't have a chance to eat breakfast this morning, and I looked around for the host of all of this so as to immediately seek permission to stuff my face. I spot a gentleman sitting across the room on a white leather couch that looks oddly familiar. He stands up and begins to walk towards my direction with a smile on his face, and hand outstretched. He appears to be in his late 50s to early 60s, and I confirm that I have seen this man before, and just as we become face to face, I realize who he is. The man that has arranged all of this to happen, and the apparent Grand Master of North America, is none other than the Honorable, Chuck Hagel, Secretary of Defense for the United States of America. I recognized this man, not from seeing him give a speech on TV, but from briefly meeting him in person in the Stan. The Sec Def had decided to make a visit to JAF during my second deployment and gave a speech to a select group of soldiers about the state of the war on terror. My chain of command selected me to be in attendance for his visit, and all that were there got the opportunity to shake his hand afterwards, and he gave all of us a Sec Def coin, which I coincidentally carry around in my wallet as a good luck charm, and a potential story/ice breaker. Although now that I think of it, the stories I have to tell lately make the coin story look like a nursery rhyme.

The Sec Def welcomes me to DC and asks if I've had a chance to eat breakfast. I say that I had not, and he invites me to 'dig in' to the room service cart, and to let him know if there is anything additionally that I should want, and he will have it brought up to the room immediately. I want to make a humorous comment about there not being any hookers, but I wisely keep that comment to myself. Of all the good first impressions one gets to make in their life, this is undoubtedly one of my most important. Chuck asks that I eat as much as I like, and we will get right to business once my stomach is full. I proceed to pile my plate high with every breakfast food present on the cart, pour myself a glass of milk and OJ, and proceed to make two trips in order to bring it all over to the table in front of the white leather couches where our apparent 'business' would take place. What started as a formidable mound of food was gone in a matter of minutes. Thanks to Basic Training, the concept of eating slowly and enjoying the flavors of my meals is pretty much a lost cause. I wash it all down with some OJ and proceed to take out my phone from my pocket and looked directly at Chuck. Before we begin our business, I inform him that the ensuing conversation needs to be recorded. I begin by reassuring him that I am quite aware that what we have to discuss goes well beyond the various levels of classified information. I inform the Secretary that the reason I need to record it is so I can write our conversation down in my journal. *They* have made it quite clear that one of my main purposes is to be writing in this journal about the events taking place in my life. I go on to explain the reason of why they are wanting me to do this has yet to be revealed. Chuck doesn't reply at first, and instead takes a long moment to contemplate what I have just said. When he's finally done thinking about it, he gives me a slight head nod, and gestures towards my phone. I proceed to start recording, and this is the conversation that follows:

CHUCK: I will allow you to record our encounter, but know that the specificity of the information that we discuss will be vague due to the interest of protecting both our society, and National Security.

Me: That is completely understandable. However, first allow me to clarify something first. Why fly me all the way to DC, when a simple phone call would have sufficed?

CHUCK: The matters that we have to discuss must be done so in person, so as to assure no one may overhear what is said. Besides, I demanded to meet you in person myself.

Me: Fair enough…. What questions do you have for me?

CHUCK: Thomas has briefed me on the conversation you two had… There is much you still do not know about the world around you. If you truly are who he says you are, you have no idea just how important you are to this world; more important than even myself. And if what Thomas says is true, then you will need to know everything. But first, there is something I need to understand. How is it that you believe *they* wish for you to keep this 'journal' of yours?

Me: Several nights during my recent deployment to Afghanistan, I dreamt about finding a notebook. They revealed to me its location in several dreams. It was on a bookshelf in the USO at Camp Warrior, on Bagram Air Field.

CHUCK: Interesting… You saw this notebook in your dream?

Me: No. I saw a glowing box in my dream.. I would walk to it and open it to find nothing. When I got the chance to go there during re-deployment, I found the very same box on the same bookshelf in the USO, only it wasn't empty. The notebook was inside.

CHUCK: … And so you simply took it upon yourself to write?

Me: Kind of… Writing is pretty much the only thing I could do with it.. I can't draw for sh- ah…. I can't draw very well, so that leaves writing. At first I wasn't sure what I should be writing about, but once I started to think about my past and all of the things that have happened to me, I realized that I did have something to write about. And from that moment on, I kind of 'predicted' that there would be more in the near future to write about... well, either that, or confirmation of insanity. But as it turns out, I was right.

CHUCK: I see... well the fir-

Me: I'm sorry Ch- uhhh.. Mr. Secretary.. but-

CHUCK: Please, call me Chuck.

Me: Chuck.. there was one more thing about the notebook.

CHUCK: Oh? And what's that?

Me: There's an inscription on the back page, written in some ancient form of Arabic. I had it looked at by someone I thought might be able to interpret it, but all they could recognize was one phrase that translated to "The father of the Son". May I show it to you?

CHUCK: Please do.

(I bring my notebook out from being tucked into the back of my pants and flip to the back in order to show Chuck the inscription. Chuck takes a long look at it and then gives me back my notebook)

CHUCK: I do believe I know someone that may be able to translate it for you. May I take a picture of it in order to be sent away?

Me: (I hesitate for a moment… the Secretary of Defense… pretty sure he can be trusted… not even sure why I'm still having trust issues… I guess I'm always on guard for something. I blame the Army.) Sure.

(I re-open the notebook and set it down in front of him so that he may take a picture of the back inscription. Chuck proceeds to take out his iPhone, and snaps a photo of the back page. He then accesses his contacts lists and sends the picture to someone with a message included. I watch him while he does this, and get the bright idea that he may be sending it to the High Grand Master… This is my chance to impress, I wait for him to look up)

CHUCK: My guy usually responds rather quickly… we may know what it means soon.

Me: I don't suppose you sent that text to the High Grand Master, Giorgio?

CHUCK: (He paused to take a sip of water from a water bottle, and upon hearing this, he chokes a bit on the water)

How… Ben.. What do you know of George?

Me: They showed him to me during a Timestretch last night. I deduced that he was the High Grand Master, and realized that I needed him for something.

CHUCK: (slightly scoffing) You need George's help… for what? Translating what's in your notebook?

Me: No... Actually I was hoping you would be able to help with that. I need him to write an excerpt for my journal.

CHUCK: On what?

Me: With all due respect Chuck, that is for me to know at this point in time. I'm still not sure why *they* wish me to write, but once I figure it out, you will be the very first to read it. (I add this last part in realizing that he may wish to confiscate my notebook, and possibly my phone.. I pause for a moment because of this thought, and ask) You are going to allow me to keep my notebook and phone.... Right?

CHUCK: Of course, Ben. They are your personal possessions. Thomas was right... you have a certain degree of paranoia about you.

Me: I would prefer to view it as allowing people prove themselves to be trustworthy.

CHUCK: And what have I done that would make you believe that I'm not? Holding one of the highest offices in the country isn't good enough for you?

Me: In a sense, you are a politician. And Politicians become corrupt, lie, and develop hidden agendas of which the American public would not approve.

CHUCK: Ain't that the god damned truth... Well spoken. Ben I'm going to tell you this once, and it will be entirely up to you to get it through your stubborn skull. If Thomas and I, and everyone you meet from now on that we send your way haven't already killed you, we can be trusted. The Organization doesn't take chances. They are ruthless, uncaring, and will stop at nothing to preserve what they see as 'peace' on this planet. Anyone they see as a threat to this, they exterminate. Understand?

Me: (Smiling) Yes. Thank you. I needed to hear that.

CHUCK: Good. Ben, as I've already stated, I spoke with Thomas regarding the conversation you two had yesterday. I'm sure you have many questions that you would like to have answered, and I would be happy to do my best to answer them. But first, let me say that it is my honor to sit in the company of one of the greatest men this earth has ever seen.

Me: (The Secretary of State gets down on one knee and lowers his upper torso and head as though he were bowing to a king) Chuck?! What are you doing?!?! Get up!

(Chuck raises his torso, and in his old age, slowly comes back up to his feet and sits back down on the couch)

Me: Why did you just do that?

CHUCK: It isn't every day that one gets to be in the presence of the Guardian. You still have no idea just how special you are. You have been assigned the duty of protecting the Prophet. *The Prophet*... Not only are we living in the time of the return of a 'Jesus' figure, but we are the men that have the honor to see it through. No one can know for sure what message the Prophet will bring, but one thing can be certain... The world will never be the same.

Me: (I pause for a moment, and I think I managed a slight smile) I can see the cause for excitement, but, to be honest, I don't really share your same level of enthusiasm. There are still many things I wish to know, and above all, I need your help.

CHUCK: That's why we're here Ben. Go ahead.. ask me anything.

Me: (I try to remember what I wanted to ask, but nothing comes to mind. I remember that I wrote down everything I wanted to know in my journal, and proceed to flip through it, towards the end of all my entries. I take a moment to read over my questions.) Thomas mentioned that I have been watched by our society for a long time, and I had already come across some of its members. Exactly who have I already met in the past that was a society member, and in what other ways have I been guided'?

CHUCK: (Brings his lips inside his mouth and looks down, slowly nodding. This seems to be a thinking expression, because he speaks a few moments later) Unfortunately, Thomas knows far more about your specific history than I do, but I can shed some light on a… a few things I suppose. I took the opportunity to check up on you during your second deployment to JAF. Obviously, it was a press event designed to showcase the Secretary of Defense supporting the troops. But that was really just a cover for me to see how you were doing. When you shook my hand, I noticed your eyes were slightly dark and sunk; evidence that you were on the right path to fulfilling your destiny. When I went back to the States, I ordered Thomas to relocate closer to your general area, in anticipation that you would be initiated in the near future. But in order for all of this to happen, you needed to go to Afghanistan in the first place…. This was a problem we faced long before you joined the service. (Chuck stands up.. begins to slowly walk towards the window of the hotel) What I'm about to tell you, is one of our government's greatest secrets.. It is not my place to question the decisions of our past leaders, but this is undoubtedly one of the hardest decisions we have ever had to make. What do you know about your ability to Timestretch?

Me: You mean, why am I able to do it?

CHUCK: Yes.. Explain to me exactly why it is you think you are able to do it.

Me: Well.. I suppose I can for several reasons… First is due to my DNA. I have a high concentration of specific traits that allow for it to happen, but only when I smoke Marijuana.

CHUCK: Correct… But have you always been able to Timestretch? That's what I'm getting at…

Me: No.. there was a change.. I suspect a change within my own brain chemistry. I hypothesize it came about after I smoked Hash in Afghanistan.

CHUCK: Yes, indeed. You see, the Marijuana plant is not a native plant to this planet. It is literally alien. *They* brought it here from their home world. They had intentions of using it to communicate with the indigenous populations, but they discovered that they needed more than just the plant. What they discovered when they got here was a planet overrun by races too primitive to use to their advantage, monkeys and apes. They realized that they needed to engineer a new species that was more intelligent. So, they used primarily chimp DNA as a base, did some experimenting with other species, (hence human racial diversity) and spliced it with parts of their own to influence some key traits they needed to change in order for servitude to happen. They made us appear somewhat from their image; took away most of the hair on our bodies, made us stand upright, and increased our brain capacities considerably. The new species that was created was dispersed all around the planet and would eventually evolve into the current races that we have today.

(Chuck pauses to look over at me to make sure I'm still following. I nod my head, signaling for him to proceed)

Once they had a much-improved race, they were then able to show us how to use the Marijuana plant to communicate. Once that was accomplished, the plant was spread across the planet to be given to the various populations for communication purposes. This worked for many years until man started to 'wise up' and wished to live freely and out of servitude. Eventually, and this part is purely based on Society speculation, they lost control of our species, and we sought to live lives free from our oppressors, forgetting the truth about our origin. Thus, enter the need for the coming of Jesus. Right around the time of his crucifixion, the founders of the organization attempted to cleanse the world of the message he was given to spread by killing all of his known disciples, and anyone that knew the truth. They then wrote the bible to be seen as the official record of Jesus. Word of his existence and his abilities spread to all corners of the planet, and they knew that many would come to the source of the story, looking for answers, but would raise questions when they found nothing. Hence the Bible; created to satiate the curiosity of the would-be traveler. This allowed for those that wanted to believe in Jesus to read the Bible and continue on not knowing the truth, and those that chose not to, bought into other various religions that were allowed to permeate. These other religions would go on to eventually become the dominant religions present in the world today. The few remaining initiates that survived, persisted on in secret, and stayed in the origin area for a long time until they had the numbers to leave the Middle Eastern area. But those that did move away from the Middle East soon discovered that the Marijuana plants they encountered outside of their homeland no longer granted them the ability to Timestretch. The plant had evolved... due mostly in part to the vastly different mineral concentrations found in the soils outside of the Middle East. It would later be discovered that the amount of THC found in the plants outside of the Middle East had been drastically reduced. A person with the right combination of *their* DNA need only to smoke Middle Eastern Marijuana once in order to 'awaken their special abilities'. Once their brain is exposed to such a high amount of the THC protein, it permanently changes their brain chemistry forever; allowing for Timestretching to occur. Does this make sense to you?

Me: Yes.

CHUCK: Good.. now, since Marijuana is generally illegal in this country, people such as yourself, from a prominent family line and possessing great potential to impact the world, may never get an opportunity to awaken your special talents. Something had to be done in order to create an opportunity for young men such as yourself, to go to the Middle East, and 'find themselves', if you will.

Me: I.. don't understand...

CHUCK: Ben.. do you remember why you joined the service?

Me: Yes.. I was in a lull in my life, and realized that I wasn't ready to settle down and become old and fat with children. I needed to go and experience at least part of the world.

CHUCK: That may be the reason.. but think further back… was there not a seed planted in your mind.. an idea, or event that made you want to join?

Me: Well.. I suppose there was. I was a senior in High School when September 11 happened. I remember a deep feeling of patriotism running through me.. I suppose that event planted a seed in my mind.. or maybe it's more accurately described as a grudge against those that would use religion to kill the lives of innocent people.

CHUCK: (slightly smiles) Yes, precisely. There are only a few hundred people with your same potential within the continental United States that are descendants of members of our society. Your family tree falls in line with these people. We had to present all of you with a way..

Me: … A way? A way to what?

CHUCK: Let me put it this way, if it had not been for September 11, do you think you would have joined the Army at all?

Me: I suppose it's possible that I would not have joined… but, what are you saying? Are you saying 9/11 happened in order to get people like me to travel to the Middle East in order to smoke pot??

CHUCK: No, no, no, Ben… Of course not… There was much more to it than that. There were many other reasons it happened… But.. presenting the opportunity.. was… a big one.

Me: Are you serious?!? (I'm borderline yelling here) Thousands of innocent American lives lost to get people to join the military??

CHUCK: (Raising his voice) Calm down Ben. You are not in a position where you need to know the whole truth. There's a hell of a lot more to it than that, as I've already stated. But yes, if it were not for 9/11, then you would have never gone to Afghanistan, you would have never reached your full potential, and you would never have been able to fulfill your true destiny… It was one of the few benefits that we could spin out of a bad situation. It was *their* wish to stop it altogether, but the powers that be had too much invested into the whole thing and would see it through to the end.

Me: Who are the "powers that be"?

CHUCK: (A brief pause followed by a long sigh) Some of the richest men in the world… but honestly, we cannot pin anything on anyone. Believe me, we've tried. The thing's airtight. It's a dead end. And that's really all I can say about that particular subject.

Me: Why not prevent all of my military woes and just hand me a bag of Afghan weed and send me on my way??

CHUCK: Because that is not how it is. It was up to *you* to make the decision to join the service, it was up to *you* to take the risk of doing illegal drugs in a combat zone, and it is up to *you* to follow your instincts and prove yourself ready to join our society. All of these decisions you made on your own. No one can force you to take these steps. New initiates must discover it on their own. That is the way it has always been.

Me: (a long pause while I mull over what I have just learned) What if I ordered you to tell me the true nature of 9/11, as the guardian?

CHUCK: I'm afraid it wouldn't matter. You may outrank me in our society and be more important than me in the history books, but who we are outside of the society still comes into play. You are asking for information that is light years beyond your pay grade, and besides, you simply do not need to know.

Me: Fine. But what if my journal should reach the public?

CHUCK: Did you just threaten the Secretary of Defense of the United States?

Me: No, I'm simply exploring every possible outcome in my mind. It's part of what makes me who I am. I'm saying, that what it if comes to pass that *they* want the contents of my journal to go public?

CHUCK: I don't see that happening.

Me: And why is that? Because you wouldn't let it?

CHUCK: No. Because release of information, such as that which exists in your journal, would cause chaos on a global scale. If that's what they wanted, it could have been achieved at any time in any century since the time of Jesus. I've been curious about the reason they want you to write it as well, but I have yet to arrive at a logical conclusion.

Me: Ah.. that makes sense. I suppose only time will tell. (Chuck gives a slight head nod) I'm not purposely trying to change the subject, but I just thought of a question I wish to ask..

CHUCK: What?

Me: You and Thomas have both mentioned Jesus' mission from *them* was to spread the truth of mankind's origin. Was that simply all there was to what *they* wished him to do, or was there more to it?

CHUCK: I suppose it's possible that there could have been more to it, but no one can really know for sure since Jesus and a majority of his faithful were wiped out. Why do you ask?

Me: I'm just trying to figure out where all of this is going. If my son does prove to be the Prophet, what message will he bring to the world?

CHUCK: That is an excellent question, and it is also for all of us to find out. But I fear in order for that to happen, some changes need to be made concerning your current lifestyle. You and your family need to be moved to a safe location. One where the Organization cannot touch you, and one where you can raise your family until it is time for your son to take his place in the world as the Prophet. *If*, that is indeed the plan they have for you and your son.

Me: Where did you have in mind?

CHUCK: I have a location in mind, but for your own safety, you are not to know until you arrive there.

Me: What? Why?

CHUCK: If you don't know where you are going… You cannot tell anyone, and therefore, the Organization cannot find out.

Me: Why should that matter? Thomas reassured me that we have nothing to worry about concerning the Organization.

CHUCK: I'm afraid that is not entirely true... You see, you were right to have Thomas look into Walter Cross.. He discovered that Walter has ties that go rather high into the Organization. Walter may not have been an actual member yet, but his older brother apparently holds a similar position in their organization to that of you and I in ours.

Me: But why should that matter? All of the necessary steps were taken to cover up all the loose ends, with the exception of the police officer that took Walter's statement... Did Thomas look into him as well?

CHUCK: Yes. He came back clear. But Walter's ties to upper tier Organization is the kicker here Ben... Family, as I'm sure you can understand, tend to be over-protective. We have confirmation that the Organization has already dispatched a Zealot.

Me: ... Which means...

CHUCK: Zealot is the term we use to describe... for lack of a better word, an Assassin. It is unknown exactly if just one person, or several are coming, but they are coming.

Me: How do you know this?

CHUCK: I received a phone call from Thomas a few minutes before you knocked on the door. He informed me of all of this. He says he was contacted by Judas, and informed me that a Zealot was on the move. Traditionally, it is just one individual that is sent.. but considering who Walter's brother is.. I would not be surprised if several are sent.

Me: Judas?

CHUCK: Yes. It's what we call our man on the inside. Judas to the Organization, but friend to us.

Me: There's a society member that's also a member of the Organization?

CHUCK: How else do you think have been able to survive in secret? We have to know what their plans and movements are in order to evade accordingly. If not for Judas, we would be sitting ducks.

Me: You're saying Assassins are on their way to kill me and my family?!?

CHUCK: That is exactly what I am saying.

Me: WELL GET THEM THE FUCK OUT OF THERE! Send someone to pick up my wife and son RIGHT NOW! Bring them to Ft. Campbell to wait my return!

CHUCK: I'm afraid that's not an option.

Me: WHAT?!? How is that not an option??

CHUCK: If your family is gone when they arrive, how will that look to the Organization? What will the Zealot report back?

Me: Fuck if I know... Why would that even matter?

CHUCK: Because Ben, it looks suspicious.... It informs them you and your family knew someone was coming, and the Organization would be forced to 'dig deeper', which could lead to the exposure of our society, and all that we have worked for would be lost.

Me: So what do you suppose we do then, *CHUCK*?? Because as we sit here, my family gets closer to death by the second.

CHUCK: You're the Guardian... you tell me. You have my capabilities at your disposal. What would you have me do?

Me: (I stare at the Secretary for a few moments, and realize that he is actually waiting for me to tell him what to do. This pisses me off, and instead of doing as he says, I go back to ridiculing) Have you already done something about this, or are you waiting for me to do your job?

CHUCK: My job? I know how to do my job son, that's not the issue here. The issue here, is that they apparently chose *you* as the Guardian, which means that you are in charge here. YOU are the one giving orders, and YOU are the one controlling the fate of this world. I suggest you quit acting like a pouty child and start acting like the great leader *they* see you as, and the great leader this planet needs!

Me: (Slightly stunned, I remain quiet for a few moments and decide to change my train of thought. What needs to be done here? What exactly do I need to do? I begin to think, and realize the answer is pretty easy…) Alright… well… I want a team of a dozen men on foot, split into four squads of three. Do you have a pen and paper?

CHUCK: Yes, one second.

(CHUCK quickly fumbles through a briefcase that had been sitting beside the couch the whole time. He pulls out a white pad of stationery adorned with a watermark of the official Sec Def seal at the top. He tosses me this and then a fancy ballpoint pen that probably costs enough to outrage the average tax-payer. I proceed to draw I-24, on the map, and then my street branching off of it, and then four way stop-sign intersection located roughly a block from my house to the left, as it would be facing the corn field in front of my house. Once these basic features are drawn, I go over what I had in my mind. I recreated a sample sketch of what I produced for Chuck on the side)

Me: Get a hold of any of the Special Forces units at Campbell and have them send 12 of their best. I want five positions total. A sniper on this grain silo here, directly in front of my house. He should be able to have eyes on everything that goes on in front of my house. I want two teams of two 45 degrees to the right and left of the sniper's position to lie in wait and converge on my house when the time comes. I want two more teams of two positioned similarly behind my house, with another sniper set up on the roof of this house here. This house is empty, so any noise he makes will go unnoticed. Both neighboring houses, however, are not. The remaining two men I want inside my house with me, positioned as I see fit. Also, get ahold of SOAR. I want an attack helicopter, an Apache or a little bird, I don't care which, to be hovering far enough to not be seen or heard, but close enough to be able to observe/and strike. Actually, make it an Apache.

CHUCK: Who or what is SOAR?

Me: It stands for Special Operations Aviation Regiment. It's *the* attack helicopter unit on Ft. Campbell. I don't know much else about it.

CHUCK: Got it. Let me make a phone call.

(Chuck gets out his phone and dials a number. Once someone answers on the other end, he proceeds to rattle off some authentication codes, which I assume are used to verify identity. He then asks to be transferred to the cell of the Commanding General's on Ft. Campbell. I wonder what number he dialed. Must be nice to have your own "oh shit" number that apparently solves all matters of National Security. At the end of the call, he reiterates this is not a drill, live ammo is authorized, and that he has reason to believe an attack is incoming from a terrorist organization with the intentions of taking out a key intelligence officer with detailed knowledge on matters that can severely damage National Security. Once off the phone, he turns to me to continue our conversation.)

CHUCK: It is done. And might I add, I couldn't have come up with a better plan myself. Let's just hope it's enough.

Me: (Already thinking ahead) Let's discuss the outcome of this really quick.. If the Zealot arrives and guns blaze, what story will emerge to the general public... Deadly Assassin sent by secret Organization to murder family? Details at five?

CHUCK: That is a matter which I will handle, Ben. Right now, I believe your presence is needed elsewhere. Your family needs you.

Me: I know... You're right.. one more thing.. What if they send an equal or greater force than what we have set up? What if we lose?

CHUCK: I don't see how that's possible Ben. The Organization has no idea that we know they're coming. They are traveling halfway around the world to die.

Me: And once the siege is over.. then my family and I will be relocated?

CHUCK: That is the plan.

Me: And what about the imminent gunfire, explosions, and witnesses that will be produced? People will hear about this.. It will be covered by the news.. National news, most likely.

CHUCK: Well… It's… looking like you are about to be one of the nation's biggest heroes… As long as the force sent is relatively small, you will be credited with killing them all.

Me: … That might work.. though, it's going to be hard to believe I took out a team of world class killers with a .45 caliber pistol.

CHUCK: .. Point taken. I will be sure the team brings an extra cache of weapons for you to claim as your own. They'll be yours to keep. Besides, what kind of Guardian would you be without the proper tools to do your job…

Me: Yea.. very true. And what about the Army? I can't just walk away from my service contract…

CHUCK: That's where having friends in high places comes into play. I will make sure that you are pardoned from the rest of your remaining service obligation so that you can focus on *their* task for you.

Me: I have so many more questions for you, but.. I've got to go. When you hear back from George, and he sends the translation of the message… Would you also forward me his contact info, so I can move along with seeing if he will write that excerpt I need for my journal?

CHUCK: I will ask him. No promises on whether or not he will agree to write it… but, we shall see.

Me: Thanks… It's been an honor, Chuck.

CHUCK: No Ben.. (with a warm smile) The honor has been all mine.

And with that, I turned off the recording, and practically ran out of the hotel room. Chuck's bodyguards were quite alarmed and attempted to chase me down, so I had to stop and explain that I needed to get back to Ft. Campbell ASAP, per orders of the Secretary of Defense. Chuck had poked his head out of his room and affirmed what I just said, and to get me back home as quickly as possible. With a trio of "Yes sirs", we were all running to the elevator, and then again out of the elevator to the Limo once we reached the bottom floor. One of the bodyguards quickly briefed the driver on what was to happen next, and then yelled something to the police officers sitting on their motorcycles. They picked up their hand mics, rattled something off over their net, and the very next moment we were speeding back to the base, lights and sirens blaring. I tried to call Michelle to give her a heads up as to what was going down, but it went straight to her unset-up voicemail box. I've told her so many times to set that damn thing up. I settle for a quick text, saying "Friends from Campbell coming over... They'll fill you in. OM." (OM stands for Oscar Mike, the words that correspond to each letter's phonetic representation from the phonetic alphabet. It's a Marine term, meaning "on the move", or as it pertains to my wife and I, on my way home.)

Once we arrived back on base, and arrived at the airstrip, I hopped out of the Limo, and ran over to the jet that brought me here. I found the pilot in the same position that he was when I first laid eyes on him; just leaning against the ladder, waiting. I told him to skip the acrobatics on the way back, and that I need to get back to Campbell, time yesterday. He smiled at me and nodded his head. He climbed up the ladder after me to assist with my harness and mask again, but I waved him off and barked "I GOT IT, GO GO GO!" With that, he climbed into his seat, secured his own harness with expert precision, and fired up the engines. He starts the procedure with the radio control tower to put us in queue to take off, but the airstrip is already on a hold, no planes landing or taking off until we depart; one last parting gift from the Secretary. Good to know that he thinks of things that slip my mind. A few moments later, we take off, and we're on our way back to Ft. Campbell airfield.

Apart from nearly losing my breakfast from the G-forces, the flight back to Campbell was uneventful. Once we land and the pilot parks the jet off to the side in front of a hangar, I notice there appears to be a small welcoming party made up of a group of rugged looking soldiers. Each is partially dressed in combat gear, and there's not a single clean-shaven face among them. They are lounging around what appears to be a mini convoy of a HUMVEE as a lead vehicle with a .50 cal mounted machine gun, a large troop carrier in the middle, and a rear HUMVEE mounted with a CROWS/240B machine gun combo. (The CROWS system basically being an advanced machine gun system operated by a soldier seated inside the vehicle by way of camera and infrared optics) These boys must be the Special Forces help I requested with Chuck. Sec Def coming through yet again. This guy doesn't mess around. I take a quick glance at my phone to see if I've received any messages since I left DC, but there are none. I walk towards the group of soldiers, and one of them sees me coming and leaves the group to meet me. This soldier outranks me, but with me being in civilian clothes, it really doesn't matter. He proceeds to quickly inform me that the plan he was briefed was complete garbage, and that he will be positioning his men how he sees fit. I attempt to object to this statement by saying it's my house, and I am familiar with the area, but he informs me that he and his team know the area as well. Before I can ask how this can be, he answers the question for me by stating that they fly over this exact area all the time on training missions. He went on to say that he agrees with the sniper positions I suggested to the Sec Def and appreciated that part of the intel brief. I think about what he has just told me.. Helicopters do fly over my house all the freaking time, and it's entirely possible that he has seen my house and the surrounding area many times. My house is exactly a mile away from I-24, and I've always assumed the pilots flying over my house use I-24 for navigation purposes while flying around the local area, only they do not fly directly over the highway... they fly roughly a mile away from it... Hence the reason why they know the area. I tell the leader to do as he wishes, and proceed to ask if he is planning on having a man inside my house. He said that he changed that part as well, and only wanted one man inside the house with me and my family. I ask if he already selected who that was going to be, and he replied with "You're looking at him". The Sergeant then went on to tell me to get in my car, and to fall in line behind the troop carrier in the convoy. I give him a head nod, and proceed to walk out of the passenger processing center, and get back into my car. After I start up the engine I look to my right to notice the trucks have already pulled up in front of the building, and there was a space behind the troop carrier already made for my little Honda Civic. We roll out of the base, fighting the usual lunchtime traffic, and head towards the highway to my house.

While we're driving, I realize that my unit might want to know that I'm taking the day off, as well as the rest of my career. What I wouldn't give to see my 1SG's face as he learns one of his best NCO's was being "dismissed" from his contract. The thought of knowing that I would never have to stand at parade rest again for his toxic ass again gave me a smile that lasted all the way home.

Once we reached my exit, the convoy pulls off to the side of the road to do a bit of staging. The NCO I spoke with earlier hops out of the truck behind me, walks up to my window and asks me to pop my trunk. As I comply, I notice two soldiers have hopped out of the troop carrier in front of me, and they both reach back up to pull down a tough box. I assume this is the "supplies" the Sec Def said he would give me to account for the potential mini war zone that may be created. Two soldiers carry the box to my trunk and attempt to push it in. I unlock my car doors and wonder how long it will take them to realize there's no way it's going to fit back there. One thing you give up with having a decent fuel economy, is trunk space. A few seconds later, they are placing it in my backseat, and the NCOIC gets into my passenger side as I watch him awkwardly try to decide where to put the M4 he's carrying. An M4 itself is small, and manageable, but this guy has every gadget under the sun attached to his. I can understand modifying it for the purpose of increased utility, but that's extra weight that makes for tiring out your arms faster. I'm sure he's used to lugging it around, but give me an ACOG sight, and I'm good. Once he's inside, he instructs me to proceed to my house. I ask if we are proceeding without the other trucks, and he says that they are staying behind to finish staging, and to move into position. I ask him how long he and his team were planning on being out here, and he tells me that they are to guard the target area until the movers have come and finished packing up my house. He looked over and saw the puzzled look on my face and proceeded to explain that Eagle 5 (commanding General of Ft. Campbell) had arranged movers to come to my house and pack up all my things. The soonest movers could be arranged to get here was tomorrow, so once they got here and the job was done, he and his men were heading back to Ft. Campbell. After this explanation, he went on to say that he wanted my car parked in my garage, and to leave the garage door open all night. He would be setting up shop in my garage overnight. I informed him that this was acceptable, and I asked if there was a radio that I could use to keep in contact with him, or if he just wanted me to poke my head in the garage if I needed anything. The NCOIC went on to say that I was to keep the garage door locked at all times, there was a functional radio already set to the freq. he and his team would be using in the tough box, and to not leave the house under any circumstance. He hesitated for a moment, as though he were debating telling me something, and then proceeded to be quiet. Once we got to my house, he helped me carry the tough box inside. We dropped it a few feet inside my door, and he gave me a head nod saying that he needed to go make sure his men were getting into position. And with that, he pulled out his radio as he walked out the kitchen/garage door and closed it behind him. I walked over to it, locked the door and turned to see Michelle holding Colin, apparently watching us the whole time. I give them both a big smile as I walk over to give them a group hug, and Colin approves with a joyous "Daddy!" I spend the next few minutes filling Michelle in on the plan at hand, and I do my best to emphasize that we are heavily protected, especially with a helicopter in the air, watching our house at all times. She raises a few good questions like what happens when the bird runs out of fuel, and if all of this is even necessary. I'm no expert of the procedures of aviation units, but if they have any sort of intelligence, they would split this assignment between two helicopters with two sets of pilots. Once the first helicopter is nearing the point of needing a refuel, a second would take to the air and relieve the first once it reached the target patrol area. The first bird would then head back to Campbell and refuel/rest. As for the 'is this necessary' question… well.. all I could say was that I hoped it was not. I told Michelle that when I proposed the plan to the Sec Def, I was thinking that he would claim it to be overkill and shoot it down, but he went right along with it. I reminded her that there is much we still do not know about the Organization, and it was most likely for good reason. If the Sec Def didn't think my plan was overkill.. it was because it wasn't. Which is a scary thought, but I didn't share that with Michelle.

Once she was more or less calmed down, I went over to the tough box that was sitting in my kitchen and took a gander at what the Sec Def left for me. Once opened, I found an arsenal that would make any gun enthusiast smile. The Sec Def apparently bought the M4 my company had assigned to me, complete with the ACOG scope I had attached to it, and two boxes of 10k rounds of ammunition. This would be particularly useful because I have already gone to the range and zeroed the scope to this particular rifle. There were a dozen HE grenades, an MP shotgun with several cases of ammunition, and a helmet mounted night vision scope commonly referred to as 'NODS' in the Army. Overall.. I'd say it was easily about twenty thousand dollars' worth of weaponry here. The only thing missing was a safe place to store it all. I need to remember to ask the Sec Def to make sure there's a large safe in the house for all of this wherever it is we end up. Hopefully the Apache won't have to fire any missiles, because it's going to be hard to convince the general public that the damage made by a rocket was in fact done by a grenade. Sure, the general public would not be able to tell, but there's always that one analyst with nothing better to do than to study the effects of various weapons used by our military.

I spent the rest of the day/evening enjoying time with my wife and Colin, trying to forget there were a dozen rifles pointed at my house, ready for whatever may come. I setup the shotgun and M4 in strategic positions around my house and spent the rest of the time horsing around with my son in-between watching the same Pixar movies we always watch. I tried to initiate a conversation with Colin, to see if there was any insight that he or match may be able to offer before putting him to bed. Colin enthusiastically said "Match says; tim-stret Boose, now!" I can tell he is imitating either his mother or me telling him to do something right now, because he takes his right hand with his forefinger outstretched and points to the floor as we would have done. I give him a kiss, and say 'Ok buddy, night night.' I turn and quickly walk to my piece, load it, and head to the bathroom and close the door. I crack open a window and light it up. I smoke it a little too quickly, as is evident by the uncharacteristic coughing fit that follows. A few moments later, that familiar feeling of warmth and racing thoughts revving up begins to take place in my brain. Almost instantly, I am taken to a time when I was out on my front gravel driveway, looking up at the stars, smoking a cigarette. Michelle was gone for the weekend, and sometimes I'm in the mood for a cigarette, because they prolong the high felt from Cannabis. (That is, as long as you're not a regular cigarette smoker) I'm looking around, and there is no one in sight. Not a sound to be made, not a person for miles. Granted there were houses next to mine, but it was only a short line of about 5 of them, and nothing but cornfields everywhere else. It was a peaceful and joyous moment. One seldom experienced in the suburbs, or by those that live in the city. I remember thinking in the moment that this is why country folk like to be country folk. This peace and serenity can be pretty relaxing. I snap out of it and I'm back in my bathroom. I'm slightly puzzled as to what this one meant…. That wasn't anything really.. It didn't show me anything, I wasn't thinking anything particularly important during the memory... Why bring that up? I think for a few moments more and realize that I had already realized the point. The point was the complete absence of a point. It was a peaceful period of nothingness. Nothing... As in, there is nothing outside. Nothing... or.. no one? I turn off the light, open the bathroom and run to my garage door. The NCO had turned off the light and was nowhere to be found. I ran to the tough box, grabbed the NODS the SEC DEF had provided to me, and ran back to the kitchen/garage door. I unlocked that bitch, and ran over to the far right wall, and put my back to it as I slowly inched along the wall towards the entrance to my garage. I turned on the NODS, and looked out to the corn fields. I'm looking and looking, and I do not see anything. No low silhouettes of soldiers watching a target, the top of the silo in the distance is perfectly round and unobstructed. I ran back to the garage door, turned off all the lights inside my house, and used the NODS to look out the window over my kitchen sink that gave a view of the backyard and the cornfield beyond that. Again.. I discover the same thing.. no soldier silhouettes, and a whole lot of nothing. They all left... as a matter of fact, I'm not even sure they were ever out there to begin with. I remembered just then that the

NCO said there was a radio in the tough box, but now that I think about it, I do not remember seeing one when I went through it the first time. Sure enough, after a second inspection, I confirmed that there wasn't one in the tough box. I was black on comms, and I hadn't checked to see if anyone actually went out to their positions. I took it for granted that there was someone out there because that fucking NCO told me not to leave the house. He most likely hung around here until it was dark and walked off to be picked up by his team. It doesn't matter what happened, what matters is(are) the Zealot(s). Is/are he/they still coming?? What do I do??

I begin to think about all the possible places I can lie and wait in an ambush in my house. But the problem with that is I have no idea what weapons the enemy possesses. I need help.. I need.. Match! I try my best to relax and clear my mind and see if I can Timestretch once more to see what weapons they have. I'm trying to focus and bam, I'm taken back to OP 6. The exact moment when I saw a man stand up from that truck bed and raise an RPG to my direction. I snap out of it. RPG. This guy has an RPG... And the more that I think of it, he most likely is intending to use more than one. One would decimate a little less than half my house, but another fired to the other side, and possibly even a third… We're talking 95% destruction, at least. Chances of survival would be slim. I need to be in a place where I can see him coming, and strike just before he fires the first round. The best place to do this would be from a rooftop. My neighbor's rooftop would be ideal, since prior to firing he would be focusing on the target and most likely wouldn't notice an obstruction on a neighboring rooftop. Though if he's got any sort of Military background, he would think to scan all the houses. I decide to use my own, and to not bring put my neighbor into unnecessary harm. I run to the bedroom, wake up Michelle, and quickly tell her to grab Colin and stay in the bathtub until I tell her it's ok. She tries to ask questions and get an explanation, but I squeeze her hand as hard as I can to get her to wince in pain and to stop talking. I explain that there's no time, and to just do it. I run to my garage and grab my ten-foot ladder to use to get on top of my roof. As quickly as I can, I bring it into the house, drop it and proceed to swing open the back door. Once I'm carrying the ladder again, I guide it out the back door, prop it upright on my deck, and lean it on the gutters. Once it's ready to be climbed, I run inside, grab my body armor out of my trunk, and grab my M4 that I had stashed underneath my couch. I make sure I've got my NODS on me, and head out to the back porch. I put on my body armor, sling my M4, and climb up the ladder with NODS in hand. Once on top of the roof, I climb my way up to the apex, and position myself so I can look over and out to the front and need only to simply roll over to look down the backside of the roof to see the back. I've got eyes on 360 degrees around my house, a full combat load of ammunition for my M4 (I always keep the spare mag pouches on my body armor ready to rock with personally bought ammo), and hopefully decent battery life in my NODS. I begin scanning all the possible directions of approach, keeping in mind that the enemy could very well walk up to the target on foot, by way of cornfield. Once I have developed a rapid scanning routine, I allowed myself to calm down a bit, and to think about what was happening.

Despite how movies depict them to fly once fired, RPG's travel in a fairly straight line, for quite a distance. The best place to fire one upon my house would be from the Silo directly across from my current position. I estimate that it's a bit over a quarter mile away, but that's nothing for an RPG. A house is a huge target, and a blind monkey could destroy it. I would have to be quick and precise with my shots. The shots themselves wouldn't be too hard, but given that it's night-time, and I've been to all of one night range in my military career, I was almost firing blind. But the key to this situation here would be to eliminate all targets as soon as possible, firing until I am certain that they are all eliminated. If I let loose too soon and there is more than one, they can seek cover and possibly get away. If I wait too long, there will be a rocket fired directly at me…. I continue scanning and scanning until I calm down yet some more, and allow my thoughts to wonder… While still scanning, of course. How did this come to be… The SF NCO must have been instructed to not guard my house. But why go through all the trouble of making it seem as though they were doing the job? I begin to think about how things could have gone awry and who is responsible, when I notice a car approaching far down the road to the front of my house in the distance. It's over a mile away, and it's the first one I've seen this whole time. While driving, I notice the driver turns off the headlights and I lose sight of it. This is odd… Suddenly I've stopped thinking about who was trying to screw me over, and all my focus is on trying to rediscover this car. I do quick half scans to my left and right and rear, making sure this is not a diversion. I look straight ahead towards where I last saw the car and still see nothing. I bring up my nods to see if maybe I can spot them… Still, I see nothing. The car must be right in line with the Silo/Barn combo. I can be confident that it wouldn't drive off the road because there's about a 6-foot ditch on either side of the road that would be hell to try and get out of, not to mention the damage that would be done to a vehicle. It was like this on a majority of the roads in this area. I quickly roll on my back, unvelcro my magazine pouches on my body armor, and place them all beside me. Four out of the six slide down the roof and into the gutter, but I manage to stop two of them. This leaves me with only 90 shots to fire off before I'd have to scoot down to the gutter to get the other 120.

I bring my NODS back to my face again, and this time I see that a dark SUV has backed into the gravel turnoff right by the Silo and stopped. They are sitting there, most likely looking at my house with some sort of observation device. I can tell that the windows of the SUV are darkly tinted, and it's going to be hard seeing anything out of those things at night, unless they have an IR device, in which case they would see my round little face propped on top of my roof. I get a gut feeling that they do not, and half-jokingly thank Match for the update. I keep watching for what seems like an eternity, and then both the driver and rear driver doors open. Two men get out and head to the back hatch of the SUV, which has apparently been opened. They are met by a third individual at the back that appears to have gotten out of one of the passenger side doors. I can't be 100% sure, but their upper torsos are looking pretty bulgy, which is a body armor indicator. They are pulling out rectangular cases that are a bit smaller than that of a guitar case... RPGs. Three long cases in all, with a fourth case that is fatter and more square: the carrying case for the rockets. I watch as the RPG tubes come out, one of the men passes them out to all. Once they each have one, another one of the men opens up the rocket case and starts to hand out the rockets. At this point in time all three are relatively close together.. one is bent over pulling out rockets, the other two are talking amongst each other. I have a clear shot on all three. With my right thumb, I flip the switch from safe, to semi. I decide the order is going to be left, right, then the one in the middle. I experience a brief feeling of doubt as the third target, the one in the middle, will have enough time to potentially run to the other side of the vehicle and hide.

I place the top of the ACOG arrow a hair above the head of the man on the left. At this distance, provided I didn't jerk during trigger pull, the rounds would drop right to the center of his face. I couldn't help but find an eerie correlation to this moment and the moment when I was running down the sideline during that high school football memory. Then I had to run faster than I ever had before.. and now, I had to focus and hit a very small target with precision and expert skill, or most likely face failure and death. I smoothly, yet rapidly squeeze the trigger three times. I know at least one hits the mark, because he falls straight back onto his back, dead. Upon the pull of the third, I quickly and ever so slightly pivot my arms to the right target who had just started to run towards the passenger side of the vehicle. I aim for the same location just above his head, and squeeze the trigger three more times. He falls to the ground as I pivot back to the third man in the middle. This man was climbing into the back of the SUV when I got my sight on him. I placed my sight slightly above his ass, the largest exposed part of him and managed to get one shot off before the lower half of his torso also disappeared into the vehicle. The one shot I fired appeared to be a hit, because a decent amount of blood splatter appeared on the upholstery of the small amount of trunk space that I could actually see. I waited a moment to see if the truck was moving from someone moving around inside, but it was too far away to tell. A brief moment of panic came over me as I thought this man might be able to drive away, and I adjusted my aim to the rear driver side tire. I shot five rounds into the sucker, pivoted to the front, shot what I had left in the magazine into the front tire. Once I was out, I dropped the mag, reached for another, slammed it up into the feeder, hit the bolt release, two taps on the forward assist, and placed the rifle onto automatic. I pointed the triangle at the engine block and let loose the entire magazine in four controlled bursts. Once this mag was done, I grabbed the third magazine, loaded it, and stopped to look for movement. The first target lie on the ground motionless. The second, however, appeared to be slightly moving around, but in a manner, you could tell that he was badly injured. No signs of anything from the third. I carefully aim at the second target, and fire four shots into him, taking a couple second pause between each shot to be sure each round hits an area not covered by body armor. After the fourth, he is no longer moving. I continue to stare at the SUV. What now? No movement. Once the silence returns, I can hear one of my neighbors hysterically chattering. Shit. This gives me 10-20 minutes before police arrive. Again. I need to be at the SUV, but the third man may still be capable of attacking if I walk up. I need help.. Thomas.. I need to call Thomas. He shouldn't be too far away and should be able to help. I flip over on my back to see if my phone was in my front right pants pocket. It was. I get it out, tell Siri to call Thomas, and she does. As I'm waiting for the phone to ring, I look over at the SUV and notice there appears to be a sound coming from it's direction... The sound of an engine trying to start.. I reach for my M4 and carefully fire several rounds into various locations on the driver side. I stare at the SUV and the man has stopped trying to start the car. Either I got him, or he has given up, or he is possibly escaping out of the passenger side. All I can do is scan with my NODS for someone trying to run or crawl away. I keep scanning and glance at my phone to wonder why in the hell Thomas hasn't picked up yet. I see I forgot to hit speaker, and tap the button real quick to make audible Thomas' concerned voice. I tap the volume up button to enable my app to record the call.

THOMAS: Ben?!? Are you there?

Me: Yes, Thomas.. I'm here…

THOMAS: What's going on?? What are you shooting at?

Me: The Zealots Thomas! They came, and my fucking Special Forces detachment is nowhere to be found.

THOMAS: What? What do you mean?

Me: They left! I don't think they were ever in position to begin with…. Their leader dropped off the weapons box in my house, told me he had to go communicate with his team, asked me not to leave the house, and that's the last I saw from him… I assumed he and his men were in position the whole time, but my son told me …. He told me to Timestretch, and they-

THOMAS: Your son told you to Timestretch?

Me: *They* told him to tell me.. Yes.. He told me to, and I was shown empty cornfields, where the men should be. I went out to investigate, and sure enough no one was there. They fucking left me and my family to die!

THOMAS: Where are you now?

Me: I took a position on my roof with my M4.. They had rockets Thomas. They were going to fire at my house. Our friends.. they showed me.. the rockets.. that they had rockets… I knew they would try to blow up my house… I can't.. wait.. I don't know what…

THOMAS: Keep going Ben.. tell me everything.

Me: Ok, ok... I-I saw them getting ready to fire them at my house. I shot them.. I shot them all.. But one managed to climb back into the SUV they came in… I disabled the vehicle, but I don't think the third man is dead. I need to go over to the SUV before the cops get here.

THOMAS: No!.. Ben stay where you are.. well.. get down from the roof, and wait for the police in your front yard. Make sure your family is ok first. Then take your M4, keep eyes on that SUV, if you see the third man, shoot him. Stay in your front yard and wait for the police to arrive.

Me: Ok.. ok.. Thomas.. stay on the phone with me until they get here..

THOMAS: I will Ben. I will meet you at the Police Station again, and do what must be done to clean all of this up. Ben.. When the police get there.. Right before the police get there, you need to not be holding a weapon in your arms.

Me: No shit Thomas…I'm slightly versed in the R.O.E. Hang on.. (As I climb onto the ladder to come down, I grab the three magazines that fell in the gutter and thrown them onto my deck. Once down from the roof, I pick up the magazines, and head back into the house)

Me: MICHELLE… MICHELLE!!

MICHELLE: (Slightly muffled from being in the bathroom) BEN!! What's going on?? Are you ok??

Me: Yes, I'm fine. I need you to stay in the house until the Police arrive.

MICHELLE: You fired so many times Ben… What was happening out there??

Me: Three men came, they were going to fire rockets at us, but I got two of them. The third is wounded in their SUV some 300 meters in front of our house. I'm going out front to keep eyes on, and to wait for the Police to get here. Once they do, wait inside and tell them that you are not fucking moving until they can guarantee that third man is eliminated.

MICHELLE: What are you going to tell the police?

Me: I don't know… Thomas will help, but whatever you do, think about what you say. Do not give away any information that the Police do not need to know, about our son, or any of this shit. I have to go out front

(And with that I quickly walk out the garage door while MICHELLE tries to speak with me some more, but I need to get back to watching for the third Zealot)

(I climb on the hood of my car, and kneel down on the hood so I can raise my NODS and look over to the

SUV. Everything seems to be just as I left it, until I notice a dark area beneath the SUV that I do not remember seeing. Before I have time to take a closer look, a burst of semi-automatic rifle fire comes cracking through the air, and the bullets whip by me to my right, with one hitting me in the right shoulder, and another hitting the chest plate of my body armor.)

Me: Fuck... SHIT... This Mother Fucker.. FUCK! GOD DAMNIT..

(I continue to swear in pain as I lay on my back on the hood of my car... At this point in time, I hear Thomas yelling something on the speaker of my phone. I bring the phone to my face and tell him I will call him back and hang up. I need to block his line of sight.. The quickest way to do it would be to close the garage door. I look over to the button on the wall, some seven feet away. Seven feet of death. I notice in my peripheral vision that my right shoulder is starting to get pretty dark with blood, but I don't have time to treat my wound right at this moment. I need to either find something that can reach the button or run over and push it and duck for cover. Both seem like shitty ideas. Then a third option crosses my mind. I reach for my phone and call Michelle. I tell her to come and open the garage door as quickly as she can, without exposing any part of herself, and then to go back into the bathtub. I hang up right after I say this, not wanting to clarify or hear any protest. I wait a few moments, and as requested, the garage door flings open. I do a soft count to four. During this time, the Zealot will adjust his aim to the garage door, if he is still aiming at all, looking for a target. After about four seconds of not seeing anything, he is going to go back to me. It is in this aim adjustment that I need to move and hope I don't get shot… again. Once I reach four, I not so gracefully slide down the hood of my car into a crouched position and proceed to run and dive into the cover of my house. I hit the wooden floor with a hard thud, and instantly crawl out of sight. Either my plan worked, or he wasn't aiming at me, because no additional shots were fired. I immediately got up and went to the back door to climb on my roof again. I have to sling my M4 around my neck, because my right arm has a weight support capacity next to nothing. I go to the far right side of my roof, and peek over the apex. I reach for my NODS, but they are nowhere to be found on my person. They're somewhere between the garage and the roof. I lug my M4 in front of me, pointing outward, and scan all that I can. Right then, I spot him… He had crawled, or bear-crawled, or used some sort of low profile scooting across the corn field. The corn was about 3-4 feet high, as it should be this time of year, and he had not made a single trail through it as he made his way up to the side of the road. He lay on the top of the embankment, sprawled on his back. I look at him through my ACOG scope, and I can clearly see his entire upper torso. I aimed right at his head and was about to pull the trigger when I stopped. He was mouthing something over and over.. After studying for a moment, I discern that he is saying 'Don't shoot'. I look at his hands, and notice that he is not holding a weapon and I'm thrown into an internal struggle. Do I kill this fucker, this.. scum of the earth low-life terrorist piece of shit that attempted to kill me and my family. Or do I let him live and try to use him to get information. While the second option could be viable, I envisioned the Organization secretly whisking him away out of whatever hospital he would be treated in, allowing him to make a full recovery, escaping all charges, and going back to his evil way of life. No.. nooo this man cannot live. Again, I've got the sight right on his head, and then I think about how it's going to look to the police.. There's no way I can retrieve his weapon in time and plant it on him. I'm bleeding out, he's bleeding out. Time is of the essence. And just as I'm thinking about letting him live for a second time, I hear sirens in the distance. This gives me about 30 seconds to make my decision. I have to do something, and I've got to do it now.. And right then, as though he knew why I was hesitating, the man pulled out a handgun, and was blindly aiming it over his head, pointing it in my direction with a severely shaking hand. I flip the switch to semi, put the cursor on his head, and squeeze the trigger twice. One round goes straight into his head, while the other hits the area where his neck meets his chest. The mans arms fall to his side, and blood begins to leak out onto the grass and into the road. The sirens are getting louder and closer. I climb over the apex, and let my M4 slide down the roof, out of reach. I lay there on my back and look up into the sky. Good god my shoulder is killing me. I remember thinking that I just wanted to be away from all of this.. to be free of war and violence, and to live my life in peace with my family. That's all I want. But I know… if I make it through this, nothing will ever be the same before all of this started happening.

Two police cars arrive at the same time, each with two officers getting out of either door, pistols in hand. I move my torso sideways so I can get a better look at them, and I see apparently one of them has an Assault Rifle, for added accuracy and power. Whomever called the police must have mentioned automatic weapons during the call, and they were authorized to bring that bad boy along. Too late boys, I've already taken care of it.

They start barking commands at me, show us your hands, is there anyone in the house, are you wounded, blah blah blah. I raise my right palm to make the stop gesture until they notice and stop yelling. I take a deep yet painful breath and yell out that my wife and son are in the house, my right shoulder is wounded, and they'll find the bodies of three men that attacked me and my family out in front of my house. One by the road, and two 300 meters out, next to a dark SUV by the silo. Once all of that is said, the weight of all my recent efforts, and … most likely due to blood loss, I felt extremely tired and exhausted. I remember looking up at the sky, and slipping into unconsciousness.

When I finally regained consciousness, I awoke in a hospital bed. My right shoulder had been bandaged and thoroughly wrapped. I looked over at my left arm and expected it to be handcuffed to the bed, but it rested free and clear from obstruction. I wore nothing but a hospital gown and was introduced to the discomfort of having an active catheter up my urethra. At least I wasn't awake for the insertion. I look around my room for anyone that may be around, and I spot Thomas sitting in a chair to my left. Per the apparent norm, he is smiling at me with that ever so evil/awkward grin. Thomas informs me that I had been unconscious for just under 24 hours, and that it was the evening of August 1st. He went on to explain that my wife and son were here, in a waiting area, and as soon as I was released from the hospital, I would be escorted to the Police station for questioning. He then handed me a tan envelope and said to look over the contents before heading to the police station. Once I was done reading whatever was inside, I was to hand it back to him and ask any questions that I may have concerning the matter at hand. I took out a few sheets of white paper, looked them over and gathered that they were a police report, detailing my statement on what had happened the night before. Before I began to read what had been forged for me, I asked if this was the actual report, or if I was just to memorize the facts and spit them back out to the Police. Thomas went on to explain that this was to be the report the Police would make regarding the statements I would give them in the near future. He went on to sarcastically say that it would be helpful that what I tell the Police, match what was written on these papers. I nod in agreement, and right at that moment, I remembered the question that had brought me much strife right before I went unconscious. Why did the SF detachment leave? As I angrily bring this question to Thomas' attention, he nods his head as though he were waiting for me to ask.

Thomas went on to express his understanding of how upset I must be, and that the explanation for what happened would not be what I expected. Once I was released from the hospital and escorted to the Police station to 'make my statement', the High Master and Grand High Master, as well as Thomas, would all be there to explain what happened. This, of course, only made things worse.. I wanted to know everything right then and there and demanded that Thomas tell me. Thomas explained that the only resolution to all of this was to hear it from the other Society members. They would explain everything and answer all my questions. But before that could happen, I needed to read the contents of the envelope he handed me. I continued to protest, but Thomas would not budge, and I was left with the envelope sitting on my lap. I opened it and began to read.

I do not have a copy of what was written on the documents within the envelope, but I will do my best now to bullet point the important facts the papers contained:

- My family had been receiving death threats from the Taliban due to the tower incident that took place over in Afghanistan during my first deployment. The families of the fallen Taliban had essentially demanded my head on a pike, and they were actively pursuing me here back in America. Despite it being a small victory, it was seen as one of the most humiliating defeats of their war efforts, and they deeply sought vengeance.
- The Taliban used social media to recruit devout extremists that lived here in the states. They flew them over to the Middle East, taught them everything they needed to know, and gave them the proper funding in order to pull off an attack here in America once they came back.
- The US Army informed me of these threats, and secretly (to the public) had a rotating detachment of Special Forces that were monitoring my house 24/7. When the terrorists decided the time was

right to attack, the detachment was in place and ready to defend me and my family.
- The incident concluded with three dead terrorist attackers, and one American wounded (Me). I apparently went out to help the detachment before all of the enemies had been killed and proceeded to get wounded. Credit for the kills was going to the SF NCO that left me and my family high and dry.

The rest of what the report said were statements given by various detachment personnel, as well as what the neighbors reported to have seen. All of it was a bold-faced lie that I had no intentions of supporting. Of course, I did not tell Thomas right then what I was thinking. I simply read each page front to back and put it back in the envelope and handed it back over to Thomas. He looked at me and asked if I had any questions to which I answered no. He then went on to quiz me about various aspects, as though he were some over-curious bystander, or even a TV reporter. I was highly annoyed at this, but played along, and correctly answered everything he threw my way. Once he was satisfied that I had a grip on the lie that I wasn't going to tell, he said that I was then ready to see 'this'. He got up, went over to my bed controls and sat me all the way upright and then walked over to the window to pull the blinds back. My bed was positioned in such a way that I could see most everything that was outside. I was apparently on a lower floor of a Hospital in the city. I take a closer look at the city, and I recognized it to be Nashville. I must have been flown to Vanderbilt Hospital due to my excessive blood loss. I remember thinking this and being warmly satisfied with my own logical deducing prowess when I finally noticed exactly what it was Thomas was attempting to show me.

There were people… an enormous crowd of people out in front of the Hospital. TV vans, reporters standing in front of cameras, people holding signs, Police holding people at bay… It was a madhouse. Thomas noticed the confused look on my face and interjected; I was the wounded victim of a terrorist plot that took place right here in America. The fact that I was wounded wasn't what was bringing them here.. Thomas went on to explain that it was the individual attention the Taliban had given me; specifically singling me out right here on American soil. People were scared more attacks would come. Everyone seemed to have an opinion on the matter; some were screaming cover up, that I was a hero, a fraud, and everything in-between. He explained that 'SGT Bruce' had become a household phrase overnight. What sweetened the pot in terms of the public eye were the heroic deeds I performed downrange, and now only a year and half later, I was being targeted for them. I was 'SGT Bruce, Hero under fire' or so went the title given to the situation by the media. The entire nation was waiting to hear news about my medical condition and ultimately wanted to hear a public statement, which Thomas informs me that I am going to have to make shortly after making my statement at the Police station.

    I turned to Thomas and ask if I was being charged with anything. He shakes his head and stated that the local police have been in contact with several high ranking people at Ft. Campbell, and they provided them with the now need to know information regarding the attack. The Sec Def had the threats fabricated by the CIA, and handed off to the Army as recently unclassified information. The Army then provided the faux information to the Christian County Police Department, the local Police division that held jurisdiction over my area of residence. Once they learned the report came from the big wigs at Campbell, and from the Sec Def before that, they dropped all charges, and hopped on the hero bandwagon that my comrades had created thus completing the full circle of protection the Society had been trying to set up.

Around this time, Thomas asked if I was ready to have my family sent in, and this made me realize that a non-family member had been given permission to be by my side while I was unconscious. While this was a credit to the persuasiveness that Thomas undoubtedly possessed, I remember feeling annoyed at the time. I told him that I wanted a nurse to come into my room, and to bring me some non-hospital clothes, to take out this catheter, and wait a half hour before letting my family come in to see me. I then added to the end of this, that I needed some time to think on my own. With this, he nodded his head in understanding, got up, and walked out of the room. A short time later, a nurse had come in holding some clothes that could have only been brought by my wife and proceeded to leave them on the table off to the side, and per my request, proceeded to remove my catheter. I'll spare the details of that experience, but I will say that it was very unpleasant, and left me with an uncomfortable burning sensation paired with the feeling of having to constantly urinate. Not fun.

Once the nurse had left, Thomas poked his head back inside and said that all I need to do is yell for him meaning that I was ready for my family. I gave him a nod and proceeded to fall into thought. My thoughts immediately addressed something that had been growing in the back of my mind. There were many things that I was not being told about what was going on around me, and this drives me insane. One thing that I absolutely cannot stand is a surprise. Granted, unforeseen things are going to happen all the time, that's the way life went, especially in the Army. But it's the things that other people know about, and choose not to tell you for whatever reason… Oh it was classified, or you didn't need to know, or it was a test, or I didn't think it was important to tell you… Whatever the bullshit reason, I was getting sick and tired of all of it, and was going to set the record straight when I was eventually face to face with the other Society members. If these people want me to be the Guardian, and be their leader, some things needed to be changed. No more secrets kept from me, no more cover ups to the eyes of the public. No more using smoke and mirrors to divert the truth. This is what has been done for decades in this country, and if I have anything to do about it, it's going to stop.

I come down from atop my righteous horse when I begin to focus on my life and the lives of my family. I want these changes to take place, but I desperately need to go off the grid to raise my family, and this apparent attention I'm getting will hinder this. Although, there is an opportunity present.. They are expecting me to make a statement. This statement will be reported across the country, and depending on just how popular this incident has become, it could travel around the world. Actually, now that I think about it, an American war hero being attacked by the Taliban on American soil sounds like at least a global main headline. They would air the facts, go over what happened, and play a clip from my statement. This... feels like more than an opportunity. It feels like the culmination of an elaborate plan. It's feeling like all of the recent events that have happened are leading to this one moment in time.

At that very moment, I could not come up with exactly what I wanted to say in my public statement. Now that it's two days later as I bring this journal up to speed, I have a decent idea of what it is I'm going to say. But that came to be only after I met with the society members at the Police Station, followed by a Timestretch shortly after. I digress back to the Hospital...

Shortly after realizing the importance of the statement I was going to make, I called for Thomas to bring in my family. My wife and son met me with an enormous hug that rivaled the embrace we shared after returning from a deployment. Once the level of emotions had subsided, Michelle filled me in on some important details concerning what happened during my unconscious time. As it would turn out, the man that had crawled up to the road, through the cornfield, whom I shot six times in the head and upper and lower torso area, did not have a gun in his hand when I shot him. He was holding a small metal box with contents unknown. Michelle stated that the police confiscated it as evidence before Thomas arrived on the scene. The police were chattering about homicide this and that until Thomas rolled in and pulled out a badge and some papers which he shoved into their faces. She didn't comment on the papers, but I assume it was the faux evidence Thomas mentioned that came from the Sec Def. This struck me as a bit odd since Thomas said the papers came from the higher-ups of Campbell. Thomas must have been posing as a liaison for the Army, and shown the police some rather convincing proof that he was who he said he was. Or perhaps Thomas is a rather humble man, and shirks taking credit for certain things. Regardless of the reason, I called for Thomas to come back inside, and told him of the box that Michelle mentioned. His eyes lit up, and he left immediately to go and see if he could secure the box and it's contents. As he was leaving, he stated that it sounded like the Zealot meant to give this box to me.. He had an idea as to what might be inside, but he did not wish to say at that time due to the high probability that what was inside could really be anything. This came off as an odd, yet, true statement. I yelled for him to bring it to the meeting at the station as he turned around the corner and disappeared down another hallway in the hospital.

Shortly after Thomas disappeared down the hallway, two Nashville Police Officers appeared to apparently take Thomas' place. They saw me dressed and walking about and pause in anticipation as though I'm about to make a run for it or something by placing a hand on their firearms and yelling for me to freeze. I give them a disbelieving look and say that I'm just greeting my family, and I'm ready to leave to the station with them whenever the hospital is ready to release me. With this, one of them leaves to retrieve a nurse while the other takes a seat in a chair outside my room as I go back in and take a seat on my bed. I'm lying on my back, laughing and tickling Colin with my non-slung arm when a couple nurses and a doctor come in to do the final once over. I awkwardly sign some papers with my left hand, they look over my bandage/sling and give me parting care instructions, and I receive their approval stamp to leave. I say goodbye to my family as I'm escorted out by the officers. I begin to greatly anticipate meeting with the Society members and all the questions I have for them as we walk through the Hospital. I get so preoccupied thinking about exactly what it is they're going to tell me that they've been withholding from me, that I nearly forgot about the crowd outside. Just before we exit the building, the Officers stop and turn to me to ask if I am prepared to make a statement, or if I wish to head to the SWAT van to be escorted. I tell them I would like to make a brief statement. They nod their heads, and we walk outside.

As soon as I step out of the main doors it was like hearing an entire stadium react to their favorite player walking onto the field. People were chanting, cheering, cameras were flashing, a dozen questions were being yelled at me all at the same time. I walk about a dozen paces out of the front door and I'm completely surrounded by people on all sides, save for a path made clear by officers in riot gear before me, leading to the van. I hold my good arm up in the air with my palm facing forward, gesturing that I wish to say something. It takes at least twenty seconds for everyone to settle down and prepare to receive what I'm about to say. I remember in the last few seconds, a couple reporters had to get in their last few questions as though their question would be the last thing I heard before everyone was quiet, and I would therefore answer their question first. These people are worse than drama-thirsty teenage girls. I tell them that my injury is healing, my family is doing fine, and my official statement on the matter will be forthcoming. With that, I look at my escorts and give them a nod to let them know I'm ready to go into the van. They close in on either side of me, and we walk down the path the other officers have made for us. As soon as we started walking the crowd erupts again with a roar of chatter and more questions. I couldn't help but smile as I climbed into the van, thinking that this is what it must be like to be a famous actor, every day of their life. My escorts close the door behind me, and I take a seat on the open bench across from a single uniformed officer that is apparently there to be my company to the station. As we pull away,

I look out the window at the faces of all of the excited people, beating on the van, and cheering and chanting my name. Once we had pulled away from the crowd, I turned my gaze to wonder around the inside of the van, and then to the Officer sitting across from me, and I realize that he has a familiar face. I casually divert my eyes, so as not to stare, and eventually bring them back to take a closer look. This man has kept his gaze on me the whole time, so I throw aside all politeness and stare right back at him.

It took a few moments to recognize him, probably due to the different uniform, but the man that sat before me was the same Special Forces NCO that had been assigned the leader of the detachment that was supposed to guard my family and me. His demeanor seemed to be non-threatening, and his hands were where I could see them, resting across his thighs and clasped in front. I scoot back in my seat and lean forward, allowing body language to show that I am ready to engage in inevitable conversation. We stare at each other for a few more moments, and I decided to be the one to break the tension by cutting right to the chase and ask him why he and his men left me and my family to die. Right after asking the question, I think to myself that I'd love to have this conversation recorded, so I lean back to make it easier to reach into my pocket at some point to slyly do so. With a slight smile, the man said that if I'd like to take my phone out, to go ahead and do so. With this comment, I freeze and just stare right into his cold and dark eyes. Did he correctly read my body language and guess what I was trying to do? Does he know that I have a tendency of doing this as of late.. or, is he somehow able to tell what I'm thinking. Without a moment's hesitation, the man simply says 'the latter'... And with that, I deliberately take out my phone, push the volume up button, and proceed to realize that my phone hasn't been charged since I entered the hospital and was completely dead. Of all the conversations I would like to document for this journal up to that point, this one is *the* one. I will do my best to generalize what was said between us.

    The man was in his 30s, possibly mid-40s. It was rather hard to tell due to the amount of facial hair he had. His demeanor was solemn, yet intense. Everything he said seemed to be charged with purpose and permanence. I was extremely anxious for the entire conversation due to not knowing if he was going to shoot me, but as it went on, I saw that this was not the case. In fact, it was the opposite. The man (He never gave his name.

I asked, but he said that it didn't matter because I would hopefully never see him again) went on to explain that he had in fact come to my house that day to kill me and my family, but after meeting me a few days ago, he changed his mind. Instead of going directly into why he decided to let his cohorts in crime try to kill me, he gave me what can best be described as a morality/history lesson. Though, I did not mind because it turned out to be the other side of the story in relation to everything the Society has told me.

He started off by saying that everything the Organization does is in the best interest for the human race. The high ranking members know about the truth behind man's origin and do whatever it takes to keep it a secret from the rest of the world, but for the most part, the Organization's main mission is to secure the future of mankind through his own means. Religion, faith, government, freedom, culture; all basic principles that vary depending on which geographic region is being discussed, but one thing they all have in common, no matter where one lives, is that they are all man made. Man rules this planet through his ideologies, and the Organization has seen to it for hundreds of years that this is the way that it stays. In the past few centuries, with the evils of man on the rise to a level never before seen, mostly due to technology, the top tier leaders of the Organization have debated whether or not the world would be better off knowing the truth. Every time the matter resurfaces during their 'council', or what they call their meetings between their top leaders, there has never been a viable vessel in which the truth could come forth. The Organization feels that far too many populations around this planet are using religion for purposes which were not intended. They wish to do something about it, but an alternative plan that would be worth pursuing, has never come to fruition. Revealing the truth has always been an option that has never been put into action, but they all keep their eyes and ears open for an opportunity.

Then, in the 1950's.. This guy's grandfather, whose name he did not share, prophesized that the second coming of the messiah would happen, and bring an end to the world. (The apparent origin of the Prophecy, first mentioned by Walter Cross) While this prophecy is known to all members of the Organization, this guy believes that it sounds too cataclysmic. Some things are not as cut and dry as they appear to be, or in other words, are not to be taken literally. This guy believes that what his grandfather meant was that the messiah would bring an end to the world as we know it. This does not need to happen through mass genocide and death. It can happen through mass revelation… Revelation of the truth. That is the purpose of this man's life, or so he told me. But this begs the question, which I then asked to the man, if the Organization seeks a new world through revelation, why didn't they let it happen when Jesus tried to do it, millennia ago…. The man replied that the world was not ready for the truth then. Its people were either captivated by it, or deeply offended, and the majority of the world's population were the latter. Ok.. so then I asked him… What makes him so sure that I am the answer, and if that's what he thought all along, why let the other Zealots try to kill me..

To this, he pulled out a small silver box. As I continued to look at it in his hand, I realized that this was the object that I mistook for a gun in the last Zealot's hand before I lethally shot him twice more. In my defense, up close, it doesn't really look like a box. It's silver, yes, but the edges are not flat like a box. It looked like a small three-dimensional piece of some cubist painting, or a hunk off of some otherworldly wall, or possibly even a small piece of a machine. As a matter of fact, it's not entirely obvious that something is actually stored inside of this object. I asked the man what it was, and he said that it was a holy vessel taken from your 'Society', as I have come to call them, long ago. He went on to explain that he is aware of the existence of the Society. Apparently, a member of the Society mistook him for a potential recruit and gave away our existence. After reporting this to the rest of the council, some wanted to actively pursue members of our society for questioning and imprisonment, but he brought up the point that we have existed for hundreds of years without the Organization being aware, and the world is no worse for it, or at least, as far as they could tell. That seemed to curb the council's lust for blood, and the two have coexisted ever since without any incidents between the two. Until, the man informs me, one of their recruits (Walter Cross, apparently) gets badly injured after he informs a member of the Organization that he was up to something big. This man in front of me was sent to investigate and came across me and my family. He reported back that I was a possible fit to the prophecy. The Organization then told him that if he confirmed that I was a fit to the prophecy, to deliver the silver vessel, and if not, I was to be terminated for attacking an Organization initiate. After he told me this, I asked him two questions back-to-back; what's so special about the vessel, and how was he able to confirm that I fit the prophecy through the few sentences we exchanged on the day I drove him out to my house.

His initial response was that he asked me if I was aware of latent abilities from our ancestors. I clarified and asked if he meant *them*, and he gave me a single head nod. I told him that I was aware, and that I was under the impression that these abilities needed to be awakened. Again, a single head nod, but he countered by saying that was more or less true, however, there are some that do not need to awaken their abilities. I asked him what he meant, and he gave himself as an example. Through years of meditation and inner reflection, this guy has apparently developed the ability to read the thoughts of those that can communicate with *them*. That day, when he sat in my car, he was aware of the internal struggle with which I had been burdened. My focus was upon truth, justice, and love… All values that were held high by those favored by 'the light' as he put it. He said that I possessed tremendous light and potential, unlike any that he had encountered before. This meant that I was to receive the Vessel, but something inside of him couldn't just hand it over. He went on to say that the vessel once belonged to Jesus, and contained an object of great power, and no one knew what it was, or how to activate it if it could be activated, or how to use it if anyone were ever able to open it. But before he could just hand over such power, he needed for me to demonstrate that I was worthy of receiving it. Once he decided that he was not going to kill me in my house, he would allow for his backup contingency plan to carry on. The three Zealots were to approach my house to see if their attack was a go. Once they got close and could see flashing police lights, smoke rising from a burning house, etc. they were to abort mission. If the house was not lit up, then they were to fire rockets at it as a backup plan. And if for some reason they were compromised, they were to hand me this Vessel in exchange for their lives. In this guys mind, it would have been impossible to defeat these enemies without guidance from a higher power. The fact that I was able to defeat them proves that I am indeed favored by a higher power, and worthy of receiving the vessel. It was at this moment that he handed me the silver box.

Once I had the object in my hand, I began looking at every corner and crevice, studying it like an amateur holding a Rubik's cube. There were corners on top of corners, and some edges even seemed rounded like little pipes running around this object. There did not appear to be any latch, hinge, or crack that would indicate the object opened at all. I was about to set it aside when I spotted an inconsistency. There appeared to be a round little crater, almost like an imbedded fingerprint scanner, but it was too small for an adult to fit the full surface of a finger in it. Something round, and smaller than a fingerprint could be placed into this area. Perhaps maybe a ball bearing, or a stone… A stone like the one resting in the setting of my ring. I looked down at my fingers and saw that my ring had been placed on my left hand, instead of my right where I usually wore it. I tried to remember putting it on my left hand, but I could not, and I came to the conclusion that I could not remember doing it because I never did. Someone else must have while I was unconscious. The only person that would care to do that and had access to me before my family did was Thomas. He must have had the foresight to make sure that it stayed on my person. Little things like that make me more and more certain that regardless of what happens, Thomas will be my right-hand man. As I continue to think about it, I become more and more certain that my ring will in fact open this object, and I began to feel quite excited in anticipation. Then I look up into the stranger's eyes sitting across from me, and remember that he knows everything that I'm thinking, and now knows that I've already figured out how to open the box. As though I were asking the question out loud, the man assured me that he was not trying to trick me into telling him how to open the box. He informed me that he was sincere about his promise to let me keep the box and its contents, and was truly fascinated to see that I had figured out how to open an object in seconds that no one else has been able to open for thousands of years.

I placed the box to my side and the conversation between us came to an awkward halt. I took a moment to look at the passing surroundings through the back window to place where we were and noticed that we were only a few minutes from the Christian county Police station. I also noticed, about 5 cars back, that there was a news van following us. I turned to look at the man and pointed out that we were nearly there, and he only had a few more minutes to tell me anything else he wished to tell me. The man reminded me that now that I had the vessel, the Organization would always be watching me. And if I ever changed my ways and were to head down a path of darkness, they would essentially kill me and retrieve the vessel. Not the kindest of parting words, but that was it. I climbed out of the van, and the man stayed seated in the back as I entered the station. I turned to look back, but the van was pulling away.

I still have to go over the events of the Police station, but I'm done writing for now. I need a break. Will continue tomorrow.

AUGUST 4, 2013

Just when I thought I was getting close to being completely caught up, more shit gets put on my to-write list. I'm referring to my smoking session last night, after I was done writing. But, I will get to that. So the Police station… Upon entering, it was similar to the previous routine. They took me into a cell to await questioning, where I sat for a few minutes. I was allowed to keep all the objects I brought into the station on my person, and considered looking over the box, but thought it best to not to until I was in the interrogation room. A few minutes pass by, and I am escorted to a room for questioning. Once there, I was questioned by an interrogation officer concerning the attack on my house. I went over the events as best as I could remember, and hoped the officer's level of curiosity would be low. Once the story was over, I made it a point to try and distract him with unrelated questions in an attempt to stammer his prying of details, but it didn't really work. He seemed very interested in how exactly it came to be that I was on top of my roof, ready and waiting with my rifle for this incoming attack. This was the line of questioning I was trying to avoid. The best way to go about it, and I suppose this applies to anyone not wanting to reveal a hidden secret, is to answer as arbitrarily as possible. I told the officer that I had a bad feeling creep upon me, and I took it upon myself to sit on my roof and wait. Short and simple; no details to be asked about, and who can argue with a feeling felt by someone? Pretty much every other prying question after that can be deflected by playing dumb or simply saying 'I don't know'. A cheap explanation, but it worked for the most part, because eventually the interview was over, and the tape player stopped recording. The officer stood up and was about to exit the room when he turned back and said that he didn't believe that I was up there on a feeling. Whatever it was, I was a hero, and lucky to be alive. I gave the man a slight smile and a head nod as a response, keeping it arbitrary. He informed me to wait here to be escorted out of the station, pending release, and turned to leave the room. Not even a minute later, Thomas, the Sec Def, and the Grand High Master all enter the room, as promised, with two of them carrying chairs for themselves. I stood up, greeted them all, (the GHM for the first time), and we all sat down and commenced our first meeting.

The Sec Def started by saying that I was up for the Medal of Honor, awaiting final approval from Congress, per the submittal from the commanding General of Ft. Campbell. It was to be awarded by the President of the United States on Live television in a few days. I couldn't help but snicker at this as I thought about the logistics of getting such a medal approved. Awards in the Army are as far from simple and painless as possible. Drafts upon drafts, on top of revisions and approvals are needed for every single award, which could take weeks to a few months, depending on how high the award needs to go to get final approval. This award should have been no exception to the rule but throw the President of the United States into the mix, and suddenly, shit that takes months to grind through the clockwork of the Chain of Command gets reduced to days. Such bullshit. Case in point, I once recommended an award for a soldier from a different unit that came out to help my soldiers, and his contribution pretty much made the success of the mission possible. The following week I wrote his award and submitted it. The award got kicked back three times; the first time was for the guy not being in our unit, which is irrelevant, and the other two were for the bullet points within the award not being strong enough…. Really? Who the fuck are you to judge what I said about this person? I was there, saw what he did, and described it adequately. I know what I'm doing, and the guy saved our butts. But nooo… my Chain of Command had to throw a wrench in my spokes, and the process took so long that the window for the award to be approved (90 days from the date of the actions deemed worthy of recognition) passed, and the soldier ended up getting nothing. Stupid shit like that makes me want to punch Colonels, Captains, and Sergeant Majors in the face. More often than not, your subordinates are better than you, smarter than you, and simply need you to do your job. But shit goes to people's heads, and they start feeling awfully special/high and mighty, and all of the sudden it's rabble rabble bullshit blah blah blah because I said so for no good reason. I digress.

I bring up the point that this medal would be going against the minimal attention that my family and I needed, considering.. well… *them*. Thomas counters with the point that it's far too late for that, and those destined for greatness will receive just that, and people will be sure to notice along the way. So true. He went on to say that the world is expecting a statement from me, regarding all of this, and all three of them wish to hear what it was that I was going to say. I informed them that I had an idea, but I wasn't entirely sure at the time. They attempted to insist that we all figure it out right then and there, but I quickly changed the subject by taking out the silver object the man from the van gave me and set it upon the table directly in front of me. All three of them gasped and fell silent with mouths hanging open. Giorgio, (the GHM), softly whispered slightly under his breath, 'The Holy Grail'. I turned to him, ready to negate and question, but he beat me to it by asking how it came to be that I had it. Before I could answer Thomas spoke up by saying that he suspected the object that I described to him earlier in the hospital was the Grail. He came here to recover it from evidence, but someone had beat him to it… I could tell that he wished to go on, but he knew that anything he said after that would be guesses at what happened, and I apparently already knew the truth. He fell silent and allowed me to tell the story of how I obtained it.

Once I finished telling them how it came to be in my possession, they all looked at one another uneasily. All these years they thought they had covered their tracks and remained unknown to the Organization. The news barely phased me, but I suppose it took a much bigger toll on them; finding out thinking you were protected by secrecy all your life and having it turn out to be false. On top of this, the man that gave me the Grail, according to the Sec Def, is one of the most wanted assassins in the world. He has been credited with over a hundred kills; all of his targets carefully selected by the Organization in order for them to advance towards whatever goal they have on their agenda. Apparently, I am the only one to ever have seen this man and lived to tell the story. This point left us in an awkward silence, and I took advantage of this to inquire about the Holy Grail. I turned to Giorgio, expecting an academic type of his caliber to jump on this sort of question that was right up his alley, and sure enough, he didn't miss a beat and powered into his explanation. The Organization could not leave out the Holy Grail from the Bible due to many people personally witnessing its power. The Grail was part of the reason why Jesus' popularity was so formidable. During his lifetime, it belonged to him, but it had once belonged to numerous other Prophets throughout history. This can be assumed due to the evidence that can be seen around the world.. The most notable being the Pyramids of Giza. Scientists, and the rest of the world for that matter, rule out the existence of aliens, and therefore, alien technology, which makes the creation of such amazing structures awe-inspiring. People have spent hundreds of years trying to figure out how they were built, when the explanation is quite small, short, and simple. It was done at the hand of the prophet, wielding this object. So, it apparently has the power to move large and heavy objects? That doesn't make much sense. It makes more sense for the object to be an extension of the technology that would allow the movement of heavy objects.. a glorified TV remote, if you will. I was tempted to ask them more questions about it, but I realized that anything they said would be speculation based upon ancient speculations. The nature and destiny of the object is now currently my own, and any future revelations regarding its use, or anything else for that matter, would come from me.

This led into the part of our discussion where we figured out exactly what the next step should be. At that time, I knew that I wanted to be relocated to Colorado. On the surface, there are several reasons why I chose this place. Marijuana is legalized, and I can continue to communicate with *them* as their 'master plan' unfolds, if there even is one. I also believe that there are other reasons why I am choosing this place, but I am not aware of them at this time. I know that most of my actions, and the actions of 'chosen people' are partly not their own doing in that *they* plant subliminal messages in our minds. I have no doubt that relocating to Colorado will have some sort of significance in the future that cannot be seen by the four of us just yet. I informed the Sec Def to make preparations to move me and my family to Colorado, but to await further instructions to be received tomorrow. He begins to reply with that is not where he has selected and to change my destination would be great of a setback. I quickly reply with it's either we do this my way, or I walk from all of you and the Society right now. I am the Guardian, I am in charge here, and right now, I am ready and willing to work. With the acquisition of this new object, I expressed to them that I was in great need of a Timestretch, and what will be shown to me tonight could be of great significance, or it could be nothing at all. After all parties left the meeting, they were to await my guidance and do what was needed for my family in the meantime. I also asked the GHM if the Sec Def had informed him of the task that I was wanting him to perform. The GHM said that he was aware and was currently in the process of gathering research and writing things down. I informed him that this was no longer needed. The acquisition of the Holy Grail changes everything. The Holy Grail makes the allure of the words of man on paper, obsolete. This object and whatever it does, is the key to everything. I simply needed time to figure out what it was to be used for, and how. The last thing I said to the four of them was to await notification of my next step from Thomas. Since he was originally assigned to reside in close proximity to me in order to keep tabs on me, I will give all information to him so that he can relay the information onward as he sees fit. This keeps me from having to go through the undoubtedly complex process of sharing highly sensitive information with people holding highly sensitive positions.

Once everyone was clear on their instructions, we all stood up to wish each other farewell, when suddenly, Giorgio's eyes lit up. He informed me that he had translated the inscription that was written in the back of my notebook. It loosely translated to the following: 'All of God's children will look to Bruce, the father of the son, to ascend to heaven, and prevent God's holy wrath.'

Needless to say, none of us were able to apply this translation to anything real or practical. We may come to better understand what it means in the future, but right at this moment, it just sounds like the rattling's of some religious kook. However, I did feel as though a significant weight was lifted from my chest upon finally hearing the translation. This entire time I was sure that it would be something dark and ominous but was relieved to find that it really didn't make much sense.

And that about covers our meeting at the Christian County Jail. Overall, I thought the meet and greet with the GHM was going to be far more significant and memorable than it was. He came off as highly intelligent and confident, and of course I was thankful for the translation, but at the end of the meeting, he was just one set of three pairs of eyes looking to me for guidance. As I left the station, I couldn't help but feel lost and shaken. *They* would really have to deliver tonight during my Timestretch. I felt like my association with the Society, and my position of leadership was all a sham. What had I done to deserve their respect, or to prove that I am worthy of my position? How was I to figure essentially everything out that evening? I couldn't help but feel like I had set myself up for failure as my wife drove us home from the station for a second time. But then again, I did have a new variable to introduce into the mix.. This Holy Grail. I had no idea what kind of a difference it would make, if any at all.. Though, the more I thought about it, the more sense it makes for it to do something. The rest of the car ride I spent planning the evening with Michelle. We'd put Colin down to sleep, and then we would both see about unlocking the secrets of this Grail.

Jumping right into it: I opened the object with my ring, just as I suspected I could after receiving it from the Organization member. Nothing special to report about the opening process, and the 'Grail' itself, is about what I expected. It is a small black disc, concave on one side, and apparently made to sit on top of the wearer's head, much like one would wear a Yarmulke. Exactly what the disc is made out of is unknown. Considering it's literally a piece of alien tech, it could be safe to assume it's made from a substance not found on this world. Learning more about this substance would only cause questions to arise and unwanted attention.

With my arm still in a sling, I had Michelle prepare my glass piece for this Timestretch. Once we were feeling good and blazed, I placed the object on top of my head and cleared my mind. At first, nothing happened. No images, no biblical miracles, nothing. I turned to my wife and said that perhaps the object doesn't work anymore. Just then, images of electrocuting the disc via toaster in a bathtub, putting it in the oven, and hooking it up to a car battery all raced through my head. Then I saw my wife putting it on her head, only for her to discover that nothing happened yet again. 'Holy shit', I remember saying. Then I could see myself talking to my wife about some amazing revelation, but my mouth was moving without any words coming out. At this point I reached up to grab the object off the top of my head. The visions stopped coming. I thought for a moment, got an idea, and placed it on top of my head again. I asked Michelle to think about the happiest moment in her life. She closed her eyes and as I looked at her, I could see our son through her eyes. Looking down at his beautiful and precious face for the very first time. The moment was so joyous that I couldn't help but feel it too, and tears began to fall down my cheeks. I took the object off my head again and excitedly shared my conclusion with Michelle. The grail allows you to see the thoughts of other people in your own mind. It's exactly like projecting another person's imagination into your own brain. The object must be able to pick-up the electrical signals that a person's brain is making and translate them into whatever thought or memory the person is imagining at the time. I handed the object to Michelle, and told her to try and read my mind. I asked her to see if she could picture exactly what it was that I was thinking about. In an attempt to make her blush, I thought about the first time we tried anal sex. It was an interesting experience, one that we would be willing to try again, but overall, not as good as the traditional love canal. With a sly smile on my face, I looked into her blank face, and she continued to look into mine. I asked her what I was thinking about, and she just shrugged and said she did not know. I swapped memories to the embrace of her and Colin after my second deployment, a particularly powerful memory for me. If there was any memory that would light up my brain like the 4th of July, this is the one. Again, I asked her what I was thinking about, and again, she could not tell. She suggested that perhaps she did not smoke enough, and brought up the fact that she had never smoked Afghan hash, and had a similar 'awakening' experience as I had had. I thought about this for a moment, and the logic made sense. I suggested that she go ahead and pack another bowl to have all for herself, and to go ahead and make it large. She turned to reach for my glass piece, but before she could grab it, the pipe flew off the table and hit her in the face, just beneath her right eye. For what seemed like an eternity, her hands were pressed against her eye as she keeled over in pain. As soon as she hunched over, the grail fell off her head and landed on the floor. She didn't cry or scream, but she did make a hissing sound with the air that she was slowing inhaling, as some do when in great pain. I thought for sure that when she pulled her hands away, her eye would pop out and there would be blood and brains to follow. But when she finally did, all that could be seen was a bluish-reddish mark surrounded by some decent swelling. I scooped up the grail in order to make sure it was not damaged from the fall to the floor (which it wasn't), and ran to grab some ice for her to hold over her eye, and proceeded to inquire about what had just happened.

At first, she assumed that I threw it at her, and was demanding to know why. After letting her calm down a bit, I proceeded to explain that neither of us physically touched my pipe. It flew off the table and smacked her right in the eye. At first she did not believe me, and kept going on and on about why I would do such a thing and how people would think I hit her in the face, and so on. Once she had calmed down yet again, I informed her that I had an idea, and that I wanted her to remain calm and quiet, and that I would try to explain what happened. I handed her the grail, and asked her to place it back on top of her head. Once she did, I picked up my piece from the floor, and placed it on top of the table, some 4 feet away from her. I instructed her to close her eyes, clear her mind, and once her thoughts were peaceful and blank, I asked her to open her eyes. Then I instructed her to look at my piece resting on the table. I asked her to imagine it slowly floating towards her outstretched hand and to think of the kind of care one would use when catching a tossed child. She listened to all my instructions, and sure enough, the glass piece, much slower this time, floated directly to her outstretched hand. She turned and looked at me completely astonished, and I'm sure the shock on her face matched mine. I asked her to hand me the Grail, and to let me try. After several attempts, I could not get the pipe to budge. Michelle even tried to regurgitate the coaching tips I had just given her, and I even had her pack me my own additional bowl of weed, but no matter how little or hard I tried, I could not get it to move. I gave her back the grail and let her continue to experiment. To make many trials and errors short, she had the ability to move anything that was approximately the size and weight of an apple, approximately four-six feet. Everything that was larger, or possessed more mass, she was unable to move. Also, whenever she moved something that she could move, it could only be moved four-six feet before falling off like a battery losing its juice. Once this second experimentation session was over, I came to realize exactly what it all meant.

Within each of our DNA, lie different latent abilities. Mine is that of mild telepathy, and hers is that of minor telekinesis. I'm fairly confident that if she were to go through a similar awakening process as I did in the Stan, her abilities would be greater, and she would be able to move larger and more massive objects. But, that is not the rub. The results of these early Grail trials reveal that within some people of this planet, there are two latent alien abilities. Telekinesis, and Telepathy. It just so happens that my wife and I, each possessing different alien alleles that correspond to their two greatest talents, got married, and had a child. A child, that was both an accident, and not at the same time. A child that *they* made sure would occur and chose gametes that would be sure to express both latent abilities and eventually could make what we just witnessed amongst each other seem like cheap magic tricks. A child with the power to literally change the world as he saw fit, which would make him the most powerful human ever to walk the face of the Earth.

After sharing this realization with Michelle, her first instinct was to wake him up, and to see what he could do. To that, I said no. Colin was not to know about the Grail, or any of this. He is too young to understand any of what is going on. Besides, I informed my wife that it wasn't entirely clear that we would be the ones to tell him in the first place. It may be that *they* will be the ones to make Colin aware of his purpose. Or it could be us, or a combination of both. But the bottom line was, here we were in our late twenties, just now discovering all of this on our own and many things had to happen before both of us could come to this realization, and it only seems logical that the same will need to happen with Colin before he is made aware of his true potential. This seemed to quell Michelle's lust for discovery, and shortly after, I suspect that using the Grail made her exceptionally tired since she went to bed and passed out hard. This left me free to Timestretch and see what else *they* intended for me to learn on that particular evening. I found my piece, clumsily packed it with my one good arm, and brought myself back to that perfect balance of telepathic chemistry. I cleared my mind and awaited the ensuing roller coaster.

The first thing I was shown this go around, was me sitting on my doorstep in the old house where I grew up. The T.V. was on in the living room, and visible from the front door. On the screen, billows of smoke poured from both towers of the World Trade Center, after two planes crashed into them as a terrorist plot. It was September 11, 2001. I had already been sent home from school and was to spend the rest of the day with my family as the notorious day unfolded. That memory fades as quickly as it started, and I am sitting at a table in the DFAC of JAF. I'm having lunch with the guy that found my lost bag after that flight back from Bagram. This is where he tells me about the Special Forces member that told him about Bin Laden. These two events are connected somehow? Well at first glance, Bin Laden was to blame for the September 11 attacks, but that co-relation is too easy. It's never that easy with *them*. This is going to require some looking into. I await for something else to come, but nothing does. I think to myself, what about the Grail? What about Colorado? They have to be aware of my concerns and wonders.. most likely at all times. Do they give any consideration into easing my burning curiosity? No. But then again, more answers usually leads to different questions that I didn't have before. One thing at a time I suppose.

After the Timestretch, I got onto my computer and began looking up 9/11. I wasn't entirely sure what I was supposed to be looking for, or why. For me, the event played a large part as to why I joined the Army in the first place. I felt vulnerable. I felt as though something needed to be done. I think it's safe to say, that that day gave birth to an itch in my mind that could only be scratched by joining the military and doing my part to get back at those terrorist bastards. It would take me the better part of 10 years to scratch it, but personally significant, nonetheless. At first glance, searches for 9/11 turned up the usual. Pictures and videos of the event, and of course the conspiracy theories surrounding the whole thing. I had already seen a video called 'Loose Change', and found it to be rather interesting. But the only real argument that held any weight in my mind from that video was the scrutiny of the towers collapsing. They gave numerous examples from fires across history that burned buildings, and the buildings never collapsed. Many of these examples were damaged far worse than the towers were, and of course, built to a fraction of the standard that the Towers were. And yet, they remained standing. Peculiar indeed, but at the time I passed it off as wild theory, and clearly a bunch of pissed off Muslims attacked America, and we retaliated accordingly. Thus, when I came across the same video, I bookmarked the page, and kept searching. A few minutes later, I found what I had apparently been looking for. Another conspiracy theory website, but this one had several videos that were over an hour in length. This site was newer and had links to various other frequently debated aspects of 9/11. Of course, I did not know at the time that this is what they were meaning me to find, but it became clear about halfway into the first video. Once I had devoted a few hours into this site, and quickly exhausted all of its points and research, the gravity of my latest Timestretch finally sunk in. But before I get to that, let me go over what I discovered on the site, and led to my latest revelation.

The site itself: Septemberclues.info. In their primary video towards the top of the page, the main focus held within is a direct criticism of what exactly was shown on

T.V. From this video, there are four emphasized points that it raises that I find to be irrefutable evidence of an actual conspiracy. First and foremost, is what they have labeled as the 'Nose Out' shot. There was a video feed from a Helicopter owned by Fox-T.V., where their gyroscopic camera underneath the craft does a 3 step zoom in seconds before the second plane hit the other Tower. As the video shows the plane colliding with the tower, the nose of the plane can be seen coming out the other side of the building, followed by a brief 15 frame blackout. (Quick side note; I watched all of these videos without sound, allowing me gather my own conclusions, and preventing any and all bias that was most likely present in the video) Once the feed resumes, there is a fireball going through its lifecycle from the crash, and smoke begins to billow. The video goes on to examine that the nose is fully intact as it exits the other side of the building, and that the nose itself must be computer generated since it is exactly the same shape and size as it was right before the actual collision. Due to this, they conclude that the shot must be a failed computer graphic. Definitely open to discussion, but, in my opinion, they fail to examine the most important part about this clip. There is an amateur video appearing towards the end of this movie that shows this exact moment filmed from an angle that is essentially opposite the angle of the Fox helicopter. If the nose did indeed come out the other side of the building, intact or not, it should have been seen here. In this opposite vantage point, the nose clearly does not exit the other side of the building, which further proves that the nose coming out of the building from the Fox shot was indeed a computer graphic. Not only does the nose not being present in this shot, or any other shot for that matter, prove that it was a computer graphic, but none of the five news corporations reporting that day ever discusses the fact that the nose went through the building and out the other side in the first place. No matter how many cameras film the same event, and no matter what perspective or angle they are filmed from, they should all show the same exact event, down to the smallest of details. The nose coming out of the building should be seen in several videos, but the fact of the matter is that that particular detail is exclusive to only the Fox helicopter shot.

The second thing that stands out to me is another facet of the 'Nose Out' shot. After the third zoom in of the gyroscopic camera underneath the helicopter, literally less than 2 seconds pass before the plane hits the tower in this highly zoomed in shot. The video does a great job of pointing out that in the three shots following each successive zoom-in prior to the plane hitting, the plane cannot be seen in the sky. Once the camera hits maximum zoom, the plane appears, and it is rather dark, but clearly a plane. But, in the six seconds prior to the three step zoom in, this dark plane should have been clearly visible as it approached the Tower, yet, there is nothing. Nonetheless, something hits the Tower, and something explodes.

The third thing that stood out to me, is related to a point that I made in the 'first thing' paragraph, and that point is 'that every camera filming the same event should show the exact same thing'. There is a shot labeled the 'Divebomber Shot' that most clearly conflicts with the 'Al Qaeda' shot. The 'Divebomber' shot illustrates that the second plane took a steep dive from an altitude greater than that of the Towers themselves, before leveling out approximately two seconds before impact, and then strikes the tower. The 'Al Qaeda' shot (named thusly since it appeared on their network) clearly shows a non-diving Plane flying level in the last six seconds before it collides with the Tower. The same plane travels two distinctly different paths in these two shots, which can allow us to assume that at least one is fake. In addition to this, the 'Al Qaeda' shot is not the only shot to show a level flying plane in the last six seconds before impact, just as the 'Divebomber' shot is not the only one that shows that the plane took a steep dive from a higher altitude in the seconds prior to impact. In order for these videos to be authentically showing what actually happened, they would all have to have the plane taking the same flight path right up to the point of impact. The fact of the matter is, that they do not.

The fourth and final thing that stood out to me while watching this video were the camera shots themselves. As I think about how I wish to convey this point, I cannot help but think about the end of the movie 'Anchorman'. Towards the end of this movie, news crews from all around San Diego go to the Zoo to try and film a rare birth of a baby Panda in captivity. Veronica Corningstone realizes that if she stands on top of the ledge in front of the Kodiak Bear exhibit, she is able to get a glimpse of the birthing process going on in the adjacent and walled off Panda exhibit. Of course she falls in and Ron Burgandy and his crew soon follow, but that is not the point. The point is this; that vantage point, had she gotten it, would have been exclusively hers. She would not have shared it with the other cameramen there, and her news network would have been the only one to air the footage. That is the nature of news networks. They all have independent crews, and anchorpeople working to bring a news feed exclusive to their news network. However, this is not the case during 9/11. The video points out several instances where the news feeds being displayed from different news networks is actually a rehash of a single common video feed. It is one thing for news networks to try and fight for space and all of them line up in a row in front of, for example, a courthouse hearing a major court case. (This would provide multiple similar shots, from slightly different vantage points, but none of them would be from the exact same vantage point since the vantage point that they would show on their network would be from their own on site news team.) But the fact of the matter is that several different news networks used the same vantage point, and tried to mask this fact by purposely picking and choosing which parts of the common foreground and background they left out in order to make the shot seem unique to their network. The bottom line is that while news networks should be working independently of one another and providing unique video feeds, this video proves that there were many shared feeds, which means that several, if not all of the news networks, were working together. And why is it that people, teams, or even news networks would work together? Well, that would be to achieve a common goal. What common goal?? In this case, that common goal was to use coordinated deception to hide what really happened.

AND, if that last point needed further clarification or evidence, there just so happens to be more on the front page of the very same website. Towards the bottom of the page is another video entitled 'Synched Out'. This is a shorter video that simultaneously displays the news feeds of all five news networks that were reporting that day from 8:52AM to 9:03AM. Those news networks are ABC, CNN, CBS, FOX, and NBC. At 3:36 seconds into the video, it can be seen that all five briefly display the exact same image provided by a single camera source. Prior to and after this moment, several instances also appear where two or sometimes three networks use the same shot simultaneously. The only way that this could happen would be for all of the news networks to have access to the same camera feed. And since news networks are independent of one another, with their own equipment and people, the only way multiple networks could use the same feed would be to share feeds, or in this case, pull from a pool of feeds available to all news networks during 9/11.

Now, there are many other discrepancies that arise as a result of watching these videos, however, I am choosing not to include them here since I can see weight in counter points given to refute certain claims. Part of being a good leader is being a skilled devil's advocate. However, the four main points that I listed are the strongest ones to which that even I have trouble refuting. Outside of these points and videos, there remains the victims from the attack, the Pentagon attack, the collapse of building 7, and the failed hijack attempt resulting in the 'Plane crash' in Pennsylvania. The only point worth discussing additionally are the victims. (The complete lack of any evidence that an actual plane struck the Pentagon and the complete absence of plane debris in Pennsylvania are proof enough that planes did not crash at these sites. How are a plane's wings going to supposedly penetrate the steel columns of the world trade center, and not penetrate the walls of the Pentagon? There should have been evidence of the wings striking the pentagon, and there should have been a hell of a lot more plane debris in the ditch that was discovered in Pennsylvania. Clearly, something other than a 'plane crash' happened at these sites. And as far as building 7 goes.. considering how far it was from the towers, and that it collapsed from practically nothing, then the entire city block should have been leveled if it's collapse was logical. However, this is the only other building besides the towers that collapses, and I cannot think of a single logical reason for it's collapse, other than controlled demolition.) The website goes on to claim that the list of victims and their pictures are all digital forgeries, many of which used one person to create several similar looking spin-off people, similar to the concept of changing certain aspects of a camera shot to make it seem authentic during the actual broadcast of the event, and then distributing the slightly altered video feed to other networks, making it appear to be genuine to that network. Many of the people really do look similar, and I find this explanation to be completely plausible and fascinating. All things considered, this website does a fine job of pointing out the blatant flaws that exist as a result of apparent poor video editing, as the powers that be moderately pulled off the greatest hoax in history. Which leaves one last topic that I have been saving for last: the collapse of the Towers themselves.

I am not a building demolitions expert, nor am I an expert on the burning of fuel, or the creation, use, and placement of explosives. But, that doesn't mean that one cannot use logic to deduce whether or not what happened was logical. So, here goes. Consider just one of the towers. Assume that this tower is completed, and has stood tall and firm for over 25 years. Consider the base of this tower during these 25 years. The base would have been built in order to perform the function of supporting the rest of the tower. In addition to this, the base must also be able to support the factors and strains put upon the rest of the tower through added walls, office supplies/furniture, employees, tourists, and external atmospheric forces placed upon the tower by the weather. Additionally, per my own general knowledge, skyscrapers have to have a foundation that extends underground in order to help withstand all of the forces I just mentioned. (If I recall correctly, the ratio is something close to 1/3 of the total height of the structure extends underground) Enter an airplane, striking the tower in its' upper 3/4. How would this affect the structural integrity of the base? It wouldn't. The base would continue to support the full weight of the tower, just as it had for the last 25 years. The added weight of the airplane to the total weight that the base of the tower is supporting would be miniscule; the base can and would support the added weight of an aircraft. Now, let's assume that through the impact, the Plane was able to affect the structural integrity of the core of the building at the very level of impact. So, the tower's core integrity is compromised 75% of the way up the length of the tower. Does this change the amount of weight that the base needs to support? No, it does not. But, what has changed, is how the weight of the tower above the crash point is distributed. Before, the weight distribution was flawless up and down, for the full length of the tower; now, everything above the crash site has become compromised. (If the weight of the overall structure remained relatively the same before and after the plane collision, there is no reason to believe that the base would not be strong enough to continue holding the full weight of the building indefinitely.) Due to the compromised core at the crash site, is it possible for a collapse to happen? Well, in order for that answer to be a yes, the core would need to be damaged to the point where it was essentially severed in half. So, let us assume that the plane strike did highly damage the core, and was made worse to an unknown degree by the fires created as a result of the crash. Does this change the amount of weight that the base needed to support? No, it does not. The base is still strong as it has ever been. So could a collapse have occurred at all? Yes. If the core of the building, at the point of impact, were to essentially be severed in half due to impact and pending fires, the portion of the tower above the point of impact would essentially be free standing. This could lead to a partial collapse where the upper ¼ of the building falls off to the side, and may even crush a few floors in the process of falling, but it would not completely collapse the building. Depending on the nature of the impact, if the upper ¼ were to fall at all, it would take the path of least resistance, which in this case is not straight down through the fully capable and non-compromised base, but rather sliding off to the side and falling through the air to crash onto the streets below. Consider a large tree. If one were to cut the trunk of the tree ¾ of the way up to the point where everything above that point were to collapse, it would fall off to the side, and most if not all of the remaining ¾ of the tree would remain standing. Why? Because THE BASE AND ROOT SYSTEM STILL EXIST! The same concept is applicable to the base of both towers. If either tower were to collapse, at the very worst, they only would have above the point of impact. The rest of the tower would have remained standing. The only way that both towers could have completely collapsed, as they did, would be if the integrity of the core, from the bottom up, were to be completely eliminated, allowing for the base to be unable to support the weight of the building. And this, ladies and gentlemen, could only have been achieved through the use of planted explosives.

Now, this last point is a slippery slope in that a couple points could be, and have been raised to argue against a demolitioned collapse. Several experts have gone on to claim that the outer shells of the tower were vital to the structural integrity of the Towers. Is that possible? No matter which way I look at it, that claim has to be a bold faced lie. Logic dictates that in order for any structure to collapse into itself like the towers did, the inner core, or backbone if you will, has to be greatly compromised or made to be so ineffective that it becomes non-existent. A tree with a diameter of two feet, for example, is not going to keel over from a gash that only goes into it's bark a few inches. The core of the tree remains uncompromised, and will continue to support the tree. Just the same as a person receiving a major gash to their abdomen will not collapse into themselves due to their spine being uncompromised. Sure they'll collapse in pain and shock, but unless that backbone is literally chopped into pieces, it will continue to perform its primary functions of protecting the spinal cord, and keeping the upper torso in an upright position. The core of said person, tree, or structure will continue to perform its duty unless it is deliberately weakened in order to purposely make it collapse upon itself. (Keep in mind that I realize that the cores of the towers were not comprised of a singular solid beam extending upward like a spine or trunk of a tree. They were comprised of four dozen or so beams spaced out, all attached to each other, and extended up the center for the full length of the tower. All of these beams working together comprised the 'core' that I speak of.) From here, this debate then turns to speculation on the placement of the explosives themselves, and how it would have been impossible for them to be placed without people knowing about them. It could have been that they were built into the entire length of the inner core during initial construction in order to facilitate its future demolition, or any number of schemes could have been planned in order to get the placing accomplished. But the purpose of this particular entry is not to establish every facet of the conspiracy.

(hopefully that will be done in the immediate future) The purpose of this entry is to realize exactly what it is that *they* wish for me to realize. Moving on..

The second part of the Timestretch was that of the lunch with the Contractor and I where I learned about Bin Laden not being killed over several opportunities. I already have mentioned the vast problems that I find with this, but what correlation does it have to 9/11? After sitting upon this thought for a while, I believe I have the answer. The creation of the 9/11 hoax can also be seen as the birth of a vast trail of lies. The foundation that 9/11 created for our government was one where they could use this event as propaganda in order to accomplish essentially whatever they needed in the years to come. Exactly what has stemmed from this elaborate fabrication is nearly impossible to determine without a government confession, but on the surface, it allowed the US to declare a war on Terror and use this guise to travel to the Middle-East to wage wars. These wars allowed for the creation of countless military contracts amongst ourselves and foreign countries, and ultimately provided the ability to carry out years upon years of corrupt hidden agendas. What this contractor actually revealed to me, was a brief and current glimpse into the trail of lies that was created all those years ago with 9/11; choosing not to capture Bin Laden is just one example of a lie found along the trail. But all of this begs one question... Why? If this is the reality which we face today, why would any of this be allowed to happen?

9/11 happened because the American people unknowingly allowed it to happen. The leaders that we have elected, which are supposed to hold true faith and allegiance to our country have long since become corrupt. Our leaders have taken to placing greater importance on making decisions that will benefit themselves and their benefactors over those that would be best for the people of America. 9/11 is the ultimate proof that the political and corporate elite will use anything and everything, including mainstream media, to portray our foreign and domestic policies to be exactly what the American people want them to be, when in reality, once the camera is off, they use their free reign to go about achieving their actual agendas behind the backs of American citizens. This essentially justifies any and all hatred that foreign countries have against us. American citizens are being victimized by the decisions made by the corruption and greed of our political and corporate elite. Our government goes about abusing the powers we have given them to achieve agendas that they have not shared with our citizens. It's hard to say exactly how long it has been this way, but one thing is certain, it's not going to change. It's not going to change.... Unless. Unless the American people do something about it. No.. Well... yes, but no... This corruption of our country must end. And in order for there to be an end, there must be a beginning of said end. Nothing will end unless *I* do something about it. Nothing will change unless *we* do something about it. And the only thing that we can do.. is to carry out a Revolution. R.E.V.O.L.U.T.I.O.N.

Jesus, could that be my mission from *them*?? To end American tyranny and liberate our country of the corruption that is polluting the US? Possibly, but one thing sticks out in my mind.. Why would *they* care so much about the state of affairs in America? But.... it's not just America is it... It's the entire world. Our problems can be seen as a drop in the bucket compared to the problems that are currently ongoing in other countries.. So why care so much about the US? I'm usually able to connect the dots, but right now I'm drawing a blank. What does a revolution in America have anything to do with anything? There has to be some sort of big picture that that would contribute towards which I am just not seeing. The more I think about it, the less sense it makes. I want to figure this out NOW… After sitting on this for a few minutes, I can only come up with one solution. Timestretch. But not as I usually do. I need to achieve the state I reached in the Stan. No, I need to surpass that state… and I need to be using the Grail. That's it! If this doesn't work, I'm fresh out of ideas.

Alright, as it currently stands, my plan is to essentially smoke myself to borderline unconsciousness, and then to keep going until I guess I actually do lose consciousness. I am currently wearing a PT cap with the Grail underneath so as to make sure it stays on the crown of my head where it needs to be in case I pass out. Correction: *when* I pass out. Whenever I awaken, I will continue writing what I saw, or at least, what I can remember seeing.

AUGUST 13, 2013

It's taken over a week to recover from what can only be described as the greatest revelation of all time. The aftermath of the experience left me with the worst headache of my life that lasted over a week, and nausea that lasted for 2 days. Today is the first day that I feel well enough to write since August 4th. As always, I will do my best to describe what happened.

I vaguely remember the lead up to the revelation. I remember getting sick, and puking into the kitchen sink. I continued to smoke until I got head spins. Once those subsided, I continued to smoke even more. Eventually I ended up on the floor in a pseudo fetal position. I stayed there on the floor until I felt like I was going to puke again. I attempted to stand up, and upon reaching an upright position, I felt an enormous head rush coming on, and I essentially collapsed right back to the floor.

That was when it happened. The voice that I heard in Afghanistan.. It had finally returned. Only, this time, given my extreme state of THC overload, and with the presence of the Grail, we were able to openly communicate.

The voice introduced itself as the 'Residing Overwatch' of our species, but that I may refer to it as 'Match'. It then informed me that I had entered the fourth dimension of existence that was being projected and supported by the Time Fragment, or as my species had come to call it, 'The Holy Grail'. Match went on to explain that we were connected both through the energy of the cosmos, and to the energy of the cosmos. It explained that this meant that we were everywhere all at once, and could see everything as it currently was, and also anything that had been experienced by anything else connected to the realm. If at any time I wished to communicate, all I had to do was think the words, and be heard as though I were physically speaking. All of this was happening in a black void of seemingly empty space, similar to a 3-dimensional phone call I suppose, until Match brought our consciences to a dark, deep purple planet. The planet itself was enormous, dark and stormy. But the backdrop set behind it was truly a sight to behold; Asteroids as far as the eye could see. Most of them were just floating by; some bounced off one another, some were getting pulled into the giants purple planet's atmosphere and crashing down upon its surface with a barely noticeable flash. And some… were being pulled by the planet's gravity and not crashing upon its surface.. but rather, having its trajectory altered as it vectored onto a new path placed before it by this planet's gravitational pull.

Match pointed out that the largest and brightest star that could be seen from this planet was a star that we referred to as our Sun. It explained that this planet was once free floating through our galaxy but was picked up by our Sun's gravitational pull and orbits our Sun on the very edge of its gravitational reach. The planet is 10 times larger than the planet known as Jupiter by our species, and our planet will have revolved around our Sun 7,510 times before this planet completes just one orbit. Match informs me that the existence of the planet is already known to our species, but that members of a system known as the 'United States Government' have chosen not to share this knowledge with the rest of the planets inhabitants. Match then goes on to say that since the creation of our planet, there is an event that has happened only 31 times and is now in the process of being carried out for the 32nd time.

Within the reaches of the Milky Way, there is a massive chain of Asteroids orbiting the galaxy in a manner that is similar to the way a planet would orbit a star. The path of this massive chain of Asteroids just so happens to intersect with one particular arc of the orbital path of this deep purple planet on the very edge of our solar system. If the planet and the chain were to be within this region of intersection at the same time, the gravitational pull of the planet would literally send thousands of asteroids hurtling through the middle of our solar system. Match informs me that this very event does occur every 65 million of our planet's years. During the last occurrence of this event, one such Asteroid that was sent through our solar system struck our planet, and wiped out a majority of the life that was present. This very Asteroid was pulled by the planet during the peak of the event, or the time when the two bodies are closest, and the greatest amount of Asteroids are pulled from the belt.

Match informs me that part of his task as the Residing Overwatch of this particular sector of the cosmos, is to monitor any and all potential threats that would lead to an extinction of life on any planet, to include the Asteroids pulled by this planet. Match has informed me that a few of my planet's days prior to this present window of time, one such Asteroid was pulled by the Purple Planet, and Match calculates that is has a 96% chance of directly impacting our planet. Match then went on to show this very ominous Asteroid to me as it was pulled by the planet, and then through what I can only describe as rapid fast forward, projected the path it will travel which led directly to our planet, 25 years later, with only a 4% chance of course variation from start to final impact. Match informs me that this Asteroid is significantly larger than the last one that impacted our planet 65 million of our planet's years ago, and that 98% of all species living on the planet would be eradicated. Match paused for a moment after sharing this news and requested that I ask any questions that I might have. The first thing that I asked Match was whether or not he could stop this from happening. Match replied that logistically he could stop it, but it was not a decision that he alone could make. To this statement, I asked the question of 'what exactly needs to happen in order for this to be stopped by his kind?' The following is my own summation of what his response was.

Many Residing Overwatches ago, one being in Match's current position secretly allowed other beings of his species to come down to our planet and alter the

DNA of the most intelligent of the primitive life forms present, in this case, monkeys and apes. From these lifeforms, they experimented by splicing their own DNA into ours in order to catalyze the evolution of mankind. Once they had a desirable result, they sought to enslave the beings as a work force in order to harvest one of the most valuable resources in the cosmos; gold. Of all the elements in existence, gold is the one that most efficiently stores and transfers energy and most readily abundant, making it the key to traveling through space. This was the first time in the history of their species that a lifeform was engineered on an alien planet through the use of splicing their own DNA.

At that point in time, I was wondering why they would need to enslave an engineered race when they most likely had the technology to quickly mine the gold themselves. Momentarily forgetting that thoughts and speech were one in the same on this plane, Match answered by stating that I was correct in that they could have easily mined the gold on my planet, and for the most part, they did. These beings were also drawn to the power of being worshipped by lesser creatures and sought pleasure through being deified. I then asked Match how it was that this symbiotic relationship came to an end… Match replied by stating that as time went on, two groups began to form within his race; those that believed the humans should be freed, and those that wished to keep things the way they were. A huge civil war broke out across the planet between the two groups of his race, and eventually, those that fought for freedom of the human race won and gave humanity the freedom to do with their lives as they pleased. As a response to the outcome of this war, mankind, with a population of just under a million, decided as a whole that their 'other-worldly' creators go back to their planet and leave our civilization to fend for itself. Contact between his race and ours became strictly prohibited and limited to observation only. This rule was never to be broken by any member of his race save for one exception; the Residing Overwatch, If the Residing Overwatch were to ever assess a potential extinction level event that could end the human race, he would then be permitted to once again engage with the human species. Match explained that he has been 'setting events into motion' for decades, leading up to a series of pivotal points, one of which was unfolding before my very eyes, the Revelation. Match then began communicating the most important words ever heard by any human being ever.

The technology to stop the Asteroid existed. On our very moon, Match's species built a formidable underground research/observational facility that housed the technology to completely stop the event from happening altogether. However, Match cannot simply turn it on, alter the path of the Asteroid, and save our race and planet. The technology on the moon can only be turned on by the beings present on his home planet, and in order for them to turn it on so Match could use it to save our species, there would first need to be a vote, approximately 24 years from now. I asked Match to tell me as much as he could about this 'vote', and why it was to be 24 years from now.

Match explained that at the Asteroids present rate of speed, the Earth would revolve around the sun 24 times before entering the final stages of its collision course during the 25th year. The vote needed to be 24 years from now for two reasons. The first reason was because his home planet would not even consider making a decision on the matter until it had become pressingly relevant. During the final year of the Asteroid's approach, the margin of error for the body not to impact our planet would virtually become non-existent, and both the request to consider the matter and the resulting decision would be considered relevant, and all outcomes would be expedited in accordance with the sensitivity of time. The second reason why this 'vote' would be 24 years coming, would be because of the changes that would first need to take place across the entire planet. What Match told me next made my heart sink.

Since Match and his kind have seemingly 'left the picture', in terms of human interaction, we have been free to create/destroy our world as we saw fit. One of the first things that took place after their departure, was the task of satiating the curiosity of the immediate future generations of mankind. Man took it upon himself to rewrite the story of his creation, picking and choosing which facets of the truth were to be included and which were to be left out and forgotten completely. As a result, man told the story of his creation the way that he wished it could have been, and not the way that it truly was. This resulted in the creation of the world's religions. While it would take many years for each religion to develop and grow accordingly, too many people had witnessed the actual events that took place, which accounts for why there are a certain set of events that can be found in common across many religions. (A heavenly figure coming down from the sky, an immaculate birth, sacrifice and resurrection etc.) These religions hold these events in common because they were all once based on a common truth, or upon the actual event of *them* coming down to create us. But, this train of thought is irrelevant. The eventual point that Match was trying to make was this; mankind distorted the truth of his creation just enough to hide the real truth of what happened. From there, the major world religions were born, have been followed, and were constantly being developed for thousands of years. Eventually, mankind would come to use these set of beliefs (religions) as justice to commit evils against his fellow man, and are still using them as justice to commit evil against his fellow man to this very day. Because of this, the vote to save mankind would never pass, and we are doomed to our fate.

In an effort to rehash Match's last bombshell piece of info, I asked Match to confirm the statement of 'Because select groups of religious extremists exist across our planet using religion as a way to justify their crimes against humanity, your race will refuse to save us?' Match answered yes and no, yes to the previous statement being accurate, and no due to another reason; the nature of our planets' ruling governments. Match explained that to his race, the concept of government is cut and dry. There are no secrets, and everything is decided in a logical manner with the intention of making the best possible decision on behalf of his race. As it currently stands on our planet, an elite minority already have knowledge of the planet's pending doom, and they are choosing not to share the information with the rest of the world. On top of this, only a small percentage of the overall population is aware of the truth of how they came to be, and countless members of our species use beliefs based upon lies that trigger a chemical/emotional response to justify committing horrible crimes against the sacred lives of fellow members of our species. Because of these reasons, if the current course of events remains unchanged, mankind will lose this vote, and be faced with likely extinction. To this, I asked Match, 'what would you have me do'.

Match paused for a moment, and then replied. Even if the world were to change for the better, all religions disappearing, mankind uniting under the common causes of universal peace and species betterment, and the nature of government received a radical overhaul, there is still no guarantee the vote will pass due to the controversial nature of our creation. Our civilization as we know it should never have been created, and for that reason, Match stated that there are those that would vote against our salvation based upon the simple fact that our existence in the first place was unsanctioned. An un-sanctioned creation most likely leads to a barbaric outcome, which many would argue is an accurate description of the history of our race since they broke contact with our species. Because of that, even if radical change were to take place over the next 24 years, there is no way to be sure that salvation will occur at all. But, as Match put it, that does not mean that we cannot and should not try… The exact details of what needed to happen were up to me to discover and fulfill within the future timeline of events, and he therefore could not give step by step instructions. But he did leave me with a list of goals that I needed to achieve, and before the vision ended, informed me that there would be help along the way. Around this point in time, I started to sense that our time together was coming to a close, so I asked him one last question; what can you tell me about my son, Colin? Match informed me that he was the key to success, and his potential to change our world would be entirely dependent upon his own efforts. Match paused and added that my wife and I would help him the entire way, but it would be through a means that I could not yet understand. Shortly after this, my memory of the vision becomes hazy, and the next thing I remember after that is being shaken awake by Michelle. The movers, along with private transportation, had just arrived to relocate my family to Colorado. I vaguely remember securing the grail and being escorted to an SUV with my wife and son where I proceeded to pass out for the first four hours of the trip. Once I came to, I had a long conversation with Michelle where I slowly and painfully laid out the details of what had just happened through a throbbing migraine, to include the list of goals, or milestones, that were to be achieved along the way to man's salvation. At the time that we had this particular conversation, the goals were just words describing a seemingly impossible-to-achieve mission. And what was with that last tidbit he mentioned… I wouldn't be able to understand how I would help Colin?? What is that supposed to mean? Michelle didn't have any ideas on that one as well, but we both agreed that it did not sound good.

But now that we've been here for a week, the milestones are beginning to look less impossible. I suppose from this point forward, I will mention the milestones and simply comment on their progress as notable events take place... I get the feeling that the opportunities I will have to write around what's going on will be few and far between. So, with forthcoming explanations of how these milestones become achieved, I will simply now just write them down, and briefly discuss each.

> The Invitation
> The Societal formation
> The Construction
> The Destruction
> The Broadcast
> The Revelation
> The Unification
> The Coup
> The Transformation
> Salvation

As I look over this list of steps, the lines that distinguish each phase become less concrete, and therefore, they all seem to make up a singular timeline of events. Some steps are essentially single actions that will take place and be over within minutes, while others will be ongoing for years to come. As I've already stated, I'm assuming my entries from here on out will be status updates on progress of this plan, but for now, I think the best course of action is to get the plan itself down on paper. However, generally speaking, Murphy's Law has a way of taking even the best laid plans and reducing them to rubble. (My life in these previous pages, being no exception) But for logistical purposes, a basic course of action needs to be plotted. I will do that now.

During the next couple decades, I am going to be putting together a massive team of the best minds available to me. These minds will be the expert knowledge I need to cover my own lack of knowledge on certain tasks to come. Gathering these minds is the second task, and one that will be ongoing for years to come. The 'Hook' if you will, or how exactly I am to get these people on board and believing, will be 'The Invitation'. Somehow, I will come up with a way to safely and secretly recruit the minds that I will need, with much of this task being performed by Match. As far as exactly how Match will go about doing this, he did not say. But once the first few begin to come, I imagine how this will go about being accomplished, will become clearer.

Once I have what I need to form a minimal society, I can begin 'The Construction' phase. Using the Grail to expedite construction, we will build an exact replica of one of the World Trade Towers. It will be built using the original blueprints for the Towers, and will be exactly the same, down to the placement of the very last bolt. Exactly how long this will take, is unknown… But, it took approximately five years to build both towers with a labor force of thousands of men. Considering that I will have access to a technology that will cut that labor force needed down to a fraction of the original amount, I really don't see the construction taking more than a couple of months. I suspect the hardest part about that whole aspect will be acquisition of the parts and materials. One tower, including labor and materials, took about $450 million dollars to build, in the 1960's. Obviously, I do not have half a billion dollars just sitting around in my bank account, but I suspect because of the grail, and for reasons unknown to me now, this cost will also be drastically reduced. There are a few problems that I can foresee now.. such as shipping all the materials to Colorado, and producing steel that is chemically identical to that which was used in the 1960's. Both of these problems will keep the cost high just because that is the nature of how things are. Plus, I'm sure there are scores of other problems that I wouldn't even know to think of because I'm not a Skyscraper Architect, or a

Steel Engineer, or a whatever else I'm not thinking of at this time. These issues will need to be thought of and addressed by key members of my Society; hence why it must be formed prior to construction. But that is a bridge I will attempt to cross upon arrival.

The next step will only take minutes, and really isn't much of a step at all; The Destruction. I will have a remotely piloted Boeing 767 fly into the exact impact area that the second plane did on the second tower on September 11, 2001. Once that is complete, the tower will simply be left to let come what may. As the immediate aftermath of the impact goes on, I will have my team of Architects, and Engineers compare this sequence of events to what we were shown on 9/11 on TV. Every little detail, and I mean EVERY, LITTLE, DETAIL, will be analyzed and compared to 9/11. What follows will be the next two steps combined; 'The Broadcast' and 'The Revelation'. Leading up to this point, I will need to have been documenting construction of the tower with interviews of my Architects and Engineers, as well as footage of me using the Grail to construct the tower. I would like to have the impact of the Plane itself be broadcast on live TV, followed by analysis and construction footage, but, seeing as how TV stations are controlled by Mainstream Media, convincing any of the networks to essentially expose not only our corrupt 'Big Government', but also the networks themselves, will be near impossible. The details of how this will be pulled off are unknown to me at this time, but if I can do it, if *we* can do it, the greatest Revelation in the history of the world will take place. People will see the tower still standing, hours, days, weeks after impact, and will be forced to look for answers. I will present them with the most un-biased, factual, and scientific explanation that I can provide. Much of this can be pre-written by simply analyzing what we were shown on 9/11 during the impact using a step by step/side by side comparison. Details that were overlooked and taken for granted will be made obvious as it becomes clear that my broadcast was of an actual plane hitting my replica tower, and what we were shown on 9/11 was an elaborate concoction of lies and deception.

Now, while I am more than confident that this is what will be shown come that eventual fateful day… There is a part of me that wonders that what if my tower does collapse like the ones did on 9/11… What if all my efforts will be proven to be null and void? Well, while that would be undeniably disastrous, I would still have the grail, and I would still know the most important piece of information of all. But, then again, it wouldn't be logical for this tower stunt to go wrong. Why would Match, having observed the actions and lies of our species for hundreds of years, make it a point to show me something that was supposedly a lie, only to have there not be a conspiracy? It doesn't make sense. This construction is to be the foundation of humanity's salvation. The whole fucking point is that our species is going to be eradicated, and there is an established and vast system of lies and corruption that would seek to deny not only Americans, but humanity as a whole, from knowing the truth. Knowing the truth. What will it mean to 'Know the Truth'? To know the truth, is a side effect of Revelation. In order for true Revelation to take place, it must be met with the next step, unification, to be then immediately followed by the Coup. In order for Match's plan to work, (and really, it's more of a joint effort, because after all, who is filling in the gaps here) the United States must lead the way.

There is no denying it, the U.S. is one of the dominant superpowers on our planet, if not *the* dominant super power. Many countries love us, even more hate us, but very few will go as far as to say that we have little impact on world policies and happenings. While our foreign policies are far from perfect, leaving mostly negative aftertastes in the mouths of those that would request our aid, there is no doubt that we take it upon ourselves to play a very large part in all matters that go on around the world. Many would argue that this is wrong to begin with, and we shouldn't be involved in half of the things we are. This arises a complex paradox that Americans deal with on a daily basis. Looking at the world subjectively, there are many, many issues that should be addressed on a global scale. Injustice to a certain people within a particular country can lead to an injustice upon the human race as a whole. An easy example which all can understand: Adolf Hitler. Hitler sought to rise to power, take over the world, and eradicate the Jewish people in the process. This is an example of the injustice of a certain people within a foreign country that quickly became recognized as an injustice on a global scale. Slowly but surely, countries fell into line, chose sides, and an epic global struggle to end this injustice took place. Since then, the U.S. has continued this 'justice for all' campaign, making a point to participate in chosen injustices happening to people around the planet. So good for us, right? No. On the surface, it may look like the people in these countries do need our help, and it may be that they sincerely do… But the U.S. has long since stopped helping people because it's the right thing to do. The revelation that Americans need to have, is that our country only does things and makes decisions to better itself. A more accurate statement: the U.S. only makes decisions that would result in the increase or sustainment of its current wealthy elite. No matter which war campaign we enter, or which trade agreement we make, or whatever the case may be on all foreign and domestic policy, the United States has long since abandoned its original pedestal of foreign nobility and righteousness, and replaced it with a shawl of greed, corruption, and deception. When my tower refuses to fall, when all of the little inconsistencies are found by placing my recreation side by side to 9/11, Americans, and the World, will know that I speak the truth concerning the current state of affairs. They will look to me for answers while the wealthy elite and Mainstream Media are caught with their pants down. I will show them the truth. I will display the powers of the Grail for all to see. And then, I would have them rise up, and take this country back into the hands of its people.

'The Coup', or a coup, will take place right here in America. Once this truth is brought to light, the wealthy elite and MSM will seek to discredit, defame, belittle, disprove, etc. etc. Lawyers will tsk, political experts will cry treason, and those in charge of the system will use any and all weapons at their disposal, both literally and metaphorically. But the American people will not have it. I will liberate them from this veil created by our wealthy elite as I reveal what they will realize to be the greatest deception of all, only to then shatter that reality yet again with pending cosmic doom. A sense of pride and nationality will spread like wildfire with the fiercest of roars. A sense of purpose and a newfound righteous glory will fuel every citizen as they break free from this long established system and remember what it is to be an American. Citizens of all races, genders, religious beliefs, all income brackets, all education levels; citizens of all facets of every characteristic imaginable, will rise. They will rise with a unity of purpose, to march on Washington, Congress, the Pentagon, the FBI, the CIA, media corporations, anyone who is anyone with power will be stripped of this privilege and be held under citizen's arrest. All service members will be temporarily excused from duty, police officers will rally to our cause, and my society, head by yours truly, will complete 'The Transformation' of the face of America. I will then approach the world, not as a

President, or a Monarch, or a Pope, not as Emissary, or as an Ambassador, or even as an American citizen. I will address the world as the one true Guardian, and as a citizen of humanity, and I will lay before the world the path to Salvation.

And so, begins the part where I'm supposed to write about the Salvation of Humanity. In order to give all of us the absolute best chance of survival, the people of the world will have to make the greatest of sacrifices. All current religions will have to be redefined, and an end must be put to all associated religious conflicts; for everything about these matters has been written and created by man. Our world must openly acknowledge and embrace the fact that we were created by another race of beings from another world. I realize that the chances of everyone accepting these facts are quite slim. Sure, there will always be the silent minority that goes along with the master plan even though they hold reservations, (which is still a problem since we are talking about keeping secrets from an alien race with the ability of telepathy) but the real question is, what is to be done with those that refuse to believe my message? My first instinct to that matter is to say 'fuck em', and send a nuke their way. But, that cannot be the answer, nor will it ever be the answer. That animalistic train of thought is the very reason why the world is the way it is. Yet still, a small group of few willing to stand up against the will of many is just another reason Match's council will vote not to save us. As a matter of fact, it could be *the* very reason why we are not saved. Unfortunately, that cannot be known until it's time, and if that is indeed the scenario when the time does come, it may be too late. If there does turn out to be a certain religious faith that refuses my message across the globe, right now, the only peaceful solution I can see is exile. These people will act as a tumor seeking to hang on to what they know, and combat my proposed radical change, all the while growing in size and refusing to believe the truth, even when set right before their eyes. The only peaceful way I can see is to cordon off a section of the world for these people to live in and continue their paganist ways. That way, if it did come to mankind being allowed to persist if only these people were eradicated, the problem could be solved by the push of a button. But, as I've already stated, I do not wish for it to come to that. This is why every step that I/we take now in preparation for what comes next, is the most important step until the next. If everything goes as planned, then come judgement day, the human race as a whole will live together, or die together.

To the cynic that would state, if the human race is to undergo such pain and suffering, because such a change will force much of both upon the world, only to be killed off anyway, then what is the point? Why go through all of this trouble?

To this person, I would say, it's better for the people of this world to embrace one another as a loved brother if only for a day, then to spend lifetimes killing each other over beliefs based upon lies. There is only one way forward, and that is by embracing the truth, together. That is the task that lay before all of us. *That*, is the meaning of life.

AUGUST 14, 2013

Since my family and I are here and officially living in Colorado, it marks the end of my life at Ft. Campbell, and my time with my last unit. I have mentioned a couple times just how miserable it was for me and my soldiers during this time, but never really got into why, or any of my unit history for that matter. Of course there are more pressing things going on at the moment, but allow me to paint a picture and close a chapter of my life. I will try to keep it short and sweet.

Both of my deployments were with the only 'Signal Company' that Ft. Campbell had to offer. We were attached to supporting the command footprint of the 1st BDE Combat Team, which therefore kept me on a large FOB with minimal responsibilities during those deployments. Tough leaders came and went, but overall the unit was quite good. We always excelled in every mission assignment, and life while not deployed wasn't terrible in the least. But like all good things, it did not last forever. My unit was officially dissolved by the base commander, and we were attached to an Engineering unit in an effort to create a new and unique unit with a vast array of combat support capabilities. This unit wasn't any worse or better than how we were previously, but we did get put into a brand new building with a lot of storage space, and everyone seemed happy to be there. I was as well, until I found out that I was being sent to a different unit altogether, due to personnel needs. (People in all positions are constantly being promoted or moved and replaced, it's how the Army goes.) We were over strength with people that held my job, and this other unit was in desperate need of someone in my exact position. I wasn't too thrilled to be leaving the people I had come to know over the past four years, not to mention, deployed with twice. And when I found out which exact unit it was, it became clear that from day one, I was correct to dread the move.

I was transferred to the 1-506 Infantry Regiment, Red Currahee, one of the most famous units on the base, and in the world, for that matter. If you are at all familiar with military history, you will recognize this unit to be the very unit that was holed up in the city of Bastogne during WWII. With limited ammo, clothes, ammunition, man-power and after being completely surrounded and bombarded with mortars for days by the Germans, they were still able to hold onto the city until receiving the long overdue relief brought on my Gen. Patton and his armored tank Division. (The HBO series 'Band of Brothers' is based on the exploits of these men) Well the HBO series is based on the book, and the book tells a tale of some of the most grueling and hardcore soldiers that ever walked the planet. These guys went through absolute hell in preparation. But it turned out to be all worthwhile since this hard training would present the opportunity for this unit to rise and take its place in history.

What has changed since those days? Unfortunately, not much. I wasn't directly attached to an infantry platoon, but I was in the S-6, and S-6 provides comms support for their people in the field. This unit had no pending deployment, (they had actually gotten back from one a few months earlier from when I joined them), but I soon came to discover that it didn't matter. Due to some asinine sense of tradition, or just through plain ignorance and disregard, this unit was moving to and from the field multiple times every month. When out in the field, we were expected to stay out there, with field exercises never being shorter than a full week. While this may have been a normal operational tempo for infantry, it was not for us and our signal world. Infantrymen do not hold the same level of respect for our equipment, which would lead to an incident (pretty much every field exercise without fail) where one of our major comm components came back broken, missing altogether, or missing key components. This would prompt us to begin the repair process for said broken piece of equipment, which typically went as follows;

- We would coordinate with the motor pool company since they handle all things being sent out for repairs, regardless of who wants to send it.
- Getting the paperwork prepared to send it out often took several days due to running around having to gather facts and serial numbers.
- Often times, the motor pool company wouldn't even be able to accept the paperwork, because they have their own training schedules that their own soldiers need to meet.(ie one exercise where we lost 2 of our 4 remaining good operational

radio antennas, we had to wait a week and a half just to turn in the paperwork since all motor pool soldiers were out in the field qualifying on weapons systems for the week.)
- Once the paperwork is submitted, it takes about a week for it to get where it's going, another week or two or three to get it repaired (depending on the repair shops workload and the complexity of the item itself) and then another week to be sent back to the motorpool company.

On average, it was at least a month turn-around on anything we wanted to get fixed or replaced. But as already stated, after one week, two at most, we were right back out in the field, falling victim to whatever will be lost or broken next. Once we returned yet again, if we were lucky, we had equipment to be picked up. But how it usually went is we started the second or third round of repairs being sent out before the first got back. Eventually, we began operating on absolute bare bones for equipment, meaning that nothing else could break or we would be unable to perform our duties as signal soldiers. Because of this flaw, created by our Chain of Command, my Soldiers and I and my people were considered to be the skid mark on a highly prestigious and historic unit. I can only imagine how they tsk at us and shake their heads behind closed doors, when THEY WERE THE ONES CREATING THE FUCKING PROBLEMS. How much common sense does it take to realize that OP tempo needs to be adjusted if certain groups are falling behind? Apparently more than any of our leaders possessed. I mean, I get it, it's a historic unit, they were hardcore through and through, thus they wish to continue on that legacy. But it's always going to be at someone else's expense, aka the S-6. And I know they saw us as the problem, because my Company Commander and First Sergeant both came down to give us a completely ridiculous pep talk/assessment speech to see what the hell was going on. I should have done them a favor and pulled their heads out of their own asses during this visit.

The other thing that made my life my with this unit particularly frustrating, was my job and the nature of my equipment. The Army is always releasing new and improved tiers of communications, catering to the ever-changing demands of the infantryman. This latest tier of equipment that had been released, (released to Ft. Campbell and a few other bases first before full

Army-wide deployment) was particularly bad, compared to the previous tier which had very little wrong with it. The new tier had systems relying on systems with each individual system failing on the regular, with certain systems being completely wiped of programming, reagardless if it was properly shut down or not. This provided for the beginning of every exercise to be hours of smashing our heads against our equipment trying to figure out what's not working this time. But that was how it was with my old unit. (The new tier was released before I was sent to Red Currahee) Eventually our team would persist, and we would always get it up and running on the first day, usually through civilian contractor help. Here at Red Currahee, I had no team. I only had myself.

Now of course I had soldiers under me, and could task them out as needed, but that wasn't the solution that needed to be implemented. My equipment required 4 straight months of training, 8 hours a day, 5 days a week. Each issuance of the equipment went to a comms team comprising of usually 3-4 people. At least 2 of that sum held my job, and one person was the satellite operator. A team could have a 4th person which was usually an NCO position, in charge of mission and equipment oversight. My equipment absolutely needed these 3 people to be present, because without team depth, problems arise to other problems, and instead of making progress figuring out what needs to be done, one person would essentially just make a huge, long list of what's wrong and attack it in circles with the real possibility of not making any progress at all. This is how it was for me at Red Curraheet. I was the only one that had received the required training for my equipment. The training itself was too in depth for me to replicate, and the best I could hope to do is give my soldiers crash courses on how to operate equipment. But when it came time to go out to the field, I was essentially on my own.

One field exercise stands out in my mind that should have been an eye opener to the unit, but of course, it was not. It had gotten to day 3 of the two-week exercise, and I still had not gotten my equipment up. My signal officer ended up approaching me and asking me man to man what I needed to get my job done. I informed him that I need someone else that knows what they're doing out here with me so we can work together as a team, AS IT WAS MEANT TO BE. A few hours later, one of the people from a different unit that was in the 4 month class with me showed up, and 5 hours later, we were able to salvage everything and bring the equipment up. Prior to that moment, however, I was in the eyes of every higher up in my unit. At one point my Company Commander approached me directly, not comprehending why exactly it was that I was failing at my job. I was beyond stressed out at this point, and I don't remember what I told him. But I do remember him saying something along the lines of 'his XO graduated top of his class at West Point, maybe he could figure it out'. And with that, I climbed down from my ladder and let a completely untrained person touch my equipment for a spell, without any prior knowledge. This was a huge no-no. If you don't know what you're doing, you don't touch shit. And this guy was, therefore humiliating me in front of essentially my entire unit. That was the straw that broke my back. I remember being so furious that it took all my self-restraint not to explode on my Commander and Hulk smash his face in, and I nearly walked the 10 miles back to base from the exercise field. But it was around this point that the S6 signal officer intervened and did as I requested. That extra set of expert knowledge was the difference between success and failure. I mean, is this concept so hard to recognize?? Let me bring it down a notch using terms a combat arms Soldier could understand… Consider a tank, with a 4-person crew; the Commander, the Driver, the radio guy, and the gunner/loader. If you were to train just one of these men on how to do the jobs of all positions, and then throw that one man out on the battlefield to complete all 4 jobs solo, how combat effective do you think this tank is going to be? Not very. It's the same exact concept with my equipment.

And to drive the nail home, my old unit that sent me to this current hellhole of a unit, decided to setup a 3 weeklong replication of the course I took in order to help out the units that had this equipment but lacked the trained soldiers to operate it. I found out about this close to when it was first proposed, and my old unit prepared for these classes for over a month. This was quite literally, the golden signal opportunity that would fix a lot of S6's current issues. So, did we end up sending anyone to this class? Nope. There was a month long training exercise scheduled during this time, and no one got the much needed training that my 'World Class' unit needed. And yet, the S6 continues to be the main point of failure within the unit, and my Chain of Command just cannot seem to figure it out. Don't get me wrong, Red Currahee is, and will always be, one of the best and best trained infantry units on the battlefield, but a unit, no matter the history, is only as good as the leaders in charge. And during my brief history with this prestigious unit, I figured out that truly good leaders, like myself, are so rare, that it's really no wonder that my destiny is going the way it's going. Who else do I know, or that I've met, that would be capable of handling what has been put before me? As it currently stands, there are none. But I know that needs to change, because what I have to accomplish requires, without a doubt, a team made of the best of the best, being lead by me, The Bruce, Guardian to the Prophet, and bringer of light to a world amidst it's darkest days. I have my work cut out for me.

On second thought, there is one final cherry to be placed on the famously bitter sundae that is 1-506 Red Currahee. Previously I have mentioned specific treatment of certain soldiers, and how it was blatantly unfair, but have yet to provide an actual example. Well.. I came across several instances of this happening, but there is one that stands out above all the rest. I remember I was standing outside of our company formation area, awaiting a pending formation, as one often does in the Military, and I came upon a group of infantrymen in my same Batallion, but different company, discussing the overall awful nature of the current unit we were all 'priveleged' to be a part of. This soldier, Spc Jones, started telling a tale that was truly horrifying, and to be honest, I cannot spend too much time thinking about his story, else become fired up like a bloodthirsty Valkyrie soaring on wings of justice and vengeance. Spc Jones was a relatively quiet person, black, shorter in stature, but very thick. (muscular) But he was also not afraid to tell it like it was and whenever he broke his silence, it was always to lay down a truly well aimed zinger or a quality comment that defined his personality. His story went more or less as follows:

At the time that he told that story to the various others standing there in the group, it had happened over a year prior to that exact moment, during their last deployment to Afghanistan. He and his platoon got caught up in a small arms firefight, and at one point he was seeking cover behind a wall as he could clearly see bullets hitting the ground directly in front of him, not to mention hear the crack they were making as they also closely passed by his position at upper torso level. Well, there had been another soldier taking cover behind the same wall, directly behind Spc. Jones. This Soldier physically pushed Spc. Jones out from behind cover into the oncoming small arms fire that was clearly landing right in front of both of them. By way of pure luck, Spc Jones manages to not get shot, and to sprint to another close by wall and regain cover. After the firefight ended, Spc Jones brought the incident up to his Chain of Command, and when everything was all said and done, long after the deployment was over, the Soldier that pushed him received zero punitive action. The Red Currahee Chain of Command simply swept it under the rug as though nothing had ever happened.

Needless to say, I was awestruck. What this soldier was describing to me would be labeled as Attempted Murder in every court of law in our country. The only logical explanation I can come up with as to why my Chain of Command handled it the way they did, was to avoid negative PR. Make no mistake, had this incident blown up, it would have been National news. I believe my Chain of Command recognized this and decided that 1-506 Red Currahee did not need this kind of negative popularity, because after all, this incident happened under their command and they would have also been seen in a negative light, putting a serious hurdle in their own career progression. Upon hearing this story, I was gung-ho, ready to go to JAG right there and then to seek the justice that this Soldier deserved. But Spc Jones insisted that he had let it go, that he was getting out of the shithole known as the Army and told me not to worry about it. I cannot express to you how crushed I was to hear him say this. Consider what this would do to a person; someone legitimately attempts to kill you, and nothing happens to them. I don't care how you spin it, this incident will be the direct cause of the end of this Soldier's career. Spc. Jones would have spiraled inward, and lost all hope and feeling of mental stability, or worse, spiraled out of control, and went on a arguably deserved killing spree of his Chain of Command. If it had happened to me, I would gone straight to JAG and fed that piece of shit so called 'battle buddy' of mine to the wolves at Ft Leavenworth. (Military Prison) Sure 1-506 would be the shit stain of the Army for quite a while, but that's what it means to be a leader. You must make tough decisions every day. What defines your character as a leader, however, is if you make the right ones. Obviously, my Chain of Command, who had the fucking audacity to stand in front of us all on a daily basis as our supposed 'role models', did not choose the correct decision. I cannot tell you how much I wanted to march down to JAG and file a case against the Soldier in question (who was white, making this look potentially racial) and to also request that my entire Chain of Command be investigated pending relief of Command, and Court Marshalls of their own. But again, nothing happened, and if not for this journal potentially reaching the world, no one would ever know.

After I had some time to sit on this story, and truly assess my own feelings about it, I saw a direct correlation between my own leaders and essentially all world leaders. At one point or another, all of them are faced with a decision of that magnitude, and more often than not, they fail to make the right decision. Whether that reason they choose the wrong solution is to protect themselves, their association, their own futures, or to make big money happy, it matters not. Leadership is about having the balls to do what is right when no one else will. If you hold a position of responsibility, in any walk of life, and you cannot honestly say to yourself that every major decision you made was the right one, you do not deserve to lead. And every day that you continue to lead after making a mistake on par with one I just mentioned, it serves as a mockery to the few of us that are actually trying to make this world a better place. Realize that you are an awful person, resign from your responsibilities, and allow for someone like me to perform your duties for you. Corruption is the number one problem that plagues all systems with any sort of established leadership.

Well guess what world, that shit is coming to an end, and it is starting with me, today. My work is cut out for me, *indeed.*

MAY 9, 2032

What you have just read, are the visions and aspirations as can be found in the actual journal of the late and great, Benjamin Bruce. 'Benjamin who??' you might ask. Some may remember the name from a few decades ago. Ask your Grandparents, and they may say something about some Soldier getting caught up with drugs and getting his entire family killed. According to them, that would be what the history books say. Sure enough, I went to the Boulder Public Library and was able to confirm this story, as evident from the following news excerpts that were printed in the *Colorado Daily*;

(August 24, 2013)
HERO ARMY SGT AND FAMILY FOUND DEAD IN COLORADO HOME

(Boulder, CO)- Ft. Campbell Army Sgt, Benjamin Bruce, and his wife and son, Michelle Bruce and Colin Bruce, were all found dead in their Colorado home yesterday. Local authorities received a phone call from a concerned neighbor that had not seen the family for over a week, and reported a foul odor coming from their home when they went to knock on their neighbor's door. Upon entering the house, local police found that Michelle, Colin, and Benjamin had all suffered gunshot wounds to the head had been dead for over a week. Initial investigations may suggest that Benjamin murdered his wife and son before committing suicide approximately nine days prior. Sgt Benjamin Bruce dies at the age of 30, Catherine Bruce 27, and Colin Bruce was 3.

Authorities are looking into everything from Sgt Bruce's recent celebrity status, to his medical history, in order to try and find a motive for this heinous crime.

Some three weeks ago, Sgt Bruce made national headlines when he was reportedly attacked by Taliban forces at his Kentucky home. Thwarting the plans of four would-be terrorists, Sgt.

Bruce became the first American to be individually targeted on American soil by a terrorist regime, escaping with only a flesh wound. Sgt Bruce then refused to attend his own Medal of Honor ceremony as a result and made no official statement explaining his actions.

Sgt Bruce served two tours to Afghanistan, where he was awarded a Silver Star with Valor on his first tour for successfully defending his base during a Tower guard shift against 20 attacking Taliban. Some of his other achievements include two Purple Hearts, two Army Commendation Medals, two Army Achievement Medals, and one Good Conduct Medal. Sgt Bruce is survived by his mother, Sharon Liemann, 62, residing in Columbus, Ohio.

The investigation continues.

(August 27, 2013)
INVESTIGATORS CONFIRM: SGT BRUCE AND FAMILY MURDERED BY DRUG CARTEL
(Boulder, CO)- Investigators assigned to the Sgt Bruce case have officially released a statement concerning their findings. After interviewing all

of his subordinate Soldiers, investigators learned that Benjamin Bruce had been keeping a personal journal, one that he started at least three months ago. Investigators then re-searched his house, and found the journal hidden in a wall compartment located in his home basement. In this journal, Sgt Bruce describes how he and his Kentucky neighbor, Fred Hubert, 43, came to be affiliated with the Cartel. Bruce goes on to describe his own internal struggle with drug-addiction, his violent and unstable relationship with his wife, and his plans to go AWOL from the Army in order to move to Colorado to continue pursuing Cartel business.

When asked if Sgt Bruce's recent encounter with the so called 'Taliban', was actually a Cartel-related attack, the lead investigator stated that 'at this time, there is no concrete evidence that would suggest this, but the investigation is on-going, and that would certainly appear to be a logical explanation.'

Investigators would go on to state that other than the findings indicated by Bruce's personal journal, there were no other signs in his personal life that would allow an outsider to know anything was wrong. Sgt Bruce's military medical records came back without incident, and reports from everyone that knew him suggested that he was some sort of 'pillar of morality'.

However, after acquiring a warrant to search his neighbor's home due to the evidence presented in Bruce's journal, FBI investigators found over two dozen fully grown Marijuana plants being cultivated in his neighbors attic, as well as a trunk full of stockpiled military grade automatic assault rifles, grenades, and bomb-making materials, said to be valued at over $50,000 on the black market. Fred Hubert is currently facing serious drug trafficking, and weapons charges that could land him quite a formidable jail sentence. That Supreme Court trial is set to occur in February of next year.

When asked if Investigators would be releasing the contents of Bruce's journal to the public, they stated that it would be 'some time' before that happens, 'since the journal contained various other sources of valuable information to be used in the ongoing struggle to uproot the Drug Cartels taking hold in America. Once these new found leads had been followed, and there was no one else out there to be potentially victimized by this release of information, then it would be released.'

In light of the recent findings made through the discovery of Bruce's journal, Sgt Bruce will have his Congressional Medal of Honor rescinded, his Honorable Discharge changed to a Dishonorable Discharge, and any and all life insurance payout that may have been going to his surviving family members as a result of his death during active duty, will be forfeit.

Despite the recent swell of negative press, the Army has declined to release an official statement regarding the life and actions of Sgt Bruce. Bruce's mother Sharon Liemann, has also declined to make a statement at this time.

There were many other articles that would go on to meticulously analyze the downfall of Benjamin Bruce. The world came to know him as a criminal mastermind that lived dual lives as a highly decorated soldier, and as one of the biggest Drug Lords on the rise in the early 21st century. There was even the eventual release of this so-called 'Drug Diary', containing all of Ben's supposed inner thoughts and plans, which would then lead to further documentaries, eventually escalating Ben's criminal status into legend.

Lies. All of it. Ben did none those things that the newspaper reported, and this supposed journal that was found was completely made up. But I'm not here to redeem the life of Benjamin Bruce. I will eventually clear his name of all charges, but right at this very moment, I am not interested in the world knowing the truth of what really happened to Ben.

What does interest me, however, is *the truth* that Benjamin Bruce was trying to share, *the truth* that was contained within the pages of the original and actual journal, written by Benjamin Bruce. *The truth*, which you now know, as a result of me finding Ben's journal, way up in the Colorado Rockies.

If you have read this, whether you have already realized it or not, you have several decisions to make. Do you have a part to play in mankind's upcoming struggle? Would you be willing to risk your life rising up against the country you have known and loved all your life? What would you be willing to do to save humanity?

Who am I?

My name, is Colin Bruce. I am in fact, alive, I have found my father's journal, and I have the Holy Grail. I seek to finish what my father started eighteen years ago. There is no time for secrecy and diplomacy.

Will you help me change the world?

Will you help me *save our world*?

If the answer is yes, then you already know what to do. Follow your instincts, and they will bring you straight to me. All I ask is that if you do decide to find me, do so with haste. Each passing day puts us closer to Armageddon, and ultimately to the point where it will be too late to do anything about anything at all.

If the answer is no, then know that I am well on my way to being ready to step into the known world. Pray not to false gods, but spread the truth and light that was my father's message, and gather all the hope that you can for humanity. We are going to need it.

And I promise you here and now, that just like my father, I will do everything and anything in my power to secure the future of our planet, our race, and our continued existence. I will continue to fight for all of our rights to life, and will not stop until I save humanity, or fail trying.

And in that final hour, if it comes to it, as I lay on my back, looking up upon certain death and destruction of our planet, I will try… with my dying breath.. just… one… more.. again.

EPILOGUE

During the time that I was writing this story, I was beginning to go through a major telepathic awakening. I would like to express that it is entirely unnecessary to need to use copious amounts of drugs to achieve telepathic communication. One must simply have an open-mind, curiosity, and pure spirit in order to be considered for contact.

At one point in my life, I did make initial first telepathic contact with a being known as Valiant Thor. This contact lead to me inevitably propose a Peace Treaty between galactic peoples that gained galactic attention. Ever since this approximate time, I have been in constant daily telepathic communication with the Galactic Federation. I am being groomed for leadership among the stars and invite all of you that read this story to follow in my footsteps and have the bravery to face the bold future that inevitably lies before all of us as we each find our own way to contribute to the cause of humanity ascending to our destinies.